Encoded

Encoded

A Richard Braddock Mystery

Richard Nedbal

Strategic Book Publishing and Rights Co.

Strategic Book Publishing & Rights Co., LLC
USA | Singapore
www.sbpra.net

For information about special discounts for bulk purchases, please contact Strategic Book Publishing and Rights Co. Special Sales, at bookorder@sbpra.net.

ISBN: 978-1-952269-28-8

Acknowledgments:

Thanks to my wife Linda, who quietly tolerated me during the process. That is not an easy task.

Many additional people contributed in many different ways to the completion of this book, and I am grateful for their efforts. Special thanks to my graphics designer Leah at leahjayart.com, whose creativity in designing the cover was exceptional. Several other people gave specific advice to this book; thanks to Robert Nixon and Sharon Turnoy. And finally, I am indebted to Write My Wrongs, LLC, who did the initial edit of the manuscript and made significant suggestions to its content.

Disclaimer:

This is a work of fiction. Names, characters, businesses, places, events, locales, and incidents are either the products of the author's imagination or used in a fictitious manner. Any resemblance to actual persons, living or dead, or actual events is purely coincidental.

Publications:

Dickie, Memoirs of a Mad Scientist
How to Build Max-Performance HEMI Engines.
PCAD & PCB, Making the Marriage Work

"If a fellow isn't thankful for what he's got now, he isn't likely to be thankful for what he's going to get."

—Frank A. Clark

Prologue

Valentine's Day, February 14,

Present Day, 12:15 p.m.

Newcastle, Oklahoma

Mason Branner moved quickly, racing against the Oklahoma sun to finish detailing his classic 1968 Dodge Charger. Any minute now, the few remaining drops of water scattered on the hood would dry into "sunspots." Those were not acceptable. His wife, Angie, said he was a fanatic about the car. Maybe she was right, but he was determined to maintain that beautiful exterior indefinitely. That required commitment. It required love.

Whenever Mason took his muscle car out for a spin, he liked to dress the part. Today, it was jeans, cowboy boots, and a plain, white, short-sleeved T-shirt, the kind they sold in the men's underwear department. Those had the right type of cotton that stayed up when you rolled the sleeves almost to your shoulder. He pretended not to notice rolling up the sleeves made them tight around his biceps. The effect was that his muscles looked even bulkier than they were, what some might call "babe bait." He knew most men his age hadn't seen biceps like his sticking out of their own sleeves in decades. Mason lifted weights daily to keep his hard as a rock.

He'd purchased the black Charger from the original owner's widow a few years back. The red stripe cutting down the middle of the hood and roof complimented the leather interior. In 1968, it was one of only 475 Charger R/Ts made that came with a 426 HEMI. That engine guaranteed the car would handle its own in a drag race, and Mason was sure it had been tested regularly back in the day. It was a rare specimen amongst the rare, a showpiece and a collector's item. It was sure priced like one.

Mason didn't care, but Angie had opposed spending gobs of money on a "used car." She even hinted, several times, there would be hell to pay if he went through with the purchase. He wasn't worried about it though. He just hoped she didn't demand he choose between her and the Charger. She couldn't possibly understand a love affair extending all the way back to preschool.

When Mason was six years old, his next-door neighbor had bought one of these Chargers when they first rolled off the assembly line. Every morning at 7:30 sharp, Mason ran to the front bay window to watch him start the beast. Some days, he even did a burnout as he left, leaving two black strips and a whiff of testosterone in his wake.

One late afternoon, Mason circled the car longingly in the man's driveway. His neighbor came out and asked if he wanted to "drive" it. Did he ever! With some help, Mason climbed into the driver's seat and proceeded to "race" the Charger, making all the screeching sound effects his six-year-old voice could muster. All too soon, it was time to go, but he vowed to own one someday—and now he did.

Mason wanted to take Angie out for lunch in it for Valentine's Day. He asked if she would, just this once, not complain about the car's cost during the trip. He loved her and didn't want any disagreements on Valentine's Day. She should have known that after almost three years of owning it, he was sick and tired of being nagged about the price. He wanted to relive the excitement six-year-old Mason had felt. After all, what was done was done, and he couldn't take it back. He actually felt a little proud that the widow had used the money to finance a condo she had always wanted near her kids in California.

Providence must have been smiling down on Mason. When he parked at the restaurant, taking up two spaces to protect the car, an older fellow approached him. The guy asked if he could peek under the hood, and Mason was only too eager to brag about all the work he'd done to restore it. Then the fellow asked if he would consider selling it.

Angie pretended not to eavesdrop, but she didn't miss a word. Without so much as a deep breath, the guy offered one hundred and forty thousand dollars, but Mason told him he had no plans to sell. Angie didn't say anything and remained silent on the topic throughout their lunch. When they finished and were getting back in the car, a second fellow walked up, eyes wide with lust. Mason was glad Angie was there to see these unsolicited offers. That would show her it was no ordinary "used car."

While Mason showed off the restoration and engine work again, they shared in some general guy talk and discussed the history of the Charger. The second fellow said he was interested in it for one hundred and fifty thousand dollars. Was it for sale? Again, Mason said no.

Angie wasn't stupid. She knew he had purchased the Charger for just over eighty thousand dollars. At the time, she'd thought it was an obscene price for what she viewed as just an old car. Now, she changed her tune. She looked at Mason with a new appreciation for his investment knowledge. She respected the negotiating skills he must have used to get the price down when it was clearly worth more. She even showed some affection for it, patting the glove box a couple of times like a family pet.

Mason started up the Charger for the drive home. He had taken the entire week off from his high-paying, high-stress job as VP of Southern Power for all of Oklahoma. The parent firm provided natural gas-fueled power to five states, but southern Oklahoma itself was enough of a challenge to keep Mason fully occupied and then some. He badly needed this break and was looking forward to the time off with Angie.

February was the beginning of the tornado season in Oklahoma, so good weather was always a hit-or-miss proposition at this time of year. This year, they lucked out; Valentine's Day was going down as one of the best on record. It was seventy degrees, not a cloud in the sky, and the breeze was no stronger than a sleeping cat's breath. Mason wanted to be a sleeping cat after their big lunch. He wondered if he could convince Angie to take a nap with him when they got home. He suggested the idea with a little wink.

She blushed. Mason loved that about her. He found it charming she still got embarrassed as a new bride whenever he invited her to a bedroom "appointment." Still red as a beet, she said, "Well, at least now I have an excuse to wear those new PJs you got me."

Ah, yes, the Victoria's Secret see-through babydolls. This might turn out to be one of those no-sleep naps, he thought with a smile. Tired as he was, he wouldn't mind a bit. With such beautiful weather, he was surprised to hear his next-door neighbor's backup generator running as he pulled into his driveway. Missing its muffler, it was almost as loud as the Charger. That meant there was a power failure, and the buck stopped at Mason's desk for any power problem in the state that couldn't be solved at a lower level. He hoped he wouldn't be summoned to the office on Valentine's Day, just after he'd secured a bedroom appointment with his wife.

Mason could hear their own backup generator running. If his neighbor's power was out, it made sense his would be too. But *why* was it out? The weather wasn't hot enough for everyone to crank up the AC, and there weren't any signs of a tornado. A drunk driver might have taken out a pole, but it was early in the day for someone to be that drunk, even in Oklahoma. He held the door for Angie as she exited the car. They had just started toward the house when his cell phone played his favorite ringtone, Lady Antebellum's "I Need You Now." The ID showed a call from Jesse Burke, so he signaled to Angie he'd take the call outside.

Jesse was more than his right-hand man at work. They'd grown up together and even entered local rodeos when they were teenagers, but they never competed directly. Mason specialized in calf-roping, while his friend wrestled steers. Jesse was what you'd call a man's man. He picked up street fighting about the same time as steer wrestling, which quickly morphed into mixed martial arts. Between the two hobbies, Jesse turned into a force to be reckoned with.

Jesse knew it too. Occasionally, Mason needed to remind him to tone down the machismo on the job. It was fine for protecting Mason's ass if they ran into trouble at a bar, but he didn't need to exercise his manliness on the lowly plant techs. Jesse deferred to Mason's brains when better judgment was called for, and between his brains and Jesse's brawn, they'd had a good partnership for more than thirty years.

Mason answered the call. "Jesse, wassup?"

"We got a problem, and it's not funny. We've lost the Internet between every one of our power plants."

"Huh?" Mason wondered what could have gone wrong. Each plant had a control room, and each of these was linked via the Internet to a central control station located just south of Oklahoma City. Had Central lost contact with all of them? Maybe he needed to make a trip to Central. Rather than moving to the city center to preside over the central control station, Mason opted to work out of the Newcastle station on the outskirts. It meant he was one step removed from the action, but he didn't mind. No matter where he was, everyone knew Mason was the boss. Working remotely also allowed him to enjoy living in a much smaller town with a country feel to it, something both he and Angie preferred.

Balancing power distribution between all the plants feeding the grid wasn't nearly as hard as it used to be. In the old days, bringing a local plant online was a very delicate, manual operation. The AC generators needed to slow down or speed up until their output phase synced with the grid before they could be switched online. If they couldn't sync up, a phase mismatch would cause the network to overpower the plant's generators. The consequences could be minimal or disastrous, depending on how out of sync they were. If the phase was only slightly off, the generators would groan and shake. Hearing the groans of tons of metal under stress and watching it all shake was scary enough, but a more substantial mismatch could destroy a generator altogether. At that point, all hell would break loose. After several generator rebellions and one serious burn accident, the state required them to stop bringing plants online manually. They were forced to find a safer way to do it with less collateral damage.

The Internet turned out to provide the best solution. It enabled all the plants to be phased in and controlled with precision by a computer from a central point. No more human error, no more generator problems. But if they didn't have Internet access, as Jesse was reporting, Central could lose control, and by law they would have to take the generators offline. That didn't sound good, and it didn't bode well for restoring power to Oklahoma anytime soon.

Jesse yelled through the phone, "Mason, we gotta get reconnected with Central Control! Either that, or we go back to manual, but I don't think anybody here remembers how except maybe me."

"Where are you?" Mason interrupted Jesse's rant.

"I'm at Plant Four today. We've been on emergency power since noon."

Mason's mind was still racing to take in all this information when he realized he should apprise Jesse of his own situation. "I lost power here at home, too, and I get mine from Plant One. What the hell is going on? Did you check the news?"

"The TV in the break room says, 'No Signal,' and the landline phone is dead. That's why I'm calling you from my cell. But you know what's weird? I can't get on the Internet at all, not even from my cell."

"Sounds like our Internet is down. Did you call Ok-Net? We pay enough for their damn crappy service for them to at least keep the Internet up! That custom high-speed fiber-optic setup isn't worth shit. I knew that was gonna be a waste of money when they talked us into it!"

Jesse jumped in, "But Ok-Net has nothing to do with my cell. Something else must be happening. Something bizarre!"

"Whatever else might be going on, Ok-Net is Southern Power's Internet provider. They must know something. I'll call them myself and get right back to you. Stay offline until I call back."

"Hey!" Mason had something to add. "A word to the wise, Jesse—I know how much you like to show off, but don't even think about trying to manually go back on the grid. That's too dangerous, and by law we have to stay offline until we figure this out."

"Aye-aye, Cap'n. You're the brains. I'm just the brawn," Jesse recited, as he had hundreds of times before. Despite the emergency, Mason had to smile to himself.

Ok-Net provided not only the Internet but Voice Over the Internet Protocol (VOIP) for the telephones and the cable link for the TV. If Ok-Net was down, that would explain everything except Jesse's cell phone. Not being able to go online from his cell was a separate mystery.

Mason stepped out of the sun so he could see his cell phone screen. He found the number for Ok-Net and called.

"This is Mason Branner from Southern Power of Oklahoma. I need to talk to a supervisor ASAP."

"This is Julie. I'm your Tier-3 supervisor. Nice of you to finally call."

"What do you mean by that? What's going on?"

Julie responded sarcastically, "As if you don't know. We're on backup because we lost our power—again. Our equipment's fine, but our customers are saying they can't connect."

"Customers like us," Mason complained.

"You guys are out too? Right. Well, what happened to the power?"

"Don't know yet," Mason replied. "Has anything else gone wrong today?"

Julie pondered for a second. "Hmmm, you know, come to think of it, our incoming news link and the AP wire are dead too. We thought it had to do with the power problem, but I just remembered they're just incoming lines. They don't need our power. So why did they both quit on me?"

Mason was ready to end the call. He probably wouldn't be able to keep his appointment with Angie—there would be too many interruptions. He could at least go inside and rub her feet between phone calls, but he was still stuck outside.

Julie interrupted his reverie. "Why did you ask me what else went wrong today? What's the real story here?"

Mason said, "I was hoping you could tell us."

"Us tell you? We're in the dark just like you are." Julie couldn't resist letting out a little snicker. "Sorry, I couldn't resist."

Everyone's a comedian, Mason said to himself with a sigh. He knew there was something just out of reach that he wasn't seeing. It was like the feeling you get when a word is on the tip of your tongue but you can't think of it.

"Look, I really don't know what's going on. I'll see what I can find out and let you know. Meanwhile, call me if you hear anything useful." Mason gave her his cell number.

He turned around to face the house. Angie was framed in the doorway with a towel around her wet hair and a bathrobe over what Mason suspected were the new babydolls. She took the towel off her hair, shook her hair out around her shoulders, and untied her robe so it hung loosely over her lingerie, framing her curves perfectly. She looked at Mason expectantly, batting her lashes ever so slightly.

Damn! Damn! It's always about the timing. She is not going to be happy with me.

Mason held up an open hand to hold her at a distance because his cell was ringing like a Klaxon bell. A few seconds later, an emergency alert message popped up on the screen:

EMERGENCY NOTICE
FIRE, POLICE, AND EMERGENCY VEHICLES DISPATCHED TO
SOUTHERN POWER—OKLAHOMA—PLANT #4.
MANDATORY EVACUATION IF YOU ARE IN THE AREA.
GET INFORMATION AT YOUR LOCAL POLICE STATION.

Plant Four! He immediately dialed Jesse's cell. It rang and rang until Mason was sure it would go to voicemail. Just in time, Jesse picked up.

"Jesse, you okay?" Mason asked.

At 250 pounds and more macho than Arnold Schwarzenegger, Jesse was trying to keep his voice from giving away how close he was to real tears. "I screwed up bad this time. I'm sorry, bro. I know you said not to mess with the generators, but I remembered how to sync them to the grid. I had all four of them in sync. They were begging to go back online." Jesse sighed. "I must have been off, though, 'cuz when I tried . . . shit, Mason, it just blew up!"

"Silence, Jesse. Take a deep breath. Right now. That's an order."

Mason heard Jesse gulp for air, swallow, and take a breath.

Jesse let out another big sigh, shaky at the edges, then told Mason in a halting voice, almost a monotone, "Two of the turbines let go and busted through their containment walls. Christ. Like bombs going off. The steam safeties kicked in, but it was too late." Jesse continued in that eerie, dead-sounding voice, "Mason . . . I watched Jorge, the new tech, get scalded by one of those firebombs of hot water.

He was right in front of me. It was . . . I think he's dead. It was . . ."

Now it was Mason's turn to gasp. A breach of the containment wall was catastrophic in its own right, but if that fractured the natural gas feeds, and if the transformers exploded, that could destroy the entire plant. That explained the evacuation. No one would be safe! *Dammit! I told him not to try to get anything back online.*

Jesse continued in a voice that sounded like it was coming from far away, still with that dead, monotone quality. Mason wondered if he was in shock. "We were standing so close. If it had been just slightly to the right, it would have been me. It hit him right in the face . . . you should have heard his scream . . . then the fire hit . . . there was nothing I could do. It should have been me. Why Jorge? His wife just had a kid. Jesus Christ. What the hell could I do?"

Mason was silent, not knowing what words could make things better.

"That scream, Mason, I'll never forget that scream . . ."

***

Two Days Later

February 16

Wells, England

The Internet had been down for two days when Hollis Buckley decided it was time to snoop around town. Hollis, Edna, and their goats were plenty satisfied with things just as they were before the arrival of the Internet. Even after they got the Internet for their home, Hollis spent very little time online and didn't really care when it went down. "It's all high-tech rubbish," he would say.

But Edna, his wife, was worried. And when Edna worried, she clucked and she hovered. Hollis didn't mind the clucking really—he had heard it many times—but he didn't care to be hovered over.

A townsfolk meeting was scheduled for that night, and he figured he would go for a change and find out the latest on the Internet situation. He'd like to bring Edna some good news if he could, so she'd stop hovering.

Like the rest of Wells, he used the Internet mostly to keep track of his bank balance, and that was about it. Folks weren't much interested in the latest technology in these parts. Hollis hadn't wanted to put their little nest egg in a bank. That meant he would have to monitor it on the Internet. Why couldn't he continue to keep it under the mattress, where he could count it by hand whenever he wanted?

Edna was convinced it would be safer in the bank. What if there was a fire or a burglary? The more she thought about it, the more she worried something would happen to their money in that mattress. She clucked and hovered over Hollis until he finally gave in and deposited their funds in the bank.

But with the Internet down for so long, Edna wanted Hollis to go to the bank and take their money back out. Maybe the mattress was a better solution after all.

"The bigger and more complicated things get, the more that can go bonkers," Hollis said, as he did at least once each day. "Not sure why I ever bothered to listen to you in the first place," he muttered under his breath in Edna's general direction.

"Did you say something, Hollis, dearie?" Edna chirped. Hollis didn't reply.

They finished packing a few things in their old Land Rover, including some blankets (the Rover's heater hadn't worked in years). Soon, they were on their way to Lloyd's Bank in downtown Wells.

About an hour later (Hollis didn't drive that old Land Rover over 45 kmh), they reached the main intersection of Wells. Hollis hated the town, especially when he couldn't find a parking place anywhere close to the bank.

As he rounded the last corner, he did a double take. Coming into view were at least a hundred people queued up in front of the bank.

Hollis and Edna parked as best they could, got out of the Rover, and walked toward the crowd. Hollis was about to walk by an elderly gentleman when the classic navy homburg he had on his head caught Hollis's eye.

Hollis gestured towards the man's head. "Felt or wool?" he asked.

"Felt, of course," the man sniffed, clearly insulted by the implication.

"'Scuse me, guv," Hollis offered. "Didn't mean to offend. I was actually admiring it." Hollis smiled and held his hand out. "Hollis Buckley."

The other gentleman reluctantly held his out for a weak handshake and responded, "Alastair Thompson—Thompson with a P."

"Mind telling me why all these folks are standing in the cold here?" Hollis asked.

"Well, sir, the bloody bank says we can't have our money right now. Something about the bloody Internet! They must think we're all so filthy rich we don't mind living without a pound in our pocket. I, for one, am staying put right here until they hand my money over. And they best be quick about it!"

Hollis looked at the queue. Standing outside the bank in this climate was not a good option. Hollis thanked the man and guided Edna through the crowd to the bank's entrance, only to be blocked by a uniformed bobby.

"No one allowed to approach the counters," the bobby said, then handed Hollis a flier from the top of the stack he held.

> This office carries a minimal amount of cash for security reasons.
> The Internet is required for all ATM and
> bank transactions over 100 pounds sterling.
> There is currently no Internet connection.
> Bank withdrawals under 100 pounds sterling will be handled in person
> every morning from 8 to 9 o'clock until communications are restored.

Hollis and Edna had no choice but to go back outside. Thompson was standing there. Hollis waved the note in front of him and asked, "What's all this about?"

Thompson studied the note for a minute. "That note is just to cover their arse. If the Internet is down, the banks can't talk to each other. So, they're saying we can't get more than a hundred pounds until it comes back up. Not that I'm going to let them get away with that excuse!" Thompson finished gruffly.

"But is our money safe?" Hollis asked.

"Supposedly." Thompson looked up from the note and into Hollis's eyes. "But who really knows?"

To his left, Hollis was certain he heard Edna cluck.

***

February 17

Kewanee, Illinois

Daryl Walker's daughter, Lucy, had rented the Kewanee social hall to hold a surprise party for her father's seventieth birthday.

The guest of honor was sulking in a chair still decorated with pink ribbons and red hearts left over from the annual Valentine's Day party two days ago. Daryl lived just outside of town, where he occupied himself with his ham radio most of the time.

Daryl had yet to say a single word to anyone.

His reputation as the town's curmudgeon was well-deserved. When anyone came onto his property, instead of shouting out "Hello! Who's there?", he preferred to fire a few warning shots into the air from whichever gun was handy. That habit tended to discourage socializing, which suited both him and the townspeople just fine.

Lucy knew she was pushing the envelope for anyone to come to a party for Daryl. It wasn't just his personality, although that would have been enough, but the streets were filled with six-foot snowdrifts from the brutal storm they'd had for almost a week. No one was going outside unless they absolutely had to.

Fortunately, a few people showed up, so Daryl didn't have to be humiliated. Daryl would have said he couldn't care less, but Lucy knew there used to be a heart inside the old crab. She had encountered it frequently before her mom passed away.

Five members of Lucy and Daryl's family and one local cop sat around the social hall's table. Daryl sat in the head chair, just hoping the festivities would end quickly.

Then, without a sound, they were blanketed in darkness.

Daryl stood up and turned around to look out the window. With no streetlights, he could barely see Main Street, but he saw enough to exclaim his first words of the evening: "Crap. The whole damn town looks dead! My radio gear better not be toast, or there'll be hell to pay!"

Lucy's little brother, Butch, turned on the hall's battery-operated shortwave radio to eavesdrop on the police channel. The police sounded as confused about the power outage as everyone else. All Butch could make out was that the Internet and the power were out all over.

With that kind of no-news news, they'd never be able to find out what was really going on. After ten more minutes of hearing the police rehash the few facts they already knew, Daryl snapped at Butch to shut off the damn radio. He had a few more choice words for him too.

Lucy frowned at her father, avoiding the hurt look on Butch's face. In her mid-forties and a natural peacemaker, Lucy had approached her father frequently throughout the last twenty years about the way he treated Butch. Their mom had died of a hemorrhage giving birth to Butch, and Daryl had somehow related that to the boy. Butch had mental development issues, but he was basically a good boy who didn't make any trouble.

Lucy didn't want Butch's psyche destroyed by Daryl's coldness. She had moved Butch in with her family when he was in his late teens. Nowadays, Daryl took his resentment out on the entire town instead, but when Butch was around, he was often the primary target.

Everyone said their goodnights and moved quickly to their vehicles to get home and see if their heaters were working. Nighttime temperatures in February were no joke in Illinois.

Two days passed, and Kewanee began to resemble a ghost town. A few people left to seek accommodations out of town, hoping to find power until the storm blew over, but most of the townsfolk were leery about using gasoline to drive any distance. Local gas stations couldn't operate since there was no power, and it was anyone's guess if gas stations in other towns had fuel or could access it. Would they find gas two towns away? Would they find anyone alive two towns away?

People were starting to huddle in the police station and anywhere else that had backup generators. At first, the power outage had been a change of pace for the small town, a bit of an adventure, but even though they could get temporary power from the generators and were used to heavy storms, no Internet, no television, no cell coverage, and no radio, it got boring soon enough, then frustrating.

Something one step short of panic was setting in. Losing electricity during a mid-winter storm was not uncommon, but losing all communication with the rest of the world was downright spooky.

In the police station, in front of the wall heater running on a portable generator, Officer Ken Griffin broke the silence. He said what everyone was thinking, but no one wanted to address. "Daryl Walker is a ham radio guy. I bet he could find out what's happening. He has a generator too."

Met only with utter silence and averted eyes, Ken said he'd drive out to Daryl's and float that idea, figuring Daryl wouldn't shoot a police officer—at least not on purpose. Maybe.

No one volunteered to go with him.

Thirty minutes later, Ken drove up to Daryl's place with his high beams on, beeping the horn so Daryl wouldn't be surprised. It was never a good idea to surprise Daryl.

Daryl peered out from the front door, his double-barreled shotgun slung over his shoulder like an ax. It was late morning, and the air was as cold as a mother-in-law's kiss, but at least it had stopped snowing for the moment, and the wind had calmed down.

"Daryl, Officer Griffin here," Ken shouted from his car. He hoped Daryl noticed he was in a black-and-white. "Got a minute?"

"For what? I don't have power, so no damn radio. Can't you see that? Go back to your station and leave me the hell alone."

"Hang on, Daryl. We can't seem to contact anyone to find out what's going on," Ken continued as though Daryl hadn't objected. "We were hoping you'd heard from someone by now on your amateur radio gear. We thought you had a generator."

"My generator's out too. No power means no radio."

"Did the generator quit, or did you just run out of fuel? We could bring more fuel."

"Damn piece of shit seized up. Never started when the weather was this cold anyway. Piece of imported shit," Daryl reiterated.

"We could lend you a portable generator. There's a six-kilowatt at the station. Would that work?"

Daryl thought for a moment. "Seems to me you should be willing to let me use it for a while if I get you what you want." Daryl was always ready to take advantage of any situation for his own benefit.

"I'm sure we can work something out. Why don't I just go get it? Will the six-kilowatt be enough to power your equipment?"

"Bring it, but you'd better bring someone with you," Daryl replied. "You'll have to shovel some snow to get to my piece-of-shit generator. It's in the backyard buried under a drift. You'll need to jerry-rig it to the six kilowatt. But just one other person. No more. Got that?"

Ken saluted and drove off to get the generator, some extra fuel to be safe, and someone to help him clear a path to the generator. Butch was at Lucy's house and willing. Ken picked him up in the four-wheel drive police pickup. They loaded the generator with extra fuel and drove back to Daryl's.

Two hours later, Ken and Butch had chipped through the ice and completed the shoveling, but they were so cold that all they wanted to do was plant themselves in front of Daryl's fire to defrost. Ken wasn't surprised that during the entire time he and Butch had slaved away in the cold, Daryl had stayed inside drinking bourbon.

Ken would have killed for a small shot to warm up his insides, but he knew that was stepping over the line. Daryl was just ornery enough to report him to the police commissioner for drinking on the job. Ken consoled himself that at least he was inside in front of a fire. The good news was the six-kilowatt generator was running and temporarily wired in.

Butch let out a whoop of celebration. "What's next?" he asked.

Daryl snapped at him, "Hold your damn horses, for Chrissake. This old ham gear has vacuum tubes. They've gotta warm up. Jesus, you better learn some patience, boy, before you piss off someone dangerous."

Butch and Ken exchanged looks.

As the vacuum tubes slowly warmed up, Daryl began tuning the receiver, listening for anything at all. He ran through the amateur radio bands slowly and methodically, one after another. All they heard were a few squeals, beeps, and hissing noises.

"Sounds like AM," said Ken.

"So what?" barked Daryl with a resentful attitude. "Nothing wrong with AM radio. Those FM and SSB guys are just appliance operators. Real hams still use AM and CW! Are you just going to sit there and bitch? And CW is Morse code for you, Butch . . . dumbass."

Butch should have just kept quiet, but he asked anyway, "What's SSB?"

"Single Side Band, but in your case, it stands for stupid son of a bitch."

Ken saw that coming, but Daryl was too fast.

"This damn receiver better not be toast. Cost me two grand," Daryl muttered to himself.

"What about transmitting?" Ken asked. "We might be able to contact somebody. Worth a try, right? Let's see who's out there."

Daryl, with a sneer on his face, just leaned back. He didn't like being told what to do. After a short delay, he keyed the button on the microphone and started adjusting a few dials. The lights dimmed just as the transmitter sucked the power from the six-kilowatt.

"All that damn snow has changed the loading on the goddamn antenna. It'll take me a bit to get the SWR right." He looked at Butch. "That's standing wave ratio, dumbass."

Once Daryl was satisfied, he pulled the microphone up to his mouth, keyed the transmitter again, and spoke. "CQ, CQ, CQ, K9DAZ in Kewanee, Illinois, calling CQ."

He released the switch and heard only the hiss again. Daryl repeated the sequence of steps several times, trying different bands and frequencies. It was mostly static and dead air.

Ken was the first to hear the voice. It was a weak signal, but it was a ham operator, which meant it was human. Maybe they'd finally get an explanation for what the hell was going on.

Excited at first, their faces fell one by one as they listened to the ham operator from the outside world fill them in on the news.

It wasn't good.

Preface

Richard Braddock here, retired high-tech private investigator. Emphasis on "retired."

After forty-some-odd years riding the roller-coaster life of a big-city, high-tech private eye, it was hard at first to adjust to the sluggish pace of retirement. I moved from San Francisco to a condo in the burbs near San Jose, where demands on my time and energy were minimal.

These days, I wake up, brew some java, get dressed if there's a reason to, check the news, read email, and maybe eat something left over from the night before. After expending all that energy, I've been known to lie back down for a nap.

Most of my home maintenance chores are taken care of for me. Someone else cuts the grass, waters the plants, and comes inside twice a week to move the dust around. They change the sheets, load the dishwasher, and send my dress shirts out to be cleaned and pressed on the rare occasion I wear one.

As I was forewarned, I've begun to experience the typical aches and pains of aging. My knees make a clicking sound sometimes if I have to squat down to pick something up from the floor, and I avoid stairs when I can. Why put extra stress on the joints? I don't jump up from an easy chair quite as nimbly as I used to either. Not that there is much to jump for anyway.

My memory is not what it once was, which everybody told me to expect, but I can't remember why. I'm in bed before ten most nights, only to wake up again at four in the morning to pee. And I've developed a strange addiction to old episodes of *Gunsmoke* and *Matlock*, which are usually on the rerun channels when I come back to bed at that hour.

Overall, though, I'm still in reasonably good physical health. I'm not so sure about my mental health, but some would argue it was never sound in the first place.

Retirement seemed like it was going to be a bit of a letdown after the life I'd led. As they say, "I used to be somebody"—at least, in my area of specialization. My fame was confined to the high-tech investigative world.

My obsession with technology began before I can remember. As a kid, I graduated from taking the family television apart (much to the dismay of my mother) and putting it back together again (to her great relief) to experimenting with semiconductors and software as I grew older. I ultimately earned a reputation as a bona fide geek.

In the sixties, I spent some time in the military during Vietnam, where I was assigned to a group that worked with cryptography equipment. That exposed me to ciphers and code-breaking and security issues that fit right in with the electronic developments of the time. Later, after I became a private citizen again, the aspect of using my software background to ferret out security breaches appealed to me. I became well-known rather quickly because I could use technology in ways other gumshoes couldn't.

While other PI's were lagging in the high-tech arena, I was hacking, decrypting, surveilling, and employing drone photography. It became a contest between my technical skills and those of the high-tech outlaws, an ever-growing, ever-smarter segment of the criminal population. To stay ahead of them, I made sure to keep current with the latest technology, as it seemed to change every six months.

Along the way, I achieved a level of financial independence. That provided for most of my needs, or at least the material ones. Like many technologists, I wasn't comfortable in social situations, and relationships with women were fun but mostly short-lived. My work was a convenient buffer. Eventually, when I was forty-five, a woman did manage to get through the parapets I had up, much to the surprise of everyone who knew me—and myself, for that matter.

Although we never married, I found I enjoyed the comforts of cohabitation (I wouldn't go so far as to call it intimacy), even if I rarely showed my romantic side. I automatically prioritized my work ahead of everything else out of habit, and the relationship suffered more than I knew. I would leave on an assignment at the drop of a hat, and due to security concerns, I may not have been able to call. Sometimes I was restricted from discussing my work even after I returned. This was no way to foster a relationship, and as you might expect, we parted ways when I was fifty years old.

After we broke up, I told myself that now I'd have more time to focus on my work, but that wasn't much consolation compared to a warm body next to me in bed every night. As I aged, the number of assignments started to dwindle. And when I wasn't working, loneliness started to rear its ugly head. Had I thrown away my only chance at real happiness?

My line of work didn't lend itself to meeting women—at least women who weren't criminals. I fumbled for conversation topics with women who were viable relationship material. Unfortunately, few of them genuinely cared about Moore's law of exponential transistor growth. I didn't expect them to comment intelligently about it, but would it hurt them to listen?

Another mark against me was my line of work: dangerous. Anyone would think twice before banking on a long-term relationship with an old risk-taker. And last but not least, I was no spring chicken either. Nope, a real catch I wasn't, sorry to say.

But I must have done something right, though, because within a few weeks of moving from the city to the burbs with an honest attempt to retire, I met Lara at the pool table in the senior club room. She was an independent woman who brought the fun back into my life. An artist and musician, Lara's creative right brain and my OCD left brain met with surprising compatibility somewhere in the middle. The clouds had parted, and a beam of hope shined down.

Widowed Lara missed adult companionship as much as I did and was happy to satisfy that need exclusively with me, but conveniently, she wasn't eager to get married—at least not yet. She had her own condo in the complex not far from mine and had turned her second bedroom into an art studio.

She quickly fell into the habit of spending more than half her nights with me, and I realized, to my surprise, I wouldn't mind if she moved in altogether. With three bedrooms, my place was plenty big enough for both of us, but she seemed to cherish her independence.

Maybe she was waiting for me to make an honest woman out of her. I didn't think so, but I didn't want to raise the question. What if she expected me to propose immediately after I brought it up? I wasn't sure I was ready for that, so the topic remained offshore and untouched.

Meanwhile, I could live with the current setup. I was never quite sure which nights Lara was going to come over and which nights she'd get caught up in her art until she fell asleep at her easel. I'd given her a key so she could come and go as she wished, and I admit I was overjoyed whenever I felt her slide into bed after thinking she had forgotten me for the night. Sometimes, after snuggling up against me for a few minutes, she would turn over and reach for me. She hadn't forgotten me at all.

When I first began to think about retiring (or so I told myself), I sold a gaming app I'd invented that had remained pretty popular. It provided enough money to build a secure, nonflammable retirement facility to work from. It was state-of-the-art for the time, with HD cameras, automatic alarm systems, full backup power, and all the expected accoutrements. Eventually, even that secure office began to show its age, as do all things high tech, but no one else could tell.

Although planning had always been a critical part of my private investigative process, I hadn't spent any time planning what I would do with this fancy Fort Knox of an office when I ultimately retired for good. It had been a hub of activity for a while, but post-retirement, I'd wake up and not have a clue how I would spend the day.

In this period of semi-retirement, during my BL days (before Lara), as I like to call them, I'd drive into town to my secure man cave. But there would be no software designs to work on, no investigation projects to plan, no meetings to attend, no phone calls to prepare for. It was beginning to feel like I was unemployed.

Then a fellow named Travis Brown contacted me.

Travis turned out to be a six-foot-five, 250-pound, burly, thuggish-looking forty-five-year-old with ample body hair spouting from every one of his exposed crevices. Crisp black slacks, a bright-blue shirt with the top three buttons open, no tie, and two Italian gold chains hanging around his neck that looked in danger of getting snagged in that chest hair (a painful thought). He was the epitome of cool for his generation and social standing, whatever that was.

He was worried his trophy wife, Trisha, was having an affair, but he had no evidence. He said he just "felt it." Sometimes, he said, he'd call her on her cell and could tell she was with someone, but she wouldn't say who. Or she would say she hadn't been out, but the hood of her car would be warm.

He showed me her picture—a beautiful, well-attired woman in her early thirties. I couldn't imagine why she wouldn't want to cuddle up with Travis, maybe comb his back hair while she was at it.

"Could you monitor her online activities?" he asked. "Maybe record her phone calls, install a GPS on her car—basically find out what she does while I'm at work or busy?"

All that was possible, of course, but some of his requests were illegal without a warrant. I let Travis know that, but he insisted he needed solid proof that the only problem was his paranoia. I told him clearly that I would not break any laws, but I would do my best to find out what was going on. I assured him that domestic issues like this can be resolved with basic investigative techniques that I would bet my reputation on. He was assured if I didn't find any sign of cheating, he could be sure I hadn't missed anything.

He was a happy guy when I gave him good news two weeks later, but first I asked him how he felt about his mother-in-law.

"That old bag? She's a real pain in my ass. I'm glad she doesn't come over anymore. I had to put my foot down," Travis said gruffly. "Trisha completely ignores me when her mother shows up, and she rushes around to get her every little thing she might want. One night I had to wait fifteen minutes for her mother to finish telling some old, stupid story about when Trisha was a little girl before Trisha noticed I wanted seconds from dinner. I don't like being in second place behind her mother."

I showed him some photos of Trisha and her mother having lunch, shopping, at a yoga class. She was never with another man.

"This is why you felt like she was hiding something from you. Your instincts were good. She was hiding something. She had to. Maybe you should just agree to let her see her mom outside the house. Then she won't have to sneak around or lie to you. Those aren't habits you want her to get comfortable with."

Travis contemplated that idea for a minute. "You're probably right. I'll think about it. But you're sure she wasn't cheating?"

"Nope. Just hanging out with her mom. Besides, a woman who pays attention to her mother when she's old is more likely to take care of you when you're old. It's a basic characteristic of a good woman."

"Okay, okay. I got it, man. Spare me the lecture."

Travis was grinning. He paid me in cash, with a nice bonus to boot, shook my hand hard, and bounced out of the office with a much lighter step than I'd seen on him before.

There were some pleasant aspects of this job, I thought to myself, especially when I could deliver good news.

It was unfortunate that soon I would have to kill two people I didn't even know.

***

My last assignment before I retired (although I didn't know it would be my last) was for a group of clients I simply referred to as "the Agency." I'm not sure how legitimate they were, but it entailed government security and various other things they said would be better if I didn't know. They hired me to get information on an elaborate embezzlement and money-laundering scheme, codenamed "Farley." Lots of PI work with a fair amount of travel kept me busy to the point of exhaustion.

The sophistication of these Farley criminals was head and shoulders above the typical local yokels. Electronic wire transfers using the latest encryption and behind-the-scenes, automatic bookkeeping adjustments made the slow drip of money into multiple offshore accounts almost imperceptible. I had no idea who was behind all this.

I managed to figure out the basics of what was going on by decrypting personal transmissions—something the official security agencies could not do without a warrant. I, however, did what I had to do and started to stack up the evidence.

Finally, as they said on the old TV show *Hawaii Five-0*, I had enough damning evidence gathered to be able to tell the agency, "Book 'em, Danno!" Some of the data I uncovered was unusual in that it came from the highest levels of government. That made me very nervous, so I was glad to wash my hands of the case, which my trusted government contacts had warned me not to take in the first place as too dangerous.

While taking a break in my office one night, my detectors showed activity outside. Usually, such action wouldn't amount to much, since parking was free on the public street, and there was a well-frequented bar down the street. Nevertheless, any movement automatically switched on my video feed.

I watched a fellow exit a car, and the vehicle drove off. No big deal, but then, in the time it took for that car to drive around the corner, a similar car drove up, stopped, and let another guy out. The vehicles never parked. They were clearly dropping the two off separately, but something gave me a sense they were together. Had they come to partner on a job?

My antennae were up.

My video cameras always automatically tracked people using AI software, but I didn't see anyone onscreen anymore. If these fellows were walking down the street to the bar, the cameras should have been tracking them, but there was no sign of these guys. It was like they had vanished into thin air.

Another video feed covering the front entrance of my building and the access to my office also showed no activity. Suddenly, without so much as a squeaky hinge, my head was slammed back and held with a rubber cord.

My arms were seized and tied behind me by a second person, and someone started barking out orders. Still, I couldn't see anyone, either on-screen or in person.

"Okay, Braddock, let's log on," a voice barked.

"Log on to what?" I queried, trying to exude a calm manner while the rope tightened against my forehead.

The goon leaned in closer, intending to project a threatening posture. Almost close enough to kiss me, his bad breath and body odor invaded my nostrils like stinky insect spray. When was the last time he had showered or brushed his teeth? A week at least, I guessed.

"You're in no position to be a wiseass if you ever want to type with those fingers again," he whispered in my face, as though he had read my thoughts. "Quit playing around. Just log on—and by the way, did we tell you? We have a record of your login keystrokes on this flash drive."

How the hell could they have recorded my login keystrokes?

But I was ready for them. I didn't have OCD for nothing! In a prior attack of paranoia, I had set up a parallel login site that looked and acted exactly like my real site. It just didn't contain the pointers to any sensitive data (pointers are what the system uses to find files). All I had to do was log on, even using my correct password, but be sure to "accidentally" make at least one small typo.

That typo would signal my system there was a security breach. Immediately, an automatic shut-down of all operations would begin. Besides shutting down, it would move files, overwrite disks with false information, and notify the authorities. I also installed facial recognition and automated armament, which under certain circumstances, would even aim and shoot unrecognized invaders. Pretty cool security system, right? As long as it could recognize me.

The best high-tech part about it was that my sensitive data wouldn't really be deleted at all. Most people don't realize deleted files are not entirely deleted; only the pointers to the files are removed. There are many examples where government officials attempted to hide objectionable correspondences by deleting files and emails, not realizing that when a savvy IT guy restores the pointers, the data comes right back. That's how Trump's hooligans (or the Russians, depending on whom you believe) were able to read emails and leak their content to the press.

The only surefire way to delete information for good is to write new data into the old space. Hard to do from outside the system, but not impossible if you know what you're doing—and I know what I'm doing. But I wasn't going to do that to my system. If the system detected a break-in, I wanted the data to look deleted, but I needed to be able to retrieve it when the danger was over.

However, these assailants had come prepared with a duplicate of the keystrokes I used to log in. If they typed it in themselves, I wouldn't get the chance to use my typo trick to shut everything down and protect the data. If they completed the sequence with no typo, the operating system would think it was me logging in and potentially open the floodgates.

How did they get my login keystrokes in the first place? That bothered me. I'd have to check into that later, because right now, it looked like it was going to be a rough night at the office.

Sure as shit, the brutes logged in using my keystrokes. When they got to a security portal, the smelly guy said he would untie my arms so I could take it from there. I still had no idea who these thugs were or what they were looking for, but he filled that void quickly.

"Once you get in, copy the Farley files to this flash drive."

Crap. The Farley assignment had exposed me to people and organizations I didn't previously know existed. I wish I didn't know they existed. This visit was something I had been half-expecting and worried about ever since I dug into the case.

"Obviously, I can't go there," was my response.

The goon who was about to untie me stopped.

"You'll go wherever we want you to go, and remember, we have a record of your previous access, so we could get in ourselves if we have to. Why don't you make it easy on all of us and just do it?"

So, even though they had a record of my keystrokes, they thought they might still need me for some reason.

Maybe they assumed there were other protocols to follow besides keystrokes—things like time limits, built-in delays, or operations that couldn't be recorded on their keystroke log. These goons were savvier than the old guys I meet at the monthly seniors' lunch.

While I remained strapped in my chair, they pushed me to the console and spun me around so I could see the screen.

The second thug untied me. I could tell his hands were thick and sweaty, and he was no better smelling than the first guy.

"Go on!" he said.

They waited for me to act while I debated with myself. Finally, I said, "Okay, but first I'm going to give you an outline of how this works, so you won't think I'm bullshitting you. After I click the close button on that red dialog box, I have three seconds to enter a code. When I've done that, I wait about five seconds until another dialog box pops up, asking for another code. I'm not supposed to click anywhere in the box. I just type the code on the keyboard. It won't show on the screen either. I'll press enter, but nothing will be displayed. It will look as though the system isn't aware I've done anything. I need you to know that this will happen.

"But if I wait for about ten seconds, the red border around the box will turn green. That tells me the server has acknowledged my request. Ten seconds is a long time, but it's to discourage high-speed hackers."

Smelly Guy was going to follow in the keystroke log. Then he barked out, "Do it, asshole!"

The other guy held a gun to my temple as I massaged my fingers to get the blood flowing again. As they watched, I stiffly typed. They followed my steps. The border eventually turned green with the cursor blinking in an open field.

As quickly as the green border showed up, it went away.

"What's up?" Smelly Guy asked, suddenly suspicious.

The other guy pushed that gun to my head harder and said, "These geeky tech guys aren't worth shit!"

I responded to both of them, "Hold on. Relax. The system was just waiting for a keyboard entry. No entry within two seconds automatically exits the routine."

Meanwhile, one of the video feeds showed the arrival of a Yellow Cab outside. Two men exited and walked in the direction of the bar down the street. The three of us watched them without alarm.

We prepared to go through the login steps again. They hit the keys this time, and soon they were pleased to be greeted with that green border. In their minds, they were within a few seconds of accessing the prized Farley data.

A thick, off-colored gas flooded the office. Then, two shots rang out very close to me. That's the last thing I remember.

When I woke up on the floor, I was surrounded by a circle of men in familiar trench coats. Agency guys, one of whom was an old contact of mine named Charlie. Didn't they know the trench coats made them look like a cliché?

I had a killer headache, my neck was stiff, my eyelids were stuck together, my breathing was rough, and the skin on my wrists was mottled. I grabbed the wastebasket in front of me and threw up last night's pizza.

That felt better.

"Braddock, you idiot," Charlie addressed me. "When are you going to realize you can't protect yourself anymore? You're old and obsolete. Five more minutes, and you'd be toast along with the data. And by the way, what's the status of the data? Or don't you know?"

"Do we know how they got in?" I asked.

"No idea. The security door was still double-locked and coded. Any chance you forgot to lock the front door like you sometimes forget to turn off your left turn signal? Old guys do that, you know."

I wasn't going to dignify that statement with a reply.

"But what about the data?" he went on. "We couldn't care less about the bugs in your lame security system."

"Don't worry. The data is secure. It was never in danger."

"What makes you so sure?"

"The goons thought they could log in with a recording of my keystrokes, but part of the login protocol is a separate operation that can't be recorded, which they didn't have. When the operating system didn't see that sequence, it went into lockdown, even though the display looked normal. If it hadn't done that, you and I wouldn't be having this lovely chat right now."

I added, "By the way, who are they?"

"You mean who *were* they. We don't know yet, but we will soon. Both shot in the head by that AI targeting system you stole from us a few years back. We'd like to know how you avoided getting shot."

"Facial recognition. My system knows me. Good thing it shut down automatically right after that, or else when it saw your face, it would have shot you. It's programmed to shoot ugly."

Charlie yelled, "Braddock, you ungrateful son of a bitch! In case you hadn't noticed, we just saved your miserable life! Maybe it's time for you to go away and get out of my hair for a while. Your jokes aren't getting any funnier. Try some fishing up north. Do something. Anything. Just disappear from our radar for a while."

"Go to hell," I responded automatically.

He had a point though. Maybe it was time for me to take it easier. I wasn't physically able to defend myself as I used to, without injury, and my technology, while state-of-the-art when I bought it at an electronics security show, was at least a decade old. In electronics, that's like a millennium. I'd come closer to meeting my maker this time than I think I ever had before, and I blamed my out-of-date equipment and my out-of-date reactions.

While the coroner's office came and collected the bodies, I completed the paperwork to transfer my data to the agency, including access to all my encrypted sites. Tomorrow, I would sign the necessary nondisclosures, debrief them on everything I knew, and shop for a new laptop. I wanted to get email at least, and they were laying claim to the laptop I'd been using the last five years.

As we filed out of my "secure" man cave, I was the last one to leave. I took a final look around, knowing this was goodbye. Then, I shut off the lights, locked the door, and handed the key to Charlie.

It was sinking in that I was closing the most significant chapter of my life, and I didn't like it. I decided to think about it more after a hug from Lara and a good night's sleep, not knowing that I'd soon get a personal phone call from the president of the United States.

PART 1

Chapter 1

I awoke to the sound of Lara snoring softly beside me—a sound I admit I enjoyed getting used to. She always slept in after working late into the night on her art.

Thinking back over the last couple of months, I couldn't say I regretted handing the Farley case back to the Agency, but I did miss my secure man cave, even though I still didn't know why my security measures didn't stop the smelly guy invasion. Moving to the burbs, then meeting Lara and falling quickly into a full-time relationship, I'd had plenty to distract me, but I was feeling some kind of restlessness in my legs as I lay in bed thinking about it all, and it wasn't restless-legs syndrome.

Maybe it was time for me to get a part-time job. Perhaps I could be a greeter at the local Walmart, or the money-taker at the car wash, or the van driver at the local Ford dealership's service department—all great old-guy jobs. Or I could try something a little more intellectually challenging and volunteer as a docent at the nearby historical museum. I wouldn't need to study much; I was probably alive when most everything happened anyway.

But all these career decisions would just have to wait until I had my coffee. I wandered past my desk on my way to the kitchen. *Any phone messages overnight?* Nope. *Important emails?* Nope. And my secure phone didn't allow texts.

Whatever emails I got were about products guaranteed to increase the size of my penis. Why would a guy at my age need that? Maybe I should get a dog. At least he'd need me to walk him. *I think I'll clean up the kitchen leftovers before Lara wakes up.*

I was feeling lazier than usual, and Lara would stay in bed for at least another hour or two, so I figured I'd let someone else do the breakfast thing. Whenever I bothered to fix my own breakfast, my method of cooking was damn efficient. Make eggs in a nonstick skillet, so all I had to do was wipe it out with a paper towel. Use the plate from yesterday left sitting in the drip tray. Ditto for the knife, fork, and coffee cup. The problem with this approach was it only took ten minutes; whereas, if I went out, I could buy a paper and stretch out breakfast for almost two hours. Then I could think about lunch.

I decided to go out.

I was back in the condo full of breakfast and news updates by 10:00 a.m. I caught the phone as fast as I could on its last ring, thinking Lara must still be sleeping.

"Richard Braddock?"

"Yes."

"My name is Gloria. I'm an assistant to President Elliot. Mr. Elliot would like to schedule a time to talk to you."

"Right! Let me check my calendar and see what time I'm scheduled to talk to the Joint Chiefs of Staff today. As long as the president is willing to work around that time, we're good. Oh, it's a conference call with two lobbyists. Darn! Guess I can't meet with the president at all today." I hung up and wondered which old buddy of mine would take the time to set that up.

Thirty seconds later, Gloria was back on the phone.

"Mr. Braddock, I assure you this is a sincere call. How about I arrange to have President Elliot call you today in just about an hour, say at eleven o'clock your time?"

"You are talking about Paul Elliot, right?"

"Yes, he's still our president."

"Sorry, Gloria is it? I hope I didn't offend you, but I have some weird friends."

"Not a problem at all, Mr. Braddock. I understand the surprise, and your response was very humorous. If you don't mind, I'll share your feedback with a few friends around here, but we'll keep it to ourselves."

"Please don't tell the president."

"It'll be our secret. Eleven a.m. then?"

"Sure. I'll be here."

Paul Elliot and I were similar in age, and, coincidentally, we went to the same high school, but we were a few grades apart and didn't run in the same circles. So, while we weren't friends, I knew who he was and vice versa. Paul was in the drama club, was active on both the football and baseball teams, and ran for class president. I seem to recall he lost. All I had were my amateur radio activities and building projects for the next science fair. Nerds didn't hang out with wannabe class presidents or even wannabe presidents.

At precisely eleven, the phone rang, and I heard, "Hi, Dick. This is Paul Elliot. I used to call you Dickie, remember? I trust you understand that this phone call may be recorded?"

"Uh, sure. Of course."

The president continued, "You know that time when I was a senior, and you were, I think, a sophomore, and we discovered my buddy Neil had a car key that fit your dad's Plymouth? And the three of us sort of borrowed it for an hour or so?"

"Ah, yeah. I almost forgot that," I said.

Obviously, the president has researchers up the ass, but this had to be the real Paul Elliot because only he would know about that episode. It was a great personal verifier and icebreaker. I was impressed.

"I'd like to talk to you, but not about grand theft auto," Elliot continued.

Jesus Christ! The president of the United States called me and wants to talk? My typical day was about to be recast—in bronze!

"Shoot," I told him.

"I'd like to meet in private and discuss a development I could use your help on."

A "development." That didn't sound good. "Ah, sure. I guess. So, how do we do this? Is a strip search required?" I was never known for laugh-out-loud humor, more like funny, wise-ass comments. I decided I should think a little harder before I talk next time.

"Very humorous, Dick. I'll have a car with two agents pick you up about two p.m. today, if that'll work. It won't be a stretch limo, so don't hold your breath. They will verify you using the 'Script' procedure you should remember from your government days. Do you still have the card?"

"Yes. Of course. Then what?"

"They will take you to Moffett Field, where we can have a light lunch."

Moffett is a military airport located in an unincorporated part of Santa Clara County, California, between Mountain View and Sunnyvale. Once a United States Navy facility that housed dirigibles. This former naval air station is owned and operated by the NASA Ames Research Center. In 2014, NASA announced it would lease airfield acreage to Google.

This fits well with Google's overall plan to take over the world as we know it. Moffett is steeped in history and would be a great place to meet the president in private.

I showered, shaved the stubble, and put on appropriate business attire. When Lara woke up just before two, I told her I had some business to take care of. She knew not to ask for details, especially if I had gone through the extra effort of cleaning up both myself and the kitchen.

At 2:00 p.m. on the dot, a black Cadillac Escalade pulled up out front and waited. No one got out. If I hadn't been watching, I wouldn't have known. I strolled out of the condo and nonchalantly got in the back seat. No one offered to help this senior citizen. Agent One and Agent Two identified themselves, checked my credentials, and we drove off.

"I don't suppose you're at liberty to tell me what's going on?" I queried.

No response.

"How about playing twenty questions?"

Nothing.

That gave me time to peruse the all-black interior of the Cadillac. I'd ridden in many Cadillacs, and they were generally pretty quiet, but this one was like a tomb. If I snapped my fingers, I didn't think I would have heard it. It was an anechoic chamber on wheels. I thought this would be a great place to test stereo speakers.

Thirty minutes later, we entered a parking lot at Moffett. There were no cars, and we parked well away from the buildings while Agents One and Two verified the area was devoid of paparazzi.

Once inside the building, they scanned and searched me, but my body cavities remained uninvaded. I had changed into clean underwear for nothing.

They then escorted me to a cafeteria where President Elliot was sipping coffee at a corner table. There was a clear view of the vacant airfield out the window. It was a beautiful, sunny California day and cool inside, even though I could feel some dampness under my arms.

Not another soul was in the cafeteria, not even Secret Service, which I thought was odd. The table had a clean, varnished wood surface, no tablecloth, no napkins—only the tall sugar dispenser with which every trucker is familiar. This looked like it was going to be an intimate brunch.

We are similar in age, but Paul looked a hell of a lot better than I. He wore a crisp blue suit. Hair coiffed to perfection. Clear, tanned skin. Bright, piercing eyes. Teeth so white I expected to hear a *ting* sound when he smiled. Plastic surgery can work wonders.

The president stood up, and we shook hands. His hand was neither cold nor clammy, and his grip was firm. I withdrew mine, which was cold and clammy. He didn't seem to be the least bit uncomfortable.

"Hello, Dick—or should I say Rich? Or Richard?" he asked me.

"I dropped Dick when the double entendre was causing issues. Richard works."

"Okay, Richard it is. As you might expect, I've been doing some homework. Your technical background and investigation record are notable, but my research tells me you've decided to cut back and maybe do some fishing."

Fishing?

Is that what he thought retired high-tech investigators actually do? Knowing he had probably already gotten all the information on me he needed, I had nothing to say. Sure, I was more than curious, but there was no protocol on how to proceed. Should I just come out and ask him what we were doing? *How are the wife and kids? Seen any good movies? Are we planning to attack any of our allies?*

Instead, I just sat there—one of the rare times when I kept my mouth shut. Well, almost shut. "No fishing, just semi-retired."

Paul retook the lead. "Richard, I want to discuss a project where I think your skills would fit well. We'll discuss it in a minute, but first, let's get something to eat."

A waiter or president's assistant drifted to the table without making a sound and without his feet touching the floor. Not sure how he did that. There were no menus. We just told him what we wanted, and he drifted away without writing anything down. Very impressive, but creepy too.

During the next forty-five minutes, we talked about nothing important. I ordered a hot roast beef sandwich with chips, and he ordered a chef salad with no meat. Well, at least he was eating hardboiled eggs. His "people" brought in placemats for our plates and napkins embossed with the presidential seal.

I wanted to ask if I could take the napkins as a souvenir, but again, somehow I managed to keep my mouth shut. Maybe I could get through this without making an absolute fool of myself.

He asked my opinions of the job the government was doing, if I voted, if I'd ever been married (as if he didn't know), and general small talk about my plans for the future.

Trying again not to be sarcastic, I bit my tongue before making a typical wise-ass remark, such as "Plans? We don't need no stinkin' plans!" Mel Brooks would appreciate my restraint.

Paul was presidential material from the time he became the leader of the high school chess club, class valedictorian, and starting quarterback. He was good-looking as well. Our lives didn't intersect, mostly because we were members of different social classes. Then he got a college scholarship back east, followed by his distinguished service in the Army as an officer during Vietnam. I was also lucky enough to visit 'Nam, but not in the same context.

We shared a story or two about our experiences in Vietnam, which overlapped only in time, not involvements. I was drafted, and he was, of course, an officer who made it to colonel in a relatively short time. Most of his tour took place further north than mine, where, in his official capacity, he visited a few cities that actually had access to bathrooms.

At the beginning of my tour, while crawling around in the mud, I called myself an MT, a Mobile Target for the Viet Cong. After the military figured out that I knew something about electronics, they trained me to handle the newer solid-state cryptography gear, which I carried into the field. That was good because I was further away from the front line, but sometimes I'd have to leave my M16 back at the tent because the gear was bulky, so I changed my moniker to MUT, which is both a scroungy dog, or in my case a Mobile *Unarmed* Target for the Viet Cong. Such is life.

I didn't have to ask him much, because the press had already painted President Elliot using indelible ink. His public image was no better or worse than any other president, with the usual 40 percent approval rating after only one year in office no matter what he did. They noted his military service to his country during Vietnam but never delved into details because that was a time the United States wanted to forget. Paul Elliot was never a POW and hadn't suffered from PTSD. Pretty unremarkable stuff, overall.

We finished our lunch, and I dabbed my lips, trying not to soil the napkin. I figured stuffing this one in my pocket was the only way I'd get that memento.

"How about an after-dinner drink?" Paul asked. "Maybe a Drambuie or a nice wine?" The waiter was a well-trained servant to the president who continued to drift around the table unheard. His shoes still didn't make noise even though the floors were hardwood.

Drambuie? I hadn't tasted that since the seventies.

Not wanting to appear undecided, I quickly told the waiter, "A glass of merlot sounds good."

I had stopped drinking merlot after watching the movie *Sideways*, but I had to say something. Unfortunately, the waiter asked if I had a favorite brand or vintage. Back in the eighties, I would have been able to handle that question, but lately, my wine selection fell into three categories: red, white, and screw-top.

"I'll trust your judgment," I said to the waiter, congratulating myself on my cleverness in sidestepping the question.

After he was out of the room, Paul leaned closer and, in a more subdued voice, said, "Richard, I have to ask that you keep this conversation totally private and off the record. Discretion is imperative. Can you do that for me?"

"I can do that."

"I can tell we are in agreement that the late sixties was a strange time to be fighting a war no one could explain in a country no one knew much about. As Richard Nixon said in 1969, 'No event in American history is more misunderstood than the Vietnam War. It was misreported then, and it is misremembered now.'

"I was young, eager, and confused, like most of us were. Well, Richard, to get right to the point, I met a girl while I was in Vietnam. Her name was Hau Thom. We never married, but I fathered a daughter."

Holy crap! This was totally unexpected. How could the president of the United States have fathered a daughter no one knew about? And worse yet, why was he telling me? I never liked being the only guy with the key to the ammo box. Oh, waiter, better change that merlot to a double Johnnie Walker Scotch. Straight, no ice!

There are many times in my personal history that I tried to use humor to cover an awkward moment when I should have just kept my mouth shut. This time, I kept my mouth shut. All I said was, "Well, that's interesting."

The president continued, "My daughter's name was Thi Thom. I saw her only once, and I tried to follow her development as best I could, but it was impossible given the ridiculous situation we had created over there. After I returned to the US, I wanted to do more, but my political career took precedence. I confess the spotlights gave me an excuse to forget many things that should never have been forgotten."

"So, I'm guessing you want me to find her without involving the press?"

"Correct. And my wife, Nora—she doesn't know either. I'd prefer to keep it that way for the time being."

"Well, that can complicate things," I said, again shocked at that revelation. "And then what?"

"Honestly, I'm not sure. All I know is I have a hole in my memory that needs filling. I don't even know if she's alive. She'd be about fifty now. I'd have to see where she is and what she needs and make a judgment as to whether I could help.

I know the press would be brutal if they knew, but I think Nora would forgive me. After all, that was a long time ago, well before I met Nora, and lots of strange things happened then. I will tell her, of course. Probably soon."

"In the meantime, I want to keep this private. If and when you find Thi, please let me know immediately. I'm sure she doesn't have any idea who her father is."

"If I take this assignment, and if I do find her, someone— me or somebody working with me—will have to talk to her, don't you agree? I can't see just taking a picture and jotting down an address." I continued, "Why can't you just disclose all this and then institute a search via normal channels? You have access to many more tools than I do. American soldiers in conflict have done a lot worse, and that was so many years ago. The public might give you a pass. This isn't Watergate or Monica Lewinsky."

"It gets complicated. You see—Hau Thom, her mother, was part of Communist Vietnam—basically our enemy. I must keep these circumstances classified for the time being. So, you see using federal resources for something like this is out of the question and would never go over with the public, much less the Senate."

"Can I inform the Agency?"

"Absolutely not! This is just between the two of us!"

"But they'll wonder what I'm up to."

"No, they won't. Since that Farley operation, the deaths of those two thugs, and your decision to retire, you are off the radar. As far as the government is concerned, you no longer exist."

"So, I can stop paying taxes?"

"Still the Dick Braddock I remember."

"But how do my expenses get covered if I can't file reports?"

"That's one reason I sought you out. You've done well in your career and your software business, so perhaps you could fund this endeavor pro bono for a while, as a friend. Once I tell Nora, we might be able to contribute private funds, but I can't guarantee that."

President or not, this guy has a lot of nerve, interrupting my retirement and a potential career at Walmart to undertake an expedition to find his illegitimate daughter on my dime!

Again, without thinking first, I blurted out, "But you're picking up the lunch tab, right?"

Paul's face made it clear that he was not used to working with a wiseass like me.

"Sorry, I can't help it," I apologized. "What have you got that will help me? Old photos? Any files that show dates and locations? Where's the mother now?"

Paul Elliot overlooked my discretions and moved right along.

"That's the real problem," Paul said. "The mother, Hau Thom, was active with the North Vietnamese and the Viet Cong. She was killed in one of our incursions. What would people think once they found out I fathered a daughter with a North Vietnamese woman who was our wartime enemy?"

"I have to admit, that's not a pretty picture. I think some would call that treason," I said, then changed the subject. "Give me what you have. I'll do a little research and see what I can do. No promises. How do we communicate?"

"You can have this folder. It has some information you might find interesting and several photos of Hau Thom. You can't just call me at the White House, because every phone call is recorded, but I have set up a private secured line. Here's the number. You can also use a secure email account. You still have your encryption card and access codes, I assume?"

"Sure do."

"If those methods don't work, I have a contact who can be our intermediary. His name is Tanner. Here's his secure cell number. Tanner represents me and can make sure secure emails get processed. Later, perhaps we can set up one-on-one meetings like this one with more direct methods of contact. I'll build a cover for Tanner that won't arouse suspicion."

"Mr. President, I have to say this all sounds very strange to me. We haven't talked for fifty-odd years, and now I'm being asked to go off sleuthing for you without anyone finding out, even your wife. And what happens to me if there's no one covering my back? I'm sure you understand I'm feeling very vulnerable."

Elliot didn't respond other than to half-close his eyes and look down at the table like a little boy whose father just found out he had misbehaved. I didn't ask for any details on Tanner.

Then he said something I never expected to hear from a sitting president: "You don't have to do this if you don't want to."

So, I could just walk away? I had to stop and think for a minute while neither of us said anything. The silence and my temporary lack of sarcasm was refreshing. I had to ask myself what would become the legacy of my life? What mark would I leave? Everything had been so damn secret that there would be no Wikipedia coverage of Richard Braddock. Of course, I had to do this! Risks or not, I was talking to a human being, not just a politician. This was more important than me. I knew that once I accepted this assignment, I might have to keep Lara partially in the dark. That was the worst thing about having a companion when you were in my line of work. Sometimes you can't share details about what you're doing. If you work from home, whenever you put up that radio silence, you come off looking like you're ignoring them. However, if you have to physically go on assignment somewhere geographically far away, then you have a good excuse for being incommunicado.

No matter how much your partner might whine about your being gone on missions for long periods, I'd personally rather have her miss me than misinterpret my silence as me being an uncaring, self-absorbed asshole. I figured I could tell Lara enough to make sure she knew I wasn't doing something that would get me killed, and I saw no reason we couldn't keep in touch. All I could do was appreciate her intelligence and be as honest as I could.

I said, "I'm in love with a beautiful woman named Lara. She understands me. Some day we may even get married. How much can I tell her?"

The president replied, "I'm aware of Lara, and I'm glad to see that you are coming into the fold of what's really important in life. I'll leave that up to you. You trust her, and I trust you to be able to handle those issues. Just do me a favor. If this news does get out before its time, let me know as soon as you can."

"Thank you," I said. "I will tell Lara that I am on a personal mission for the president and that she needs to keep that to herself. I won't discuss details."

The agents shuttled me back to the condo and booted me out the door without making sure I would have a nice day. Due to my vast psychological experience, I concluded the agents were not briefed on the techniques of social dialogue.

Chapter 2

With no idea where to start, I began to look through the tattered brown briefcase Elliot had left me. It contained everything he'd accumulated thus far to find his daughter: old government records, maps of Vietnam, orders defining meeting locations, a few photos, and minimal correspondences. There were also a few lists of possible contacts with dossiers, phone numbers, emails, some dates, and locations.

I threw myself into the sorting process with gusto, but there wasn't all that much to sort. When I had completed those beginning steps, the other reason not to take this assignment reared its ugly head: images of lost buddies, destruction, and human chaos from that war were permanently etched on my brain cells in high-definition precision.

I'd been one of the lucky ones; because of my tech skills, the government had me work on cryptography equipment. Every message, every phone call—everything had to be encrypted. That kept me in the field, but off the front line.

Watching men come back injured from the field of battle after every attack and noting the many who didn't come back, I couldn't help feeling I wasn't pulling my weight. "Survivor's guilt" they called it. One day, two of my friends never returned, and another was in such bad shape; it would have been better if he hadn't come back at all. I told myself if I ever got out of that godforsaken place, I'd never come back.

None of us had any reason to be there anyway, other than following orders, and you would think that if you were lucky enough to still be alive at the end of the conflict, returning to the US would be a time for celebration—but that didn't go well either. America didn't want us back. They blamed us for carrying out an unpopular war, even though we faced prison if we refused to go. We were damned if we did and damned if we didn't. This was the first war in America's history in which the heroes were perceived as murderers or sellouts. It's no wonder the suicide rate for returning veterans was astronomical. What was the point of living if no one around you cared?

Whom had we risked our lives for? A country filled with people who would never be grateful. Instead of tickertape parades, we got a dozen different cancers from exposure to Agent Orange, maybe a strong case of heroin addiction, or PTSD that haunted our dreams until we went crazy. All this accompanied by a Veterans' Bureau that wanted to deny us treatment or compensation.

Enough! Enough! Snap out of it, Braddock! My reminiscing always took me on a journey into a rage, and I couldn't afford to go there that day. This ire was why I hesitated to take any case that might involve revisiting the war.

"I'll see how long I can last," I mumbled under my breath and looked around to see what I could do that would be productive and proactive in finding Elliot's daughter. I wouldn't have time to revisit history if I kept busy.

A simple Google search for the name "Thi Thom" yielded thousands of hits. Apparently, that was a popular name. Google images showed some beautiful women who looked like professional models. Several hours of searching and sorting resulted in about one hundred Thi Thoms who were the right age, but there was no way to find their place of birth, their parents' names, or anything substantial. This exercise was a waste of time. I knew I couldn't do in two hours what President Elliot couldn't do in fifty years, so I started calling people on the contact list instead.

After a few days, I got a call back from a gentleman who used to live in Saigon. He didn't know about Hau Thom, the mother, but he knew the location of birth records from that time frame and suggested I start with the American Embassy in Saigon.

Paul's notes showed Thi's birth month as February 1968 and her likely place of birth as Saigon. She picked a historic time to arrive in the world. The North Vietnamese launched their infamous Tet Offensive at the very end of January 1968. In later years, North and South Vietnam called an informal truce while each celebrated Tet, the Vietnamese New Year. As the most important and sacred holiday in Vietnamese culture, each side took time off to pray and to celebrate with their families.

However, the North Vietnamese had a surprise planned for the Tet of 1968. At a time when US popular support for the war was at an all-time low, and just after US military leaders were predicting the war would soon be over, North Vietnam made liars out of them. In conjunction with the Viet Cong, "The People's Army" in South Vietnam, North Vietnam began one of the most extensive military campaigns of the Vietnam War. So much for the United States' promise of an end in sight.

While it was not considered a technical success for North Vietnam, with over 180,000 North Vietnamese and Viet Cong troops wiped out, it became a significant factor in the Nixon administration's decision to withdraw from

Vietnam. "Winning" would have necessitated wiping out the communists in Vietnam completely, which we were learning was not likely to occur. It was the first world war where you couldn't tell who the enemy was. The Viet Cong had not read the rules from the American Revolutionary War when the Brits wore bright red coats and marched in a straight line.

In response to this unexpected attack, General Westmoreland petitioned President Johnson for more troops, which meant more unpopular draft lotteries. "Old Westy," as we fondly referred to him, needed to maintain his infamous five-to-one kill ratio. If we killed five of them for every one of ours, we inevitably had to be winning, didn't we?

The daily death toll was gruesomely reported every night on television. We had somehow responded quickly enough to the Tet Offensive to lose only 16,000 troops to their 180,000, and when all was said and done . . . did we win? The answer varied depending on which side you asked. One thing was certain—this was not a great time to be born in Vietnam, North or South.

Getting back to finding his daughter, I figured if Thi was born in February 1968, it might lead somewhere if I could find out where Paul Elliot had been hanging out nine months earlier, sometime around April or May 1967.

That was easy. Paul's military records showed him as unmarried and assigned to an official position in Operation Malheur I in the Quang Ngai Province. Those operations were small-scale by most military standards, so while he might not have gained any reputation points, he probably had lots of time off to explore the province.

Quang Ngai is located on the east coast of Vietnam, about halfway between the north and the south. I heard from soldiers that its beaches were so beautiful that if it weren't for the war, you'd think you were in the musical *South Pacific*, with strains of "Bali Hai" playing in the background. In a location like this, after a cease-fire, I could envision a single commissioned officer like Paul Elliot getting ideas about women.

That region was still under the strict control of the Communist Party of Vietnam, so getting into that area without raising suspicion might be a problem. In fact, I wasn't even sure I could get a visa into a country I hadn't visited since the sixties. But Vietnam was now a tourist venue. If someone had told me back in the sixties that Vietnam would someday become a tourist attraction, I think I would have just shot the guy right there and suffered the consequences.

I found my passport in the underwear drawer and started the proceedings to acquire a tourist visa. I managed to do it all online, and seventy-two hours later, I had my visa.

***

Lara dropped me off at the San Francisco airport a few weeks later, kissed me, and asked that I contact her as often as possible. I hit the bar before boarding, and even after a few stiff ones to give me strength, I still hesitated to get on the plane. Before this trip, I'd been pretty sure asking for detailed military information about Paul Elliot's assignments would only raise suspicion about who I was and why I was looking into the president's past, so I was mentally prepared to do the research on my own.

For what it's worth, I found my "tourist" flight to Vietnam was head and shoulders better than my last trip in 1965. I had thought about this before, and I knew I had to settle with the reality that memories were never going to go away. *So, buck up Richard,* I told myself. *You're committed now.* I couldn't quite understand why my inner emotions were acting up to this degree. I had always prided myself on my self-control and my ability to juggle multiple decisions in real-time with steadfast resolve, but that was a younger time and place. Now, all I wanted was another drink. I should have been contented enough with the fact that I could deplane without a wheelchair.

Of course, I could have backed out of this project. President Elliot had given me that option, but there I was, so there was no point in second-guessing myself anymore. I wanted to call Lara, and I hadn't even landed yet. Once I was on the ground, I would be able to go to Ho Chi Minh City, previously known as Saigon (it was still Saigon to me), where the supposed records were kept. Hopefully, that would get me started.

The Vietnamese people were friendly, and with my wallet full of Vietnamese dongs (no, that's not what you're thinking: one US dollar equals 21,000 dongs), all they wanted was to sell me something. No one seemed to care about the war, although after some prior online research, it was suggested that visitors avoid the subject. Buying things would have been fine if there was a price for the goods, but the price was whatever I could negotiate. That even applied to food.

"How much for the bowl of pho or the bún chả?"

"Well, that depends…" It felt strange that street people were acting like capitalists in a communist-dominated country.

Prior experiences with international travel had trained me to boil everything, never leave my cell phone exposed, and do research before asking for advice. A reasonably dressed

American looks like a walking bank account to undesirables in some foreign countries.

I stayed in an upscale hotel with a rooftop bar. There I was, standing at the bar at night, overlooking the city and the water, and enjoying an eighty-degree evening breeze even though it was early January. Technically I was working, but I was also drinking a tropical mixture of some sort (not boiled, but I risked it), and the scent of exotic flowers swimming through the moist night air made me feel like a fat koi fish in warm water after a large meal. Working or not, I had to call Lara.

"Lara, miss me yet? I'm staying at the Reverie Saigon, and to say I miss you would be an understatement."

"I was missing you fifteen minutes after dropping you off at the airport. How are you holding up? I know Vietnam was not a place you'd ever wanted to go back to."

"Well, I managed to get off the plane without help, which is about all you can expect from an old fart like me. I wish you could have come with me. It looks much better than the last time I was here."

"Any idea how long you'll be there?"

"I haven't even started the research yet. I can never predict these things. I'll have a better feel in a day or two."

Lara understood she would probably never know the specific details of this assignment, and, to her credit, she was okay with that.

"I think I'll get some shuteye," I said. "Hang in there, pet the cat, and keep my side of the bed warm. Love you."

Recline and breathe, Richard, while you still can, I told myself. *The historical images of war could reappear at any moment and block out today's realities. Focus on the work, and you'll be okay.*

***

Saigon was more inviting and pleasant than I expected. But even though people were friendly and seemed willing to help, no one seemed to know where records of births during that period might be kept. I decided to try the US Consulate.

The United States Embassy in Saigon (now called a consulate), was first established in 1952, bombed in 1965, moved into a new building in 1967, and eventually closed in 1975. The embassy was the scene of several significant events of the Vietnam War, most notably the Tet. It was also the location of the famous filmed helicopter evacuation during the fall of Saigon, after which the embassy closed. In 1995, the US and the Socialist Republic of Vietnam re-established diplomatic relations, and the embassy grounds and buildings were eventually turned over to the United States.

I went to the consulate and was surprised to find only a few people there just milling around inside. The interior was spotless—plaques on the walls and massive, round, concrete planters in front. A cute young docent noticed me and took me outside to inform me those planters were used as firing positions by the Viet Cong during the Tet. Then she led me to a large banyan tree that dated back to the nineteenth century and now stood lonely and stately in the middle of a parking lot that had no cars. The consulate building was now used for receptions, and the grounds were used for soccer practice by the consulate staff, so it was no surprise with so few visitors that they were eager to talk to someone from the United States.

The docent spoke perfect English, so we chatted for a few minutes, and I told her what I was looking for. She did not seem uncomfortable at all with my queries, but she made it clear I wasn't going to get very far in Saigon. She felt that since the mother, Hau Thom, was from North Vietnam, a better choice for finding the data I was looking for would be Hanoi. Hanoi, the city I swore my soul was never to visit unless I was under the control of Lucifer himself. How could I possibly go to Hanoi?

She told me Hanoi was actually quite safe now, and the US had an embassy there as well. I wondered how we could have an embassy in Hanoi. She politely gave me the address but warned me I would have to make an appointment with the ambassador or some other embassy official. You just didn't walk in as I did in Saigon. Also, all visitors to the American Center in Hanoi would have to undergo additional security checks and forgo taking in personal electronic devices. I could plan on a thirty-minute to one-hour delay. She gave me the names and phone numbers of people I would have to call.

It was roughly a thousand miles from Saigon to Hanoi, and even though most Vietnamese traveled by train, the train ride would take forty hours, and that was if everything was on time. It was well worth the $175 to fly instead.

Hotels in Hanoi were relatively inexpensive, but I decided to stay at the upscale Sofitel Legend Metropole Hanoi in mid-downtown. Hey! I was retired! I deserved to be comfortable. I was on a mission for the president, for Pete's sake. I called Lara later that night. I had to remind myself that 10:00 p.m. in Vietnam is 8:00 a.m. in California, and Lara often worked late, so I was pushing the envelope. But Lara picked up on the second ring as if she was expecting the call. She was upbeat and pleasantly surprised I was moving around so quickly. Now that I was away, I started to realize how totally committed I was to Lara. Who else would trust and want to spend time with a guy who couldn't even tell her everything he was doing?

My visit to the US Consulate in Hanoi was quick and uneventful. After talking to several people and being shuffled around for almost two hours, I was finally introduced to a gentleman named Peter Riggs, who also could speak perfect English. Hanoi was starting to feel like a US suburb. Unfortunately, Peter also could not help me directly, because the records I was looking for were probably in the hands of the USSR. It turned out that Peter was an American from Utah, so we talked for about thirty minutes about our upbringings, military service, and, strangely, a mutual passion for race cars. He suggested we get together later that day at my hotel and talk cars over dinner, which I would pay for, of course.

***

Over dinner, Peter said, "Please, it's Pete. Only my mother called me Peter, and then only when I screwed up. So, you said you used to race?"

"Mostly street racing," I said

"What was the car?"

I said, "I had several since I seemed to blow up engines fairly often, but one of my favorites was a sixty-seven GTO. I really couldn't tell you how fast it was because I never went to the track. All I know is that I very seldom lost a street race with it. I had swapped out the motor for a stroked four twenty-one, so no one could tell it wasn't the stock three eighty-nine. How about you?"

"Cobra replica with a four twenty-seven. The damn thing was borderline unsafe but fast as hell."

We did the male bonding thing for another twenty minutes while never discussing why I was there. After Pete found out I was a Vietnam War vet, his manner changed.

He spoke more softly, almost reverentially, when he said, "I don't run into Vietnam vets very often. That was a tough time, and I was lucky enough to avoid it. Vets just don't come back here, and the few who do don't learn anything more about that war than they knew before. So, why are you trying to find this girl?"

I told Pete, "It's pretty simple, really. I'm trying to help out a friend who wanted to find Thi Thom. She may be his daughter." He seemed to sense he shouldn't ask me too many probing questions.

He had never heard the specific name Thi Thom, but he was aware of a high-level female official for the north whose last name was Thom, but he couldn't remember her first name. Other than that, Pete couldn't be of much help, as all birth records from that time are in the Soviet Union.

I asked, "Any chance that official's first name was Hau?"

"That sounds about right," he said. "Hold on for a minute while I make a call."

Ten minutes later, Peter returned with a wide-eyed look on his face.

Pete said, "Hau Thom was not just an *official*, she was a senior military officer for the North Vietnamese Army!" She was killed in action, and that made the news because there weren't that many female officers.

Hau Thom was a high-level military officer for the enemy? Holy crap! Mr. Elliot had left out a few pertinent details.

Peter said, "So you're trying to find Hau Thom's daughter? I didn't know she had a daughter."

"Well, if she did, what happened to her?"

Pete and I were getting to know one another pretty well, and he wanted to help, so he told me about a Vietnamese fellow he warned was not recognized by the United States as a viable representative but still might be able to help me. Pete asked that I keep the source of that contact between us and told me, "Just sit tight. I will have him contact you at your hotel."

"What's his name?"

"I'm not sure, but you'll know him when he calls."

Back at the hotel, I was not getting used to the time it took to negotiate my way through a day.

"Could you please tell me where the men's bathroom is?"

"Twenty thousand dong."

Under my breath, I said, "Damn poop payment? Thanks for nothing." I paid the ransom.

"It's around the corner on your right."

A few days later, I was talking on the phone with a semi-coherent Vietnamese man who would not give his name but said he might be willing to help . . . for a price. Dongs for the data? What a surprise.

I decided to call this Vietnamese guy Hank, only because there were no Hanks in Vietnam. He chose the location to meet, which was an outdoor eatery, I guess. It could have also been a motorcycle repair shop, or a used furniture junkyard, or a graffiti test area. Anyway, I learned years ago never to go to a meeting in an unknown location with an unknown person without a few days' homework and some surveillance first.

The building, if you could call it that, was a single plank wood structure that stood out in the open with no apparent means of support. There was no front entrance or even a front wall, and the roof was corrugated tin. The entire structure slanted at maybe five degrees or so, and if the floor was wood, the dirt did an excellent job of covering it. There were no visible machines for refrigeration, nor any signs to bathrooms. They didn't need signs because there were no bathrooms. They had some electricity because bare bulbs were hanging over the tables. A few were even lit . . . dimly. The exterior walls were just the other side of the interior walls, so there were no hidden rooms unless there was an entrance to an underground tunnel. *Don't think tunnels!* Tunnels brought back memories I had hidden away. The mere thought stopped me in my tracks until I was able to breathe again. *Relax,* I told myself. *Breathe, move on.*

The next day, fifteen minutes before the agreed-upon time, I was already sweating as I strolled in and picked a table made from the same wood as the walls. No one came to the table. The smell was . . . what's the word? "Pungent," but food-based, and nothing rotting, so that was a pleasant surprise. Someone was cooking, or boiling, or whatever they did in the back of the structure. It looked like this went on twenty-four hours a day. No headless chickens were visible. There was no breeze or air movement of any kind. I guess fans weren't allowed in Hanoi. That made the air so thick that it was actually difficult to breathe. It was probably ninety-five degrees with ninety-five percent humidity. Adding to the dense air were aromas reminiscent of curry and hot rice. I had gotten sick a few years back after eating a curried something in Malaysia, so my aroma memory was about to test my body's abilities to stave off upchucking.

But on a good note, US beer was available. Go figure that out! I usually wouldn't put myself at risk with a situation like this, but I had nothing to hide and no harmful intentions, so I waved to a guy who seemed to work there and ordered a beer. He nodded, and, ironically, we didn't negotiate the price. I guessed that would come later. The beer was bottled with the cap still on. It was cool but not cold and probably safe. It would suffice.

Pete helped me find out a few things about this guy I called Hank, but for the most part, the information showed he was just a guy of no particular orientation who had assisted people from the US before, but that was about the sum of it. Where was Yelp when you needed it?

I was just sitting there, sweating, sipping, and breathing slowly when Hank rode up on his bicycle, which he propped against the wall without saying anything. He must have weighed ninety pounds at most and was dressed as if the wind blew his monocolored short-sleeve shirt over a bony skeleton. He had sweated through the clothes that clung to his stringy muscles. He was the picture of a man who was three-sigma off the low end of the body mass bell curve. He had thin, gray hair and a goatee but no hair on the rest of his body. And when I say no hair, I mean *no hair*. Hank was probably not the best name to use for this guy. He obviously carried a knife, since there was no way you could hide a knife's outline on his frame. He spoke with a heavy accent, but I could follow it.

"Want a beer?" I asked.

"You Braddock?"

"Yep."

Hank sat there, giving me a good look over. I was feeling guilty and found myself thinking maybe Vietnamese people believed fat people must be rich. By the way, I had five hundred dollars in my pocket.

Hank wanted to know who I was, if I was alone, where I was staying, and he acted as if he had never heard the term "private investigator" before. I informed him of what typical private investigator duties were, but after that, he also wanted to know who I was working for.

"That I cannot tell you," I said. I told him if he required that information, I would have to seek my information from another source, but my crash course in Vietnamese economics had taught me that money was the key to most everything in this country, including information. The sooner money was brought up, the sooner we could proceed.

"I need to find the birth records for a Vietnamese girl born in 1968," I said. "I can pay a small fee."

Hank said, "One thousand US to get access to war-related information."

"It's just a birth record that has nothing to do with the war."

Hank added, "Records of that time are *all* war-related *and* classified. It's dangerous to start digging into anything from then."

He made it clear I would not be allowed to rummage through any files. Someone might be able to get what I needed as long as I could give them accurate information, but there would be no guarantees. This was not looking good.

Finally, Hank asked, "What exactly are you looking for?"

"I want information about the daughter of a woman named Hau Thom. I have an old picture. The daughter's name was Thi Thom, and I think she was born in February 1968."

Hank studied the picture, which showed a thin, taut Hau Thom standing in the hot sun in a khaki-colored uniform stained with sweat. She wore a red band on her arm, a conical leaf hat on her head, and a .45 revolver on her belt. Her expression conveyed assuredness, and her name was written on the photo with a felt-tipped marker. Hank squinted as if the light was suddenly too intense. Hard to believe a twenty-five-watt bulb was too bright. Perhaps he was getting a headache. He put down the photo, stared at the dirt for a few seconds, then raised his head. After taking a sip of beer, he slowly turned around to check our surroundings and looked directly into my eyes. Hank was definitely taking his time to find his words. I was not comfortable with the tension.

Finally, he said, "The United States killed her. She had been very respected by her people and the soldiers under her command. It's probably better if we stop right now before you get more than you expect."

"I know what happened to Hau Thom," I said, "but this isn't about her. I'm trying to get information about her daughter, Thi Thom."

Hank hesitated, a little surprised, "How do you know what happened to Hau Thom?"

In my earlier years, I would have never made the mistake of revealing what I knew too early in a discussion. I had to scramble. "My previous research revealed Hau Thom may have been killed, but again, I have no interest in Hau, only her daughter."

"What do you know about the daughter?"

"Nothing, that's why I'm here."

"Why are you interested in someone you know nothing about?"

"I'm a private investigator; it's what I do. My client has asked me to find Thi, if possible, and see if she's alright. It's an honorable mission."

After another ten seconds of silence, Hank stated bluntly, "This meeting is over. I can't do anything for you. Maybe you should go to the American Embassy and see if the information can be found there." He stood up to leave.

"I've already been to the embassy, and they couldn't help. They don't have the information. Peter there led me to you.

I need your help to find Thi Thom. Without that, my trip would end up being a waste of time."

Hank thought for a minute. "You were in the war, weren't you? I have seen other Americans like you who come back just to satisfy their morbid curiosity, trying to find their illegitimate children. You didn't help South Vietnam then, and you can do nothing now. Scars have formed over those wounds, but they will never be healed."

"I don't know what to say, other than I'm here with no ill intent. I'm not here for any personal reasons. Can you help me at all?"

Hank sat back down and drank about half his beer in one gulp while appearing to contemplate what to do next. At least he didn't get up to leave, which I read as a positive step. I was thinking about what I would do if this turned out to be a dead end. Hank scratched his privates, clearly visible under the thin fabric, and said, "Do you have cash? I can give you a number that may or may not work."

"I have five hundred dollars US." I showed him the five one-hundred-dollar bills, which he grabbed and inspected. He pulled a piece of paper from his shirt pocket, yelled for something to write with, and scratched down a number. "Call this number, and make sure you're talking to a Mr. Lee. He's Chinese. He might be able to help."

Hank stuffed the five hundred in his pocket. I helped him with his bike, and he rode off without saying another word. I went back to the hotel to recover from the heat and to decompress. I also needed to track where Hank went after our meeting via the magnetic GPS I stuck to his bike. These new GPS trackers are only about a half-inch square, and it was easy to attach as he was leaving. I tracked Hank for twenty-four hours and saw no reason to be alarmed. His travels were all local, with no visits to any official buildings downtown. Apparently, he'd made no attempt to buy something with his recently negotiated five hundred dollars.

Paul Elliot had told me Hau Thom was part of Communist Vietnam, but I hadn't expected she was a prominent player in the North Vietnamese military. That begged several questions. Was Paul aware of that at the time? And if Paul did know, was that the reason he wanted to keep everything quiet? Although we weren't best friends, I still expected he would have told me her rank. I had to contact him directly, not through Tanner.

I called his secure number and was shocked when he answered on the third ring. "Richard, how's the search going?"

"I'm in Vietnam now, and although I never wanted to come back here, I am making some progress. The reason I called is that I'm discovering Hau Thom seems to have been an influential person in the North Vietnamese military. My contacts are not forthcoming with information about her because of that. She wasn't just a soldier; she was an officer. I am curious as to whether you knew that. I don't mean to pry, but her position might change my whole approach to accessing information."

"So, you want the details about how we met, but I can guess your real question is whether I knew the risks of what I was getting into. Correct?"

"Pretty much."

"I honestly had no idea who she was when I first met her. In sixty-seven, I had been assigned to an area in the Quang Ngai Province, a beautiful area on the coast. On an April evening, I took a long walk just north of the Trà Khúc River. This was well off base, as you might imagine, but the previous weeks had been quiet, and I was getting bored. The water was warmer than the air, which I had not experienced, except in Hawaii, and the sea breeze was hypnotic. I walked around a small hillside that was protecting an inlet, and there she was, naked from the waist up except for her cap, rinsing her khaki shirt in the surf. I immediately noticed her M1917 forty-five caliber about twenty feet away, sitting on a rock along with a bag. I could tell by the red collar badge and the yellow star she was a North Vietnamese officer. I had my Colt drawn before she noticed me."

"She was alone with no backup?"

"Yes, all by herself."

"And?"

"Well, she just stood there watching me while I walked to the rock. I pocketed her forty-five and checked the bag. She had no other weapons. Showing no stress at all, she slowly put on her wet shirt and walked straight at me, stopping about ten feet away. Then, in reasonably good English, she asked me if I was going to kill her."

"Wow. That's intense."

"I told her to sit down. She was very calm, almost as if she had resigned herself to her possible death. She told me her name and said she was washing out soldiers' blood that had accumulated on her uniform. She was no immediate threat to me, and I sensed a sadness that made me feel melancholy. She told me her name, and we talked for about an hour. She didn't understand why either of us were there or what we were fighting for. She had seen enough killing, but she was also loyal to her leadership and would fight to the end if she had to, even if her heart wasn't in it. I was impressed with her honesty and commitment to the cause, whatever that was. She was friendly and showed no personal animosity toward me. She just assumed I was following orders like she was."

"Was she trying to defect?"

"Not at all. Just talking in the night air, one human being to another. It was refreshing as hell. We met at the same spot, on and off, over the next month or so, knowing full well we would be arrested if we were caught. Then she moved on, and I didn't see her again. Later that year, after we captured a VC group, I found out their leader, a Hau Thom, had been replaced because she became pregnant. She had Thi in February of sixty-eight, and then Hau became part of what we called collateral damage later in sixty-eight during the Tet. I never found out what happened to Thi."

"Okay, I get the picture. I'm sorry, Paul, you risked a lot. Thanks for filling me in. I'll get back to work."

I could sense the frustration in the president's voice, and I was sorry I had made the call.

The next day, I called the number for Mr. Lee. I left my cell number with a short explanation of why I called and referenced my meeting with Hank. I was called back within the hour and given another location to meet. I thought maybe this time I should bring a weapon, but I decided to forgo that in case I was searched. A US citizen on an honorable mission would not carry a weapon.

I was pleasantly surprised the location was the lobby of a nearby hotel. It was air-conditioned, and there was access to a bar. Things were definitely looking up. Lee said he'd be wearing a bright-red baseball cap. I thought, *A red baseball cap? In Vietnam?* I had not seen a single baseball cap since my arrival, let alone a bright-red one.

When I arrived, the place was teeming with people. There were maybe a hundred people in the restaurant. I could see why the red baseball cap was a good idea. Lee was already sitting by himself in the back at a corner table, sipping something from a bowl. He had two drinks ready, and there was another similar setup beside him in front of an empty chair. That was probably for me. This Mr. Lee wasn't anything like I'd expected, and he was definitely not related to Hank. Lee was obviously of Chinese heritage, maybe mid-fifties, but not the undernourished type I was getting used to. In fact, he had massive arms, like a Chinese bodybuilder. I half expected him to challenge me to arm wrestle as a test before he let me sit down. One thing was sure—Hanoi had diversity!

He started the conversation before I even sat down, "It's Braddock, right? Rumor is you're looking for somebody who was born in 1968, but you have little to offer. Sit your ass down and have a drink. Well, what are you waiting for? Are you always this slow?"

Crikey! I sat down as fast as I could. Lee obviously wasn't wasting any time, and the word was getting around about me. Did these people use the Internet, Facebook, or Snapchat? Was my name coming up in a conversation over a beer? People knowing me before I knew them was discomforting. I decided to not waste any time either and get right to it.

"I just need to review birth records from February 1968. Hank said a thousand dollars would do it."

"Hank? Now *that's* funny! I'll have to start calling him that." Lee plowed forward, "Please. Just drink up. I hope you like pho. We have plenty of time, and it's too hot to be anywhere else. I was told you're specifically looking for Hau Thom's daughter. I can tell by that look on your face you have no idea who Hau Thom really was, and you are even more ignorant when it comes to her daughter Thi."

"I agree with both points. Can you help me?"

"Does Dolly Parton sleep on her back? Does a one-legged duck swim in a circle? My middle name is Help. It's just not free."

"I wasn't expecting someone from China to be so in sync with American vernacular."

"What makes you think I'm from China, dickhead? I'm a US citizen, born in New York, E-seven retired after twenty years in the Corps, and I guarantee I can kick your ass. You're old and slow, while I'm clean and green. Wanna try?"

So there I was in Hanoi, a city I never wanted to visit in the first place, sitting at a hotel/bar/café drinking I don't even know what, sipping pho from a bowl, while getting one-upped by a feisty Chinese bodybuilder named Lee who just told me he was an American. And I'm liking it! What had the world come to?

Lee added, "And, no, I don't know who you really are, and I don't give a shit either. Want to be introduced to my minions?"

Mr. Lee was starting to impress me. There was a time when almost nothing surprised me, but he had me sighted, shot, plucked, field dressed, and cooked before I knew what happened. Maybe I was too old for this shit.

I tried to act unimpressed. "Meeting your little friends will not be necessary. All I want is to see birth records from February 1968, so I can begin to track, and hopefully find, Thi Thom. There is nothing more to it than that."

Lee added, "Are you going to drink that or not? I could get you something else, like a Shirley Temple or maybe a ginger ale."

Lee was doing a great job positioning himself as the alpha dog of this two-dog pack.

After about thirty minutes of this banter, during which he ate, drank, drank some more, and talked while I listened, he finally slowed down, as if feeling sorry for me. He then lowered his voice and said, "You seem like a reasonable asshole, Braddock. I shouldn't do this, but I can save you five hundred bucks. The information I have is worth five hundred, and if you don't think so, I'll take your word as a gentleman, and you don't have to pay me. Deal?"

My word as a gentleman? Where did that come from? There was a time when I would want to hire a guy like this to work for me.

"Is this information you're referring to the birth records?" I asked.

"Birth records? That's a waste of time. You don't need birth records! You need information!"

I hesitated for only a few seconds. "Sold! What's the info?"

"Money first."

I fanned out six hundred-dollar bills on the table so they could be easily counted. Then I stacked them, folded the group in half, and inserted the money into Lee's shirt pocket, all while he sat there just watching me, with one hand on his drink and the other resting on the table. I admit this was brazen for me, given the circumstances. Meanwhile, he never took his hand off his glass. I gave his pocket a friendly, backhanded love tap while saying, "I think your information might be worth a hundred-dollar tip, but I reserve the right, per your gentleman's conditions, to request the original five hundred back if I deem the information inadequate. Either way, you can keep the extra hundred for your time."

"Braddock, you little shit. I'm actually starting to like you!"

He took a long sip from his drink. It was weirdly quiet for about ten seconds, which felt more like thirty minutes. Then he leaned over the table until he was only inches away from my face and spoke like he was telling me a secret.

"Thi Thom was extracted from Vietnam somewhere around 1978 and was housed and educated in Russia. Miss Thom was supposedly a smart little bitch. Word is, she eventually got a degree in computer science or some other bullshit and then got shipped to the US somehow. She ended up somewhere around Chicago. No one knows for sure. Anyway, birth records would be useless to you. Finish your soup, have lunch if you want, then go back to your little hotel and have another drink to celebrate that you saved four hundred dollars and were not robbed, which probably would have occurred. I'm keeping the six hundred. *Arrivederci*, Braddock."

Lee turned slightly toward me and flicked his fingers across the tabletop twice as if shooing off a fly. He was clearly signaling that it was time for me to go.

But I wasn't leaving just yet. "How do you know all this?" I asked.

"All I know is what I've been told. I already told you that no one knows for sure."

"But I'd still like to know how you were told."

"I don't have to tell you shit!"

I was quiet for a few seconds, then I smiled while I tapped his empty glass. "I'll buy you another drink . . ."

"Goddamn you Braddock! Oh, what the hell. It can't hurt anything now. Word was that Thi got married to this guy named Adrian."

I interrupted and gasped, "She was married?"

"Yeah, yeah, slow down. Adrian was killed in an accident in the early two thousands. They had already lost their first child while she was pregnant. I knew a guy who was friends with both of them, and he told me that Thi was always upset about her mother's murder, and then losing her family was just too much. So, she was thinking of working on a special project near Chicago. Next thing you know, she's gone. He never sees her again. The only Chicago I know is in the US, so . . . And don't ask me who that guy was, because I won't tell you!"

I did precisely as Lee had suggested earlier. I shook his hand—carefully—and left.

So, Thi Thom was in Illinois? I assumed she'd somehow gotten there around the mid-2000s. And she maybe had a computer science degree? And how did she get into the US if she was coming directly from the Soviet Union? And what was this "project" all about? Any possibility that this wasn't the real Thi Thom? So many questions!

Despite my hesitations, I decided to contact Tanner so he could feel like he was part of the effort and give President Elliot an update himself. I left the information on a secure server, but I didn't expect a response, nor was one forthcoming.

That night, I was looking forward to calling Lara and telling her I would be coming home. I missed cool, clean water, lower outdoor temperatures, and drier air, but the main thing I missed was Lara. She asked if I'd found what I was looking for. I had to be honest and say not yet, but this old dog was on the scent.

Chapter 3

Lara was waiting for me at the airport. It was already afternoon, but since I'd slept on the plane, I was refreshed enough to suggest going to dinner at one of our favorite spots: Stagnaro Bros on the Santa Cruz wharf.

"That's over an hour from here," Lara said. "More if we hit the usual traffic on Highway Seventeen."

"What have we got if we don't have the time to enjoy each other during my retirement?"

"Retirement? Is this what retirement looks like?"

"Okay, my error. I promise I'll cut back once this is over. Right now, I just want to smell you and the ocean and feel the cool breeze off the wharf."

We settled back to enjoy the ride while I filled her in on as much as I could. At Stagnaro's, she showed me a picture on her phone of a painting she'd been working on. I was embarrassed—it depicted a very distinguished-looking Sherlock Holmes type, only with my facial features. It was clear she not only loved me but also respected me. I was one lucky fellow.

Unfortunately, I had to tell Lara that I had to leave again soon, but this time I'd probably stay in the United States, near Chicago.

"Probably?" Lara looked a little confused.

I felt guilty. Was I taking Lara for granted? I assumed she would always be there when I returned, but maybe she thought this wasn't the life together we had discussed. After all, how could a professional private detective who spent his whole life planning and anticipating not anticipate this?

"Lara. Please understand. I have to follow through with my commitment to the president, and sometimes things just happen. I made more progress than I thought I would in such a short time, and I think I'm getting close, so I don't think this will take much longer."

She smiled but didn't say anything.

Upon arrival back at the condo, I kissed Lara, then excused myself to do some follow-up work in my new bedroom office. It wasn't high-tech, but it was comfortable. I didn't really miss my old man cave as much as I'd thought I would.

Using absolutely no information from Tanner, since neither he nor the president had gotten back to me, I started by contacting some friends and associates I had worked with before, several of whom had worked in immigration. My final call was to Brad Dempsey, who worked for the Department of Homeland Security in Chicago. After navigating around the receptionist, the automated attendant, and the personnel menu, I finally heard a phone ring followed by, "Hello."

"Brad. Richard Braddock here. Good to hear your voice again."

"Braddock, you piece of shit. What do you want now? I assume this isn't a personal call."

"Now is that any way to treat an old acquaintance living on Social Security? I go out of my way to find you, and this is the response I get?"

"Yeah, yeah. I can't wait to hear what's next."

"Maybe I should retract my potential offer for steaks at Morton's before I even suggest it."

"You're in Chicago?"

"Well, no, but I'm on my way . . . maybe."

"What the hell does that mean? Ambiguous as always."

"I'm trying to find a girl—"

Before I could even finish the sentence, Brad interjected, "Aren't you a little old for that?"

"Very funny, and no, actually, I'm not too old for that. Besides, I'm already in love with a beautiful woman named Lara. But all this has nothing to do with why I'm calling you. I'm actually calling you for help. I'm trying to find a girl who may have emigrated from Russia back in the late nineties or early two thousands."

"Are you telling me the famous and devoutly single and well-known private eye, Richard Braddock, got married?"

"No, no, no. We're not married, but who knows what the future holds."

"I can't get my head around why any woman would want to marry you. But then again, the Cubs won the World Series, too, so strange things do happen. I'm sorry, Richard. Congrats. You're becoming human."

"Thanks, Brad. I know that was tough for you to say."

Brad continued, "Now, to this girl. You are well aware people don't emigrate from Russia, Braddock. They escape." Brad started to laugh.

"Okay. Whatever. I just want to find her. She was born in Vietnam around 1969 and educated in Russia. Her name was Thi Thom, T-H-I T-H-O-M. She probably changed her name before or after she arrived in the US. Can you help?"

"Why are you calling a DHS agent in Chicago? Russia is closer to California, you know, where I last heard you lived."

"I have some intelligence that says she ended up around Chicago."

"Doesn't sound logical to me, but I'll see what I can do. But there's only so much time I can trade for a Morton's steak. What year did she come to the US again?"

"I have no idea, but I would assume it would be after about six years of university work in the mid-two thousands. She is supposed to have a CS degree, but I don't know what level."

"Where did she get the degree?"

"Somewhere in Russia."

"A female Russian with an upper-grad CS degree coming to the US post 9/11, and her name was Thi, T-H-I, Thom, T-H-O-M? I can't promise anything, but when can I reserve a table at Morton's?"

"You decide. I can be there in a few days."

"Thursday, seven p.m. at Morton's on State. Bring your checkbook."

"I'll be there, and you can choose the wine."

"I was already planning on that. Are you bringing Lara with you?"

"I can't do that because my assignment is classified. Lara knows I have to travel, but she doesn't know all the details. I have to keep it that way for a while."

"And she's all right with that? What about me? I gotta be privy to the details. And you said you were retired. You don't sound retired."

"Yeah, yeah. I'll fill you in, but I'll have to get approval from my client for that before we meet."

Brad said, "Meet you at Morton's on Thursday. Call me if you can't make it."

***

I had five days, so I decided to research what Russian universities Thi may have gone to. I found many universities with excellent reputations in computer science. Before the night was out, Brad had already sent an unsecured email asking for pictures and any other information. Unfortunately, I could be of little help while still staying secret. I sent him what I had.

I then sent a secure email to Tanner and the president that I would be bringing Brad Dempsey into the fold and needed to include him in the details of the assignment. I gave them all the information they would need to thoroughly vet Brad before Chicago.

Now that I had a break in the action, I wanted that JW I should have had with the president rather than the merlot. I was hoping Brad could dig up something that would guide me to my next step. Yes, I was pretty sure Thi was Paul Elliot's daughter, and she was probably alive somewhere, but where? And what was she doing? The amount of investigation I did was minimal at best. One competent agent could have done the same over the phone and probably not even leave the country. I had no problem with a sharp young girl coming to the US after she acquired an advanced degree; I would have wanted to do the same, but how could she do it? Did she keep her name? Why wouldn't she? More questions.

One thing in the back of my little mind was that all this was just a little too pat and easy. Easy assignments do happen; they're just rare, so there was no reason for me to make it any more complicated than it already was. *I'll just go to Chicago, have a great dinner with Brad, hopefully find out where this Thi Thom ended up, contact the president, and my duties will have been fulfilled. Then I can come back to California, entirely retired, and marry Lara. I need to find out if Lara likes to fish.*

Finish that JW, Richard, and go to bed! You overthink everything!

I slept for a solid eleven hours and felt completely refreshed in the morning. I dressed casually, and Lara and I went to my favorite breakfast place to read the paper over coffee, and maybe I'd have my favorite two-hour piece of toast. After our little sojourn, back at the condo, we caught up on what bodies feel like when they shower together. It was an excellent start to the day.

It was about two o'clock in the afternoon when I checked the secure server for news and updates.

Brad Dempsey was dead.

PART 2

Chapter 4

The secure news service said he was shot as part of a break-in at the DHS. That made no sense to me. People don't break into the DHS any more frequently than they break into the Pentagon.

I had worked with Brad ten years ago when I was more active, but I hadn't seen him recently. I knew he was happily married with a son. Although Brad wasn't a street agent, he had been a significant source of critical support information over the years. Investigation revolves around intelligence, and fact finding was all about knowing the information. People like Dempsey didn't share the spotlight or get the chance to see results firsthand, but I could argue they were at the top of the list of essentials. The intelligence they handled could be dangerous in the wrong hands, so they had to take appropriate precautions, but as far as I knew, Brad Dempsey had never been accosted or threatened in any way. I couldn't help wondering if his death was on my hands or just a tragic coincidence. There are times when I hate what I do.

My initial call to Brad was on an insecure line, but so what? Nothing classified was discussed, and if I had it to do again, I would do the same thing because I had no secure way to contact Brad since my secure communications methods had changed. Maybe this wasn't related to me at all or my casual request for information about Thi Thom.

It was time for me to develop a plan.

Later, with the only viable plan I could come up with revolving around what I was going to eat for dinner, I received a secure phone call from a Mr. Greg Dillard. He introduced himself as a lead DHS investigator assigned to the Dempsey case. He'd somehow found out how to make a secure call to someone he had never talked to. This high-tech stuff was getting out of hand.

"Mr. Braddock, if it's okay, I'd like to ask you a few questions about Bradley Dempsey."

"Absolutely," I said. "How did you know how to contact me?"

"Your call to Mr. Dempsey was logged on his calendar. It was a simple matter from there to find out who you are. The agency had your contact information. If you have the time, I'd like you to come to Chicago so we can meet. Much of what I want to talk about is best done in person. Could you be here in a few days?"

"I had already planned to be there on Thursday, but if I may ask, am I a person of interest? My call to Brad was to have dinner."

"Mr. Dempsey's calendar shows you were going to meet at a restaurant Thursday evening. That's clear. But you were the last entry in his daily activity register, and your number shows as the last phone call he had that day. That is also noted as an unsecured call. That's why I decided to call you back on a secured line. I assume you knew Mr. Dempsey?"

"I've known Brad for more than twenty years. We were friends and professional partners on several cases. I want to help as much as I can. Where do you want to meet?"

"Here at the DHS offices. Say about three p.m. on Thursday?"

"I'll be there. Please contact me if things change. Otherwise, I'll see you on Thursday."

My first order of business was to add Greg Dillard to the vetted list. I hoped Tanner and the president weren't thinking I was just spreading the word around, but it was evident that Mr. Dillard was going to need to know what I was trying to do and why I contacted Brad. I'd try to leave the president's relationship to the girl out of the discussion, but if I had to, I wanted to be free to inform Greg Dillard of all the details.

I thought I might be having an extended stay in Chicago, so I made a reservation at a unique hotel I had used many times. It's not open to the public, it accommodates extended stays, but more importantly, it's equipped to handle additional security. NSA and FBI agents frequently stay there, and I had stayed there so often I even had a favorite room. It was safe, secure, and comfortable. I packed several crates and scheduled UPS to pick them up the next day. I like to travel light, so in situations like this, I ship what I think I may need in advance directly to the hotel. Electronic instruments I might need are expensive and fragile, so I have crates with custom-cut foam inserts, just as if the container were going to an electronics trade show. My personal items were shipped the same way. This was the way celebrities traveled, and it always worked for me too.

I then brought Lara up to speed. I gotta love a woman that listened, nodded her head, and kissed me. No questions asked.

***

At precisely 2:45 p.m. on Thursday, I arrived at DHS headquarters in Chicago. I had never been to this DHS facility, and I must say, I was impressed. The floors looked like marble slabs with thin, shiny brass piping around each tile. The lobby's ceiling height had to be at least thirty feet, and all columns were surrounded by aluminum corners that harkened back to the art deco styles of the thirties. It may have been an old theatre building after a robust renovation. I asked to see Mr. Dillard. An administrative assistant arrived, introduced herself as Brenda, verified my identity in detail (without a body search), and invited me to follow her to the seventh floor.

Brenda was what you would call "a looker." It made me feel good to see a retired Dallas Cowboys cheerleader get meaningful work after retirement. But seriously, she was very professional and made no casual conversation. No "How was your trip" or "Mr. Dillard has been looking forward to meeting you." She just accompanied me in the elevator to the seventh floor and then led me to Dillard's office. Greg Dillard was sitting at his desk with his back to me, apparently enjoying a great view of Lake Michigan. He spun around.

"Richard Braddock, I presume," said Dillard as he rose to shake hands. I would guess he was in his forties, at least six foot two or more, maybe 225 pounds. His handshake left an imprint.

No office cubicles here. Dillard's office was fully enclosed with a window that overlooked Lakeshore Drive and offered a great view of the lake. His desk, definitely not military issue, rested on a carpet so thick you could trip on it if you shuffled your feet. The walls were wood-paneled, and the books on the shelves were free of dust and showed signs of being well-read. Paintings on the walls looked like originals or at least very good prints, and the chairs were plush leather. No fluorescent lights for Mr. Dillard, only gold wall sconces with green marble accents and a desk lamp that probably weighed fifty pounds. Overall, the impression was that of a home office somewhere in London. Maybe Oxford. He had to have a hidden bar in there somewhere and probably his own bathroom.

"Need anything to drink?" Greg asked. "Coffee or something?"

"No, I'm good. Thanks."

Brenda left, and Dillard jumped right in. "I've researched your background. Your history suggests you know how these things work. I know you have worked with Mr. Dempsey before, so why were you coming to Chicago to see him?"

"Correct. Prior to my retirement, Brad and I had worked together on and off for several years. All in all, I've known him for more than twenty years."

"So, if you are retired now, what was the purpose of your visit? Was it personal or business-related? It's unusual for the private sector to work directly with the DHS."

I was now part of the private sector? That was accurate but felt a little demeaning. However, I had already decided to be open and honest with Mr. Dillard, within the limits of my agreement with the president. I found out years ago that any attempt to hide or cover up information only made further discussions complicated. People can tell if you're lying or covering up, and one lie just leads to another, so it was just easier to be upfront. If I were not at liberty to talk about something, I would just say so.

I said, "I'd say it was fifty/fifty business and personal. I asked Brad if he could help me locate a girl named Thi Thom, who emigrated from Russia sometime in the two thousands and supposedly ended up in the Chicago area."

"If she immigrated here legally, it would take only minutes to find her, so I assume there was more to it than that, so you don't really know what happened. Correct?"

"That's right. I'm not sure she's even here."

"Why are you trying to find her?"

"My client has asked that I keep that private."

"Who is your client?"

"That I also would rather not say."

"Is this Ms. Thom in any way a threat to the United States?"

"I don't think so. I'm just trying to find her for a friend. I was recently in Vietnam and was told she was educated in Russia and then came to the US, perhaps the Chicago area, but I'm not sure of that. I would say I'm in the early stages of a missing person investigation." That sounded about as professional as I could be while still being noncommittal.

I added, "Can I get any details on what happened to Brad?"

Greg hesitated. It was clear that he was disappointed I was holding back information.

"If we are going to work together," he said, "I'll need to know all the details of your investigation. You understand that, don't you? I'd like you to talk to a couple of agents who have recently worked with Brad. Any concerns about that?"

"I think that would present a problem. I anticipated you would want to know more, so I've received approval from my client to inform *only you* of the details, and then only if it becomes necessary. I'm sure I would not be able to answer your agent's questions without disclosing my client details to them, so if it's okay with you, I'd like to fill *you* in personally on everything you need to know. After that, if you want me to talk to other agents, we'll figure out how to do that."

Dillard didn't speak for a moment. We were just dancing around while the tension was palpable during the silence. He was trying to decide just who this Braddock guy was and if he could trust me. Since he was under no obligation to provide anything that wasn't in the public domain—or should I say, the private sector—he had to feel me out before proceeding.

Greg added, "According to our records, you have worked with the FBI, FCC, NSA, DHS, contract work for the CIA, and the military, but you always remained private? And you've never been arrested or accused of any wrongdoing?"

"Well, I did pass gas at a presidential dinner once. Other than that, it's been pretty rewarding."

"That figures, because the record shows you are also a bit of a rogue and a wiseass too."

"I plead the fifth."

He smiled and chuckled. My humor had cracked the ice. "Okay, Braddock, or Richard, I'll share what we know with you since I think we can work together in some way. However, we must share both ways, and you need to go first. *Capiche?*"

Greg was correct. We had to share. "I agree. I was going to go over the details with Brad anyway. So, here's what I know. My client is President Elliot."

He didn't laugh that time. He just sat there with his hands in his lap. "Please explain."

"We went to the same high school. He trusts I can keep a secret, so he asked me to find his illegitimate daughter, who was born while he was an officer in Vietnam. He wasn't married at the time. This is a private investigation, not related to politics. President Elliot asked me to treat this effort as secret and keep it out of the press."

"I can see why he would want that. How many people know about this?"

"Counting you, only three so far. The president has assigned an intermediator named Tanner to assist me with communications back to him, but I haven't met him yet. On the phone, I told Brad the daughter's name, but I didn't tell him why I was trying to find her. Brad didn't know about the president. I was going to get to that when we met."

"I will comply with the president's request for secrecy, if possible," Greg said. "Can I talk to this Tanner fellow?"

"I see no reason why not. He is aware that we are meeting."

I turned over Tanner's contact information. Greg had not heard of his name.

Greg said, "Give me a few minutes, and I'll see if I can contact Tanner. Pour yourself a drink or have some coffee if you want."

I waited for about fifteen minutes. When Greg came back, he was apparently satisfied with his talk with Tanner.

After I brought him up to speed on my investigation results so far, I finally asked, "What's happening with Brad's family? Brad was a good man and a real asset to people like me in the field. I can't just sit by and watch the world go by."

"There is nothing you can do right now. We are taking care of his family and have them under 24-hour security, and we will probably move them to a secure location."

I had to go with his assessment. We shook hands. This time, my hand was not injured and didn't show any imprints. Dillard suggested that we share a late lunch together right there in his office. That sounded like a good idea not only because I hadn't eaten breakfast, but that would be an excellent opportunity to get to know one another a little better. He called Brenda.

"Brenda, let's get Mr. Braddock and me a light lunch up here. Make it a steak salad for both of us." He held the phone to the side while he asked, "I assume medium rare, Richard?"

The light lunch, if you could call it that, was great, but I started to feel very conflicted. Here I was enjoying lunch, and a view of the lake, within a few days of a friend's murder. I'm not a stranger to death, but this felt odd somehow. Greg Dillard seemed to take the death of an agent almost as a routine event.

The lunch was only light if you didn't eat it all, and the wine options were equally impressive. I was starting to get a different feeling about the DHS. Wine and steak in the Oxford office during lunch while overlooking Lake Michigan? I was wondering what a blue-collar taxpayer might say. The salad was cold in two ways: temperature and with respect to Brad's murder.

After sharing some small talk about Chicago and reviewing my personal history, I was expecting that Greg Dillard would be all business, and maybe his philosophy was that bad things happen and you have to move on. For about ten minutes, he maintained a relaxed and calm disposition, with an air of aloofness that would be intimidating if you had just met him, but after forty-five minutes of chitchat, Greg turned out to be a reasonable guy. He had a keen sense of humor, had a quick wit, and was sort of a wiseass himself. He could run for a high office since no one would be able to shake him during a public debate. Finally, after he found out more about me than most people know, he shared information about the evening when Brad was killed.

"Honestly, Richard, we know very little. We know Brad was killed late in the evening, about nine o'clock, right here in his office. That, in its own right, is astonishing, since the security level is quite high, as you would assume. Cameras are on every floor, and how the perps got by the guards is unknown."

I was surprised to hear the "perp" word, since that was more like something a street cop would say. Greg was turning out to be an interesting fellow.

He continued, "Security video shows two men casually coming up to Brad's floor and going into his office after knocking once. But before you ask, there are no cameras in his office. About fifteen minutes later, both men left Brad's office and exited the building. No fanfare, no noise, nothing to arouse suspicion."

I asked, "The news implied it was a failed burglary. Was anything missing?"

"We released that info because we didn't have anything else, but it definitely wasn't a burglary. Brad kept nothing in his office worth stealing. His personal assistant verified that, and as you know, the only thing valuable in this business is information, which is kept on several secure servers. Nothing is stored locally. Brad's terminal was untouched, and login records show no attempt was made to access the servers during that time. We are still checking phone records and personal email accounts, but so far we have a dead end."

He continued, "Mr. Dempsey was shot twice at very close range—so close that his body probably served as the silencer. Once to the heart and once to the head. His cell phone was turned off and was still in his pocket. What can you add?"

I was a little disappointed that he said *Mr. Dempsey* instead of *Brad*. A bit too remote and formal for my blood, but Greg did not loosen up quickly.

"Me? Nothing, really. All I knew was that we were going to have dinner tonight at Morton's and that Brad was making the reservations. I hadn't seen Brad for years. I just called on his cell and gave him the name Thi Thom, but I didn't tell him why I was looking for her, and as I said, I did not mention the president."

"What have you found out about her so far?"

"As I said, my research showed she was a Russian computer science student who supposedly immigrated in the two thousands to the US and was maybe in the Chicago area. That's all I told him because that's all I knew. That's about it. Back to Brad, I assume you have questioned his wife and other workers and people related to his recent projects?"

I may have made a mistake here to suggest what Greg Dillard should be doing, but he was not offended.

Greg said, "If his death was related to your call, he didn't have much time to discuss anything with anyone. Obviously, we are turning over all the rocks, but so far, we can't find a motive. We're using facial recognition to try to identify the two assailants, since they made no attempt to hide, but so far this has yielded nothing. I was hoping that bringing you into the investigation might help because you were one of the last people he talked to. I'd like you to view the videos. Maybe one of those faces might ring a bell."

"It's unlikely, but of course, let's have a look."

We spent about an hour looking at all the footage, but I didn't recognize the perps. The two men were dark-complexioned and looked Indo-European. I was taken by how calm and methodical they were—moving slowly and showing no signs of rushing, stress, or emotion. That suggested they were professionals. I was surprised to see they both wore DHS security badges, and they easily accessed the elevator.

"Don't you have to enter a badge number or code of some sort to gain access to the elevator?" I asked.

"Yes, but the badge number that they used had not been assigned. We are obviously digging into how that was possible. All the more reason to suspect burglary was not the objective. These people not only knew what they were doing, but it also looks like they had some inside knowledge of our systems. Very troubling."

I was conflicted again because, although I wanted to help find Brad's killers, I also had to continue looking for Thi Thom. "Greg (we were on a first-name basis now), if it's okay with you, and if I don't get in the way, I'd like to proceed with locating Thi Thom. If I suspect a link to Brad's murder, I will immediately share that with you. Are you okay with that?"

Greg thought for a quiet moment. "Sure, but let's keep in close touch, and don't try to use DHS help without going through me first. Agreed?"

The polite thing to do was to let this discussion settle for a while, but I am not known for political and social correctness, so I blurted out, "Meanwhile, could I see the immigration records I assume Brad was searching?"

"Brad had done a quick high-level search for that name, so I can give you those results. There's nothing in those records someone couldn't locate on their own. I'll have them printed out for you."

Greg called Brenda and asked her to print out the search results Brad had started.

Fifteen minutes later, Brenda appeared and handed Dillard and me two pages. I took a minute to scan the data. The first page listed names Brad had used in his search query. The second page showed specific information on several females named Thi Thom who were about the same age. I was surprised to see several Thi Thoms were also Russian graduates, but only one did graduate work in computer science at the University of Illinois at Chicago. Was that just luck, or what?

My "epiphany light" came on and beamed brightly.

I pointed to that entry on the second page, "This particular Thi Thom supposedly had a green card while working toward becoming a US citizen. Her student visa had been valid for only five years starting from 1994, but I guess no one knows where she is now."

"Looks like you may have already found what you were looking for. Where do I send the invoice?"

Greg may have been relaxed and calm with an air of professional aloofness, but he also had a subtle sense of humor. He was coming around quickly, and I felt like I could work with this guy. He walked me down to the lobby himself rather than delegating that to Brenda. It was a professional way to conclude our meeting.

***

Back at the hotel, I did some digging. I was well aware that the U of I is known as a premier school for computer science at its main campus in Urbana, Illinois. I thought the Chicago division (UIC) was more business-related. However, a quick search of the UIC catalog indicated special emphases in the areas of artificial intelligence, machine learning, computational biology, databases, computer security, data science, graphics, human-computer interaction, networks, software engineering, theoretical computer science, virtual reality, and visualization. Okay, that just about covers everything in the CS field. A visit to UIC should have been my next step, but if there was a link to Brad's death, I would be exposing myself, so I had to be careful. So, I did nothing while I thought about it.

The next day, I decided to call the UIC registrar rather than risk a visit. They could not find a Thi Thom with a quick search. That was unfortunate, but I knew any computer search using older software without the help of modern AI had to have the exact details of which I could not provide. I was told a more in-depth search for a student would require a personal visit, a short interview, a written request, and maybe a consent from the person being looked for. I couldn't do that, so I decided to have breakfast and read a newspaper while my mind replenished its little gray cells, many of which I had killed off years ago. Scorecard so far was Breakfast Plan 1, Progress 0.

I was just about to walk out to the elevator for breakfast when a "1-S" message showed up on my phone. Only fifteen people or so had that number, which I used exclusively for security-sensitive text messages. Greg Dillard had been the latest addition to that list, but he had other ways to contact me as well.

The "1" meant there was only one text message. That was normal, but the "S" meant it was a specially secured message. I had set up my phone with a unique algorithm for messages like this. An "S" text message could only be read once and could not be printed or copied. The message would also disappear sixty seconds after being opened. Basically, an idea I got from the old *Mission Impossible* TV show, only without the smoke. The message was probably from Greg Dillard, but I still had to be on my toes because that one-minute clock was about to start.

I prepared a sheet of paper and tested several hotel pens to find one that hadn't dried up. There's nothing more frustrating than knowing you only have one minute to write something but you have to scratch notes on torn paper. It turns out I didn't need the paper or the pen, because there were only two words in the message: *Terry Jana*. And it didn't come from Greg Dillard. The sender's phone number was unknown and not in my contacts list, and a quick return text yielded "number is not in service." However, its 321 area code rang a bell. When Brad Dempsey went to school in Orlando, Florida, we talked often, and Brad's area code at that time was 321. Did Brad have an encrypted cell used for secure text messages the DHS didn't know about?

I immediately called Dillard and filled him in on that secure text. Greg was intrigued and wanted the number, of course. He would call me back shortly. Twenty minutes later, he called back. "The 321 link was impossible to trace, but the name Terry Jana? We'll do another search for that name, but you'd be interested in knowing we were able to see several attempted hacks from the outside just after your call to Dempsey. Given this activity, I would lay low and not talk to anyone while we figure this out. Someone, somehow, was aware of your call."

I found it interesting that in all my years of working with various US agencies, they were never passive with a "maybe," or "we hope," or "we'll try." It was always "we *will*." Greg was no different when he left little doubt they would "figure it out."

Two hours later, Greg sent me a secure email asking me to come back to the DHS office the next day at 7:00 a.m., but this time a car would pick me up in front of the hotel at 6:45.

The next day, at precisely 7:00 a.m., in a small DHS conference room, I flirted with a new girl named Carla, a cute assistant who flirted back. I assume she was just being respectful to a senior citizen. Greg and Brenda were nowhere to be found. Nevertheless, Carla filled in the blanks.

"Mr. Dillard asked that I do a more in-depth private search on our offline servers for a Terry Jana, and here is what I found. In 2004, a Russian student named Terry Jana, who called herself TJ for short, was working on a PhD project that was a joint effort between the University of Illinois and a semiconductor company called American Integrated Processors (AMIP) located in the Chicago suburb of Elmwood Park. Ms. Jana worked with AMIP as an intern while she was at UIC, but she apparently never returned to her studies. We have little additional information."

I wasn't sure why Greg just didn't email me that information via a secure email. These DHS guys are strange. Anyway, I rode the same car back to the hotel. A simple Google search (I used a secure VPN so no one could track my location) showed AMIP as a twenty-year-old company whose expertise had initially been single-chip microprocessors. Their product line had expanded to include semiconductors used in all types of Internet applications. The company was privately held and appeared to be doing well. I may have a lead on Thi Thom, aka Terry Jana, aka TJ.

The Google Maps drive-by photos of the AMIP building showed no outdoor signage. It didn't even look like a high-tech commercial building, having no visible lobby or loading dock. Public documentation showed the company was incorporated in Delaware in 1999 by two engineers of East Indian descent and probably funded by international venture capital. While at Carnegie Mellon University in Pittsburgh, the CEO, Raj Matesh, had published several papers about how single-chip microprocessor systems were likely to evolve. He had predicted the microprocessor would become ubiquitous. This project was called Smart Integrated Micro-Processor Logic, or SIMPL, and wow, was he right. I think my rental car contained at least twenty microcomputers, as did virtually every electronic doodad I owned, including that Fitbit Lara bought me a year ago that I relegated to my dresser under my underwear because I didn't like what it was reporting.

I needed to talk to Greg again and discuss all this before anyone could make a visit to AMIP, Inc. I called him on our secure line. "I appreciate meeting with Carla. She was accommodating. Cute too. Her info showed that a Terry Jana, or TJ, might have dropped out and gone to work at a company called AMIP. Google shows that AMIP might be a great place to work for a CS person. Shouldn't we talk about my next move? By the way, any progress on Brad?"

"Jesus, Richard, can you at least *try* to not be so creepy? Carla could be your granddaughter, for Chrissake. Anyway, we found both the names Thi Thom and Terry Jana, and U of I records show that after her internship, she probably went to work for AMIP. As far as your next step, you should consider bringing the FBI in on this. No new information on Brad's death."

I felt a little better that Greg used the name Brad and not Mr. Dempsey.

I added, "By the way, I've been receiving warnings from my dark web security scanner. The scanner was logging that someone, or something, maybe just an Internet bot, was perhaps trying to track my cell phone location or secure calls."

"Where did you get a dark web scanner?"

"From a previous client who I won't name. This scanner doesn't leave a fingerprint of its own, but it can't track IP addresses. All it did was scare the hell out of me."

"Walk carefully, Richard. Someone is watching."

Chapter 5

I decided it was time to step up my security to another level. My host hotel has been assisting the CIA and FBI for years with clandestine support, and this had allowed me some leeway when it came to safety considerations. I was on the seventh floor, and that floor was not accessible by elevator or stairs without an access code. In addition, each suite had a wire loop behind the entry door molding, which could be used as a metal detector if the guest had the right equipment, which was in the package I had shipped to myself. Cameras were everywhere and could be monitored by any guest who had the access codes. Each room's Wi-Fi was encrypted with an untraceable VPN relocator. Maybe I could relax for the moment and think about my next move. I thought about calling Lara, but I think my heightened sense of caution would come through in my voice, and I wasn't sure if that unsecured call might put her at risk.

My phone call to Brad had not been encrypted, or, as we used to say in the military, it was "clear text," so it could have been monitored, and I did mention the girl's name I was looking for, but so what?

With all this new information about AMIP and TJ, I needed to report my status to Tanner, who I assumed would keep the president informed. Ten minutes later, after the email was on its way, the concierge let me know a man had called and inquired if I was a registered guest. He would not give his name. The hotel's protocol was to never verify. What the hell was going on?

I started to feel a headache coming on. In fact, my whole body was beginning to ache, even though I hadn't done any heavy lifting. I was the same weight I was twenty-five years ago, maybe an inch shorter, but my center of gravity had shifted. My shape was starting to remind me of that classic Weebles toy from the early seventies. I remember the tag line: "Weebles wobble, but they don't fall down." Maybe thirty minutes in the weight room would help. Who was I kidding? What I really wanted was a gin over ice with three olives. No TV, no Internet, two gins and a good night's sleep. So, that's precisely what I did!

In the morning, I was even more paranoid than the night before. I had to start changing the way I was sleuthing. That caused more stress because I began questioning everything and everybody. Twenty years earlier, it had just been part of the job, but now I was out of practice.

To explore AMIP, I needed a go-between or a proxy I could trust. I decided to call Roger Hest, an old friend from my more active days. Roger and I used to race cars together, and later in life after military service, we had occasionally worked on teams that Brad Dempsey had twice fed intel, so he knew Brad. At five foot nine and one hundred fifty pounds, it was clear that Roger was a thinker rather than a physical sort. His connections and an excellent team of ex-military guys had allowed him to run his own private security business located right there in Chicago. I would trust Roger with the keys to my Ferrari, if I had a Ferrari, which I don't. I didn't know if Roger's business was still operating, but if it was I would have to tell him all the details of what I was doing. That might not go down favorably with Tanner or the president, so I wouldn't tell them right away. I would first see if Roger was operating and interested, and if not, I was sure he would keep it quiet. Roger would know the call was classified because I would be using an encrypted voice link. It was an old number, but it went through.

After a few rings, Roger answered, "Crap. With the encryption and your caller ID, something told me this wasn't going to be a social call. So wassup, you old POS?"

"Now, is that any way to start a conversation with an old school buddy?"

"Sorry, Rich. I apologize. It's just that we said if we lived through that last ordeal, we would both retire. I'm alive and obviously not retired, but I heard that you actually did retire."

"Well, I was on that path until a few weeks ago. Then I got a phone call from good ol' Paul Elliot."

"Kiss-Ass Paul? Class-King Paul? Where-Is-My-Entourage Paul? Yeah, I remember Paul all right. But I have to give him some credit—I've heard he's done all right for himself. Why would President Paul call you? Did his old Philco TV break down, and you're the only electronics nerd he could think of?"

"Are you having a bad day, Rog? I could call back later after the drugs have worn off."

"All right, all right, what's going on?"

"Can we share some pizza and beer at Nino's on North Avenue tonight? Then I can explain."

"Sure, but you're buying."

***

We met at seven, and soon Roger and I were reminiscing about old times. I realized I was beginning to forget how great Chicago pizza was. I can forget someone's name I just met fifteen minutes ago, but my smell and taste glands time-warped me back fifty years. I might have to buy a Chicago hot dog tomorrow, or maybe a sliced Italian beef sandwich. I told Roger everything I knew and all the players so far. He was riveted. We clinked beer glasses.

With a snide look on his face, Roger summarized his thoughts. "So, if I have this right, Elliot dorked a girl during the war, had a kid, and didn't tell anyone. And now he wants you to find her. You think you may have found her here in Chicago, but as you dig in, you're getting scared, so you need a stand-in to take all the risks and do all the work, so you can take all the credit later. Do I have it?"

I laughed and said, "That's actually pretty close. Don't forget, you have the advantage of being an unknown player, and we'd be looking out for one another as always. Right? So, are you in?"

"That's the Braddock I know and love. Of course, I'm in. Fish aren't biting at this time of year anyway unless you like to freeze your ass off. What's our next move?"

"Well, first, I need to tell this guy Tanner, and Greg from the DHS, and Elliot that you're on the team. You and your background will be checked out thoroughly, so I hope you haven't done anything really embarrassing. And remember, this is classified. Dillard wants me to bring in the FBI, but I'm not ready for that yet. Then we'll need to find out if Brad's TJ is really Thi Thom, and if she really does work at AMIP."

"And I get to do all this while you watch from a safe distance, right?"

I added, "You could get started with some Internet searching, but sooner or later, someone will probably have to visit AMIP and find out what she does there."

As Roger was finishing a pull off his second longneck, he said, "Something tells me the Internet search path has already been well-traveled and won't get us anywhere, and it sounds risky too. By the way, what does this gig pay? Or do I already know the answer to that too?"

"There might be some restitution later."

"Might. I bet. But you're buying tonight! Anyhoo . . . if this TJ really is Paul's daughter, what do we care what she does for a living? Paul just wants to find her, right?"

"Maybe," I responded, "but I have a sneaking suspicion there's more to this than just a missing person, especially if it's linked to Dempsey's murder. I guess the shooting could be a coincidence, but it definitely doesn't smell like that. Why don't we get started with you stopping by my hotel on Monday morning? We can have breakfast on me, and then we can talk about a plan. Bring your credentials."

***

Rog showed up at my hotel at 8:00 a.m., punctual as usual, and ready for a free breakfast. The concierge called my room for me to verify. "Tell Mr. Hest I'll be down in fifteen minutes. Send him to the restaurant and tell him to sit at a private table."

After a tranquil ride down in the elevator, I walked into a very quiet, almost vacant restaurant. Roger was sitting in a corner booth wearing jeans and a Cubs World Series T-shirt. I greeted, "Roger, how the hell is your day going so far?" Pointing at his shirt, I said, "You know that'll never happen again."

"You know, Dick (he used to call me by that name), your abrasive character and sarcasm are really your only assets.

And to answer your question, not very well! The more I thought about this, the more it was obvious that you have nothing to lose here. You are much older looking than me and supposedly retired with no epitaph to leave for the world. I, on the other hand, have a virile life to live. Yet here I sit after being scanned and probed by the hotel's security, wondering what is deficient in my mentality that has allowed me to go this far. I feel like I'm about to risk it all while you sit in your hotel room eating bonbons and drinking gin."

"Not quite, Rog. I don't like bonbons, and even if I did, they don't go well with gin. The rest of what you say is fairly accurate. And please use the name Rich."

"Let's quit stalling and let me get a cup of coffee. There's no coffee on the El, and my first three cups from home have worn off. After that, we can talk about the task at hand."

"Did you do any digging at all?"

"I did a little on AMIP only. We know it's a private corporation, but who owns it, how is it funded, and what's their strategy? I might be able to do some background checking on this TJ to verify she is who we think she is, and if that's a positive, then what's she doing at AMIP? Then after lunch—"

"It'll take that long, huh? I guess I should assume you'd slow down as you aged."

"Asshole."

"Anyway, sounds like a good start, but just so you know, I'm feeling some heat from an unknown source I haven't fleshed out, and I have this nagging feeling telling me the game is about to go underfoot. A simple missing person case wouldn't have all these tentacles. Unless it's just a case of strange coincidences. I suggest you start by talking to UIC, somehow get a photo of TJ if possible, and then start some twenty-four-hour surveillance to find out where she lives and what she does in her private time. If we're lucky, this all could come to a head fairly quickly. Still the same team?"

"Yeah, they're still with me, but I'm not sure why. But there's no telling what they'll do after I tell them you're involved."

"You can tell them about me, but remember, don't tell them about the president. This is just a normal surveillance job."

Roger said, "I'm not so sure about that either!"

Chapter 6

While Rog went off to assemble his team, I reviewed the incoming phone records of the concierge. The phone number of the gentleman who called and asked if I was a guest came from the DHS. A quick call to Dillard verified they had indeed followed up to make sure I was staying in a secure location. I was just overly suspicious. Nevertheless, I would be watching over my shoulder, because today's technology allows a person to make a call from any area code and even from a particular number, especially if that number is a generic number belonging to a corporation or group.

Then I started to think about Roger. I have been blessed with an inner conscience or a guardian angel that instinctively speaks to me through my gut. As Edward G. Robinson said in *Double Indemnity*, "How do I know? Because there's a little man inside that tells me." When I make a mistake or sense an unresolved issue, that little man gnaws at me until I resolve it. That fellow was talking to me now and threatening to not let my digestive system process what would otherwise be considered a great breakfast. Maybe I should have gone solo on this one. Roger offered to help only because he was a great friend and I asked, but I knew he was questioning what we were doing. Roger had a family with two children and a constructive, hopeful future. Perhaps I should have called him off and told him to put the dogs back in their cages. I was in the middle of that thought when Roger called on my secure line.

"Guess what, Dickie."

I never liked that nickname, and he knew it.

"AMIP probably has links to Iran. Word on the street suggests the CEO, Raj Matesh, is just a techy puppet master. Original funding was traced to several overseas banks with historical ties to Middle Eastern governments. This was before our government shut down interactions with those banks. I haven't found out yet what exactly AMIP is making and selling for revenue, since their books aren't public. Still, I managed to locate a purchasing agent for an Internet service provider that says they've been buying chips from AMIP for years. She had no idea what the chips do, but it was clear from the volume purchased that they must be an essential part of Internet hardware. Surveillance has been set up and will start this evening, but anything more specific would require a court order, which I don't believe we are ready for. *Verstehen Sie?*"

"Yes, I got it. Once we know where TJ lives, we should be able to explore public records. Then I'll communicate back to Dillard what we found. I'll hold off for now, while we're still ignorant."

Roger said, "I'm used to being ignorant. And the more I work with you, the more ignorant I get."

I said, "Remember, ignorant is better than stupid. Ignorant just means you don't know something, but stupid means you knew, but you did it anyway." Then I pondered out loud, "Maybe we could contact some customers who are using those AMIP chips and see if there's anything there. It would be nice to get a better picture of their business. *Verstehen Sie?* Or should I say it in Czech? *Pochopit?*"

Roger replied, "Now *that's* funny. I'll see what I can do. Hey, I had another thought. From time to time, I work with a really sharp young coder. He was a video game designer turned hacker before the FBI gave him the option of voluntarily turning over a new leaf and deciding to help the authorities. He chose to accept the suggestion. We could ask him to apply for a job at AMIP. If he could get hired, we'd have a mole inside."

"I had considered that already, but I didn't have a contact who wasn't already known. What does this guy's resume look like?"

"The sensitive issues have been expunged from his record, so his documentation purports him as a sharp Berkeley grad who's single and keeps to himself. He spent a few years working for a semiconductor company in Silicon Valley, so he understands hardware as well as software. He has been thoroughly vetted and can be trusted. I would imagine he might be a good pick for a company like AMIP if they're hiring. I couldn't find any records of AMIP posting open positions on the typical job sites, but that doesn't surprise me since this level is usually filled via networking. His name is Kevin Dupree. He's not currently assigned, and as an extra boost, he has a home at Lake Geneva, Wisconsin, so he's local . . . sort of. Wanna meet him?"

"A mole. Hmmm. I'm not sure we're ready for that level of infiltration yet. But if you trust him, I'd like to talk to him. Make sure he understands—top secret! If Tanner or Paul find out I'm talking to him before he was vetted, we'd get canned, and who knows what else. When can I meet him?"

"How about lunch today? Your place? Say one thirty? I'll give him your secure number, if that's okay. You won't have any problem picking him out. He's good looking and has a ponytail."

After informing the concierge I would have a visitor for lunch, Kevin Dupree was escorted into the restaurant at 1:30 sharp. He was a dark-complexioned, late-thirty-something with dark brown hair. He was casually well-dressed, with his top two shirt buttons open, no undershirt, and a professionally quaffed ponytail. I guessed he was a little over six feet tall, but his overwhelming features were his square jaw and confident posture. This guy was confident and good-looking! I had no idea what TJ looked like yet, but I could imagine a typical female just might like a guy like Kevin.

I introduced myself. "Hello, Kevin. Have a seat and feel free to ask any and all questions. Roger tells me you have quite a background, but before we get into that, what has he told you about me and why we are meeting today?"

"Rog just asked me how I felt about getting a job as a mole."

"Well, that's pretty accurate. Have you done any intelligence gathering like this before?"

"Several times. I find it better than actually working," he said with a laugh. "When I was employed out west, I grew bored easily. I guess my attention window is only about two years, so gathering high-tech info for the good guys over short periods fits me better than attending company meetings. Now, I get an assignment, and then I take a break until the next one. I like it."

"I heard from Rog your degree is in software, but you also have been exposed to hardware. How did that come about?"

"You can think of software as the language that hardware requires. There are not as many hardware-only solutions as there used to be. You have to build a program that controls the hardware, and you can't do that very effectively unless you know how the hardware works. So, before I even got started in software, I was doing logic design for hardware systems. I built my own radio control systems, built my own amateur radio equipment, and helped design a new architecture for a microprocessor. I even had a few papers published about the pros and cons of various microprocessor architectures. You really have to know both, but my bias was the software because, as I used to say, software is what makes hardware happen. Hardware-only guys hate that."

"And the hacking part?"

"I've always been good at puzzles and math and figuring out how to circumvent access codes. Hacking that bypasses a security system is basic puzzle solving using probabilities. It was never my intent to benefit financially; I just did it for fun. But it stopped being fun when I was busted by the NSA. They didn't appreciate my hobby. I was threatened with fines and jail time and restricted from owning or operating a computer for two years. I could handle the fines and maybe even prison, but not the computer access part. So, we came to an agreement that works for both of us. No regrets."

"How long have you been doing this high-tech undercover work?"

"About ten years or so. It's a good living."

"Has Roger given you any details about this potential assignment?"

"Nope. Only that it's in Chicago and involves chips or software."

"How much time do you have today?"

"I'm here until the wine runs out."

For the next hour or so, I filled Kevin in on as much detail as I knew. I informed him of the members of our group, including Greg, Tanner, and the president. He asked great questions and wasn't too concerned about the risks. He was a free spirit who took an adult view of the decisions he had made, or was planning on making, and the ramifications therein. It was clear to me after fifteen minutes that we would communicate well together. For the most part, he just listened. I didn't have him sign anything; we just shook hands. Then he delved into some more detailed questions.

Kevin started, "So, we're not sure this TJ, or Terry Jana, is really Thi Thom yet."

"Correct."

"And we don't even know what she looks like?"

"Correct."

"And she's about fifty years old?"

"Must be."

"And the death of your friend Brad may or may not be related?"

"Also correct."

"And the president is not fully up to speed yet."

"He's a busy man."

"So, how do you propose I get hired by AMIP if they haven't posted any job openings?"

I said, "Well, maybe you could help with that. Maybe make a cold call. I could get you some names of AMIP customers. That might get you a foot in the door. And the CEO, a Mr. Raj Matesh, has published several papers about single-chip microprocessors. We've heard he may not be the one calling the shots, but it couldn't hurt if you had read his papers. That would definitely break the ice in the right circumstance."

Kevin continued, "Do we know anything about the chips AMIP sells or how software is related?"

"Nope."

"Do we have a guess as to AMIP's revenue?"

"Nope. As I said, they're private, but their main office is not anything like the Silicon Valley multistory glass palaces we're used to. They don't flaunt what they do. I don't know if other locations are involved, but I assume there must be a semiconductor facility somewhere because local zoning wouldn't allow a semiconductor fab facility within the city. They may not even have a semiconductor facility. They could farm out fabrication once the chip design is complete. However, I would think not, because farming out semiconductor processing only works for small volumes that can support a higher price, but from what we've found out so far, AMIP volume is very high. For high-volume chips, companies want to control the process and the profit margins themselves."

Kevin added, "I'd like to wait and see the pictures of TJ that Roger gets, so I at least have a clue of what she looks like."

"Makes sense. I assume you have a secure email? I'll update the president and this guy Tanner tonight about you but leave out that we are close to finding his daughter. And remember, only a few of us know about this. This is all classified. No one can know what we are doing, including the authorities."

Kevin left me his credentials that I felt would satisfy Tanner and the president.

Chapter 7

Back in my room, I just sat there wondering if I should be doing something. A martini! That's it. I needed a gin martini. A gin martini to me was gin on the rocks with three olives. No water, no spritzer, and no vermouth either. The closest vermouth has ever come to one of my martinis was when a bottle was opened in the same room—and it had to be closed quickly. My retired body can't handle gin as well as it used to, so I did as my dad used to say: "Everything in moderation." He had another phrase too: "If it burns blue, it's safe to drink." I wondered about that last one because Sterno burns blue. So much for my father's drinking philosophies.

Before finishing my martini, I sent a secure email to Tanner and the president and informed them about the addition of Kevin Dupree into the group. I also told them we hadn't found Thi Thom yet but felt like we were getting close. I blind copied the group. Within ten minutes, I received a response from Tanner stating he was coming to Chicago. I could see no benefit in Tanner hanging around asking questions and maybe shooting somebody, so I quickly responded this was not a good time for him to visit. I still didn't understand why Tanner was even involved. I told him to hold off for just a little while.

Ten minutes after that, Rog sent an email saying they already snapped a picture of TJ, and was this a good time for him to call. With only one gin down, it was as good a time as it was going to get.

One ringy-dingy later, I answered, "Hey, Rog. Waassssuup?"

"Feeling good, are we? I have photos and feedback from the guys. Now? Or tomorrow when you can buy me another great breakfast?"

"Breakfasts here are expensive. Come onnnn down now."

Right after I had reached my gin limit—two, or was it three? The concierge called and said Roger had arrived and had been cleared. I met him in the lobby, and we came back to my room.

The door-loop metal detector alarmed as soon as Roger entered my room.

"Still using the old metal detector trick, eh? That's my Nam leg plate, not a gun. They took care of that downstairs. Hey, beautiful place, Braddock. The prez must be paying you well. Got anything to drink?"

"I saw your eyes lock on that bar before your foot was in the door. And no! He's not paying me well."

We chit-chatted for ten minutes while Rog poured himself a vodka, never asking if I wanted one and never bringing up the photos of TJ. He knew I would like Kevin, and since he read my email to Paul, he found no reason to discuss it. We had our mini-team assembled—the smaller, the better—and we were operational, so I was just waiting, knowing Roger would fill me in when he was ready, and that would have to wait until after his drink.

Rog finished his vodka, then laid down some photos on the coffee table. "There are only about twenty employees at the AMIP's Elmwood Park location, so they can't be processing silicon there. These photos were taken as people came and went during the day, and there's only one female who looks Asian or Vietnamese. And because we are so damn good at what we do, we managed to get a close-up of her badge, even in the dim light from hundreds of yards away. Did I say we were good?"

The telephoto shot was a reasonably clear view of her badge showing TJ as her name and even her title: IC Test Mgr. As interesting and as pertinent as that was, it did not measure up to the overall picture of TJ herself. She was gorgeous! Slim, well-proportioned, beautiful complexion, shoulder-length hair that could be a magazine ad for a conditioning shampoo. She was wearing a white short-sleeve blouse that looked a little tight and was tucked into a black skirt that ended well above her knees. She had on patent leather high heels and no stockings, from what I could tell, but her legs didn't need them. And she was supposed to be fifty years old?

Roger looked at me with a cocky smile and said, "Kevin would be pleased."

Rog continued, "She lives in an upscale, single-family house near O'Hare. It doesn't appear she's married or living with anyone. She drives a brand-new Jaguar, and here's the plate. AMIP provides secure underground parking, so it was a little difficult to know if it was her driving the Jag, and it was no easy task tailing her through the traffic either. Did I mention we're good at this?"

"Jesus, Rog. Stop waving the flag. Today's lunch is starting to back up in my throat."

"Yeah. Well, anyway, now that we have her address, it shouldn't take long to get the history on the house. And once we get her bank information, we'll have a good picture of who she is and how she's living. But there is one thing that surprises me, and I'd like to know if you agree. She is not trying to be incognito. She also seems fairly well off with a good job, and overall, she is doing very well for herself. I don't see her interacting with undesirables unless she is hiding it very well. As far as Paul Elliot needing to help her out, I doubt she needs anything."

"Great work, Rog, and I would agree from this perspective that she is probably not directly related to what happened to Brad. Still, I'll hold off communication with the president until we know a little more. For example, we still don't know if this TJ, or Terry Jana, is really Thi Thom. Kevin will hopefully find that out if he can get hired. Pass those photos over to Kevin, but tell him not to do anything yet. I'm feeling like another martini with maybe an extra olive. Care for a bonbon?"

Chapter 8

The next day, Roger continued the detective work, uncovering all he could about Terry Jana that didn't require a warrant. He checked in about 6:00 p.m.

"Hey, Dickie (Roger never backed off—he was always just as sarcastic as I was), no big surprises so far, because I could not verify that Ms. Terry Jana ever became a citizen, not that I expected that. But we also couldn't find any record of her arriving in the United States, nor does she have a Social Security card or even a bank account, so it came as no surprise that the house and car are owned by and registered to AMIP. We couldn't find anything in her name. Even the DMV doesn't show a Terry Jana living at her address. Don't you agree this is suspicious?"

I agreed. "This is getting more interesting by the day. I'll have to sleep on that and pass on your findings to Dillard."

Roger said, "We need to get Kevin in there and start fleshing out the details. Emphasis on *flesh*."

I said, "Jeez, Rog, hold it back a little, would you? Anyway, along those lines, I've been thinking . . . don't say it! It would be difficult for Kevin to get hired. They are not in the market for someone right now, and he can't just walk in the door. I think I have a better scheme that would allow Kevin to get inside AMIP without going through the decision tree and the detailed security checks that a new hire would require.

"Remember, I spent some time working in the semiconductor industry, and I assume you are aware that a critical step in the semiconductor production process is testing the chips while they are still part of the wafer—you know, the wafer probe machines. Production stops cold when the prober quits, and with each wafer containing thousands of potential chips, the probers are usually monitored twenty-four seven. TJ's badge showed she is the IC Test Manager, so this equipment would fall under her management.

"High-end wafer probers are generally connected to a central monitoring station or the machine manufacturer themselves, which allows the tracking of how many chips were tested and total hours of operation, both of which help predict when a probe machine might need maintenance. Since Kevin has a self-earned degree in hacking, he may be able to break into those systems and cause an interruption that would force AMIP to call the tech support people at the probe machine vendor. With the FBI's help, that call could be redirected to Kevin Dupree Incorporated, master prober tech support. What do you think?"

"I like it. I'm sure I can find out whose wafer probers they're using."

Roger went to work. The next day he told me AMIP had six Zietech M300 wafer probers all online 24/7. Those machines could probe the largest wafers currently being used in the industry. They were considered the Cadillac of probe machines. Rog and I set up a meeting with Kevin, and without the slightest hesitation, Kevin said he could probably hack into the Zietech net.

I called Greg and filled him in on the plan. Greg said, "I knew we would bring the FBI into this sooner or later. I know just the guy ... Jeff Shaw. I've worked with him over the past fifteen years. Ex-military and as patriotic as a Canadian Mounty. He's our man."

I quickly sent a secure message to Tanner and the president that I would probably be adding Jeff Shaw to our group. President Elliot called me to remind me to keep the size of the group to a minimum. He didn't want me broadcasting this information just because it was easy to do.

We had a meeting already set up at Greg's office, so I told Greg I'd like to meet with Shaw beforehand. Greg said, "I knew you would want to interview Shaw. Is 'interview' too strong a word? By the way, don't be put off by Jeff's strong but quiet nature. That's just part of his persona."

"No, it's an interview no matter how you cut it. There's a lot at stake here, so being careful is just being prudent. Say, a couple of hours before our group meeting?"

Jeff Shaw showed up at my hotel three hours beforehand and was checked out and seated in a small private conference room just off the restaurant.

"Jeff Shaw, I'm Richard Braddock. Glad to meet you. Greg Dillard speaks highly of you. I'm a retired PI, but I assume Greg already told you that."

Jeff was also a big man like Greg, and I was instantly concerned if my grip would survive his handshake any better than Greg's. He stood up and shook my hand gently (he was taking it easy on this old guy) and said only four words, "Glad to meet you." Jeff was exactly what Greg implied. Tall, maybe six foot four, about 230 pounds and definitely V-shaped. I would have guessed he was a part-time bodybuilder—definitely not a lean runner. He wore a look that communicated: *Okay, I'm here. Now what?*

"Can you give me a quick rundown on your background?" I asked.

Jeff dove in with a monotone voice, as if he had practiced the narrative many times before.

"Annapolis Naval Academy, 1965. Vietnam, Marines 1965 through 1985. Raider. Top Secret clearance with Crypto access as required. Silver Star and Distinguished Service Cross in 1979. Never married, don't smoke, drink in moderation. Hobbies are hunting and weightlifting. Joined the FBI in 1991."

Where does an undereducated smartass PI go from there? I sucked it up and spent the next twenty minutes telling Jeff Shaw everything he needed or wanted to know about the mission. He listened and asked very few questions. He knew nothing about semiconductor processing or software, but he had heard about semiconductor wafer probing. He had seen a video of the process on YouTube. At the end of our talk, he asked one last question: "Is there any possibility the president could be in danger?"

Patriotic was an understatement. I did my best to answer. "No, I don't think so. Brad Dempsey's death is an unknown that is hanging over all this, but so far the connection seems coincidental."

I asked this United States version of Dudley Do-Right to attend our meeting later that day.

Greg, Roger, Kevin, Jeff Shaw, and I met at Greg's office to do some bonding and discuss the overall plan we were about to launch. It was the first time we all were in the same room, checking one another out. Adult beverages helped Kevin, Roger, and me; Greg and Jeff abstained. Kevin was absolutely delighted with the photos of TJ, and he liked the idea of impersonating a wafer prober tech support guy. FBI Jeff was quick to agree and could quickly set up a phone tap such that any AMIP calls to Zietech could be redirected to us. Zietech had a local tech support office in downtown Chicago.

I gave Kevin the parameters for the hack. "We want to stop the probers and display an innocuous message on the terminal that would force a tech support call."

"Once I get AMIP's IP address and break into the network, what do you want the message to say?"

I asked, "After you're in, do you think you could find data such as machine serial numbers, the name of the tech support person that normally handles their account, how many chips have been probed, typical canned messages, and so forth?"

"Once I get into the database, I could find whatever is stored there. If it's there, I'll get it."

I scratched out a sample message on a note pad. "Then let's assume you can find the probe count number and then round it up to the next thousand. Then the message could display something like this."

> Zietech has detected that this machine will soon approach
> xxxxxxx
> operations without maintenance or a software upgrade.
> Tracking data is potentially at risk. Contact Zietech support immediately.

"And if possible, we should shut down the probers. That definitely would force a call. Then the proxy Zietech receptionist would explain AMIP's normal tech support person was unavailable, but Kevin Dupree could be dispatched immediately. That'll get you in. We'd better get started on your Zietech badge. And Jeff, I'd like to put a wire and an earpiece on Kevin so we can follow the discussion as long as the building isn't shielded. You okay with the wire, Kevin? I won't do much talking, so as not to interrupt your train of thought."

"No problem," said Kevin. "I've worn many, and these new ones are almost undetectable."

"One potential problem," I said. "Semiconductor cleanrooms are not only clean physically, but sensitive chips being tested don't like radio interference or other sources of electrical noise either. Therefore, the cleanroom is likely to block our communications. We'll just have to cross that bridge when we get to it."

***

Three days later, at about 11:00 a.m., Kevin uploaded the hack, and the probe machines that were currently in use promptly shut down. We received a call from AMIP within fifteen minutes. Kevin wasted no time walking directly into AMIP, where a guard was waiting.

Greg, Jeff, and I were listening and recording from Kevin's microphone. I was the only one who could talk back to Kevin.

Kevin was greeted by a manager named Yalina, who politely provided escort. Kevin was professional and asked if, on their way out, he could at least say hello to one of his mentors, Mr. Raj Matesh. Yalina said Mr. Matesh was probably very busy and would most likely not be available. Yet on their way in, Matesh's door happened to be ajar. Kevin boldly stuck his head in and said, "Mr. Matesh. You don't know me, and I don't mean to interrupt you, but I was a student at Carnegie when you were doing your work on microprocessors. I just wanted to say your papers spurred me to start building my career in software. Sorry to bother you."

Mr. Matesh asked, "What did you say your name was?"

"Kevin. Kevin Dupree."

"Are you a software engineer?"

Kevin's spontaneous response was well put, "Well, currently I'm in tech support at Zietech. There's a prober problem; that's why I'm here."

"Did you say you graduated from CMU?"

"No, I went to CMU, but I transferred to Berkeley. Then I was hired by Sony to help develop a game chip and write some software. Eventually, I relocated back here."

"How did you end up in Chicago?"

"Nothing felt stable to me out west. Working in San Mateo just didn't sit well with me either. The Midwest is my home. So, I'm back home and managed to find a great position with Zietech."

"You said you did some chip development out west?"

"Yes, but I'm not an actual chip designer. I worked at the architectural level, closely akin to the work you explained in your papers, but I did logic design, and I like to code."

"Yalina, who is Mr. Dupree talking to?" Mr. Matesh queried.

"I was taking him to see TJ since the probers are down."

"That is the highest priority. You'd better get to it. Maybe we'll talk later, uh . . . Kevin."

I could hear Yalina's response, "Right away, sir. Kevin, would you follow me, please?"

I think Kevin smiled, probably waved, and said, "Great to see you again, Mr. Matesh. And thanks."

So far, so good.

**

Yalina seated Kevin in her office, then asked if he wanted a drink while she stepped out to check with TJ. In less than five minutes, Yalina came back with a gentleman named Bay Anderson, who explained that Terry Jana, the head of integrated circuit testing, was out for an hour or so and they were not able to contact her so far, but they didn't want Kevin to leave. The probers had to be tended to as soon as possible. Bay said he'd be glad to take Kevin out for a quick lunch while they waited.

Bay said, "There's a great pizza place just down the street. You okay with pizza for lunch? I've only been here for a couple of years, but I managed to find the best pizza. If that's okay, we better get going, because we'll have to come back as soon as TJ checks in."

I could clearly hear Kevin say, "I'm always in the mood for Chicago pizza. That was one thing I really missed when I was out west. California may lead the nation in many ways, but they never figured out how to make a good pizza."

"So, you're from California. Yeah, it's different here."

Bay sounded young but helpful and friendly, but perhaps a little inexperienced. He sounded like a techy who was probably too inexperienced to have developed a professional persona yet. That was just fine for us but a bit of a surprise for a high-end semiconductor vendor.

The pizza joint was within walking distance. Bay said, "Let's get our order in, and then we'll talk. Want a beer? Or not while on duty?"

Kevin said, "Normally, I'd say yes, but I'd better not drink anything while on a support call. Where's the restroom? I need to excuse myself for a pee break."

From the bathroom, Kevin made sure the wire was working. "Richard, I'm in and about to meet with TJ. No issues so far. Wire working okay?"

I responded, "I can hear you the best when you are out of the building, but I think I'll be able to hear you fine when you finally meet TJ. Take it easy, Kevin. Walk slowly and be aware of your surroundings. There's a lot at stake."

Bay should have known better than to ask that beer question. They decided to share an Italian sausage pizza. One thing Kevin learned a long time ago was that people love to talk about what they do, so he started.

"This is my first tech call to AMIP. What kind of semiconductors do you make here? I was surprised to see your account shows six three-hundred-millimeter wafer probers. Those can handle thousands of chips per hour, more than I typically see, even in Silicon Valley."

Bay replied, "I don't know too much about the technical details of our chips, but I can give you some general info. Our main product line is a series of integrated circuits that are used for the Internet. These started out as custom chips that were designed right here, and some are smart chips, meaning they have a small processor, or CPU, on the chip. But our highest volume chips are actually the smallest, and those do not have a CPU on-chip. I'm not exactly sure what those chips do, but I know they're important."

I whispered to Kevin via his earpiece, "Ask him what chips were being tested now."

Kevin asked, "Were those non-CPU chips the ones that were being tested when the probers went down?"

Bay tried to respond, "Probably, but I'm not positive. But those seem to be all we've been running lately."

Kevin moved on. "But you have other semiconductor devices as well?"

"We can do it all when it comes to Internet stuff. Most people have never heard of us because we don't sell anything on the open market. We are strictly an OEM supplier, and there would be no public market for most of our chips anyway."

Kevin asked, "Are these custom chips?"

"That's the way it started, but not anymore. Internet protocols are generic now."

I could sense Kevin stopping, thinking, and continuing. "So, when it started, an OEM manufacturer of server systems, or laptops, or anything that needs to talk over the Internet comes to you with a specification, and you design a custom chip just for them?"

"Yeah, but not so much anymore."

Kevin clarified, "Because the chips are becoming ubiquitous?"

"Pretty much."

Kevin asked, "Enough volume to require second sources?"

"Of course. We have to provide a second or third source. We have to share the semiconductor tooling with other semiconductor vendors. The industry requires that."

I let Kevin prod a little more. "So, what about the chips with an onboard CPU? What do they do?"

Bay did his best. "I'm not sure about those. They are much lower in volume."

Kevin seemed to be getting good feedback from Bay, so I asked him to switch the discussion to the wafer probers. After all, that's why he was there.

Kevin asked, "Where do the test programs come from?"

"The test routines are developed here, but I'm not sure who actually does that. I know the routines are simulated in the lab. All that is TJ's area."

Kevin said, "I see. The test routines are written and debugged right here then. In the lab?"

"You got it."

"What about software bugs in the test routines? They happen, you know."

"No bugs! That would be disastrous. But you know how fast things change in electronics. The only time we have seen bugs in the test routines is right after a new chip was designed, but we find those bugs before we go into production. Hopefully." I could hear Bay snort and chuckle out loud.

Kevin asked, "I get it. So, who's the competition?"

"Any semiconductor supplier could be a competitor. You name it: TI, AMD, Intel, and a host of other suppliers, but mostly from overseas, such as China or Korea. But this high-volume chip is a very small die and very inexpensive. Any semiconductor vendor would think twice before trying to enter this market that we essentially have owned for years and where the profit margin is small, but we still have to stay on our toes."

"That high-volume chip is that one you were describing?"

"Yep. That's one of our best-selling Internet chips. We have shipped millions of those, and who knows how many our second sources have shipped."

I try not to talk over a wire, so I don't distract, but I blurted out loud, "Holy Christ. With an M?"

After a short pause, a gulp, and I'm sure with a stunned look on his face, Kevin continued, "Where's the semiconductor facility that can support that many chips?"

I couldn't believe what I was hearing. Millions of chips? I prompted Kevin to take it easy. "Hey Kev, don't push this marketing thing. We don't want to alarm Bay with too many probing questions." I emphasized the word *probing* just for fun.

Bay answered Kevin's question, "Wafer fab is in Kansas City. Since this chip is so small and the Zietechs can handle huge wafers, the volume came pretty easy. And remember, we have second-source suppliers too. We had plans to move testing to Kansas just so we don't have to ship wafers back and forth, but since we spent a lot of development time with prototype runs and customer beta testing here, it just hasn't happened yet. IC testing is fifty percent of our facility here, and the testing equipment is expensive, as you well know, so we just haven't moved anything yet, but we will. You'd still be our Zietech support guy, right?"

They enjoyed the rest of their lunch while I pondered that Bay Anderson had only been there two years. Somehow, I would expect a technical design manager of such a lucrative business would have more seat time than that. I was tempted to tell Kevin to ask about the rest of the staff just to get his take on TJ's history, but I held off. We already knew her badge said IC Test Manager, and Bay filled in the voids, so what else did we need to know? So far, so good.

I told Kevin to excuse himself to use the restroom. Once he was in a private location again, I said I would convene a group meeting later that night and that I was pleased with how well our plan seemed to be working. He was doing a good job. Kevin was pumped and anxious to the point of enthusiasm to finally meet the infamous and beautiful Terry Jana.

***

When Kevin and Bay arrived back at AMIP, Terry Jana was still fifteen minutes away, so Bay suggested a quick tour of the facility. I could tell that the tour was boring. Kevin had seen it all before, and apparently AMIP didn't get the memo that there's a current trend away from cubicles. Kevin commented to me that everybody was crunched into their ten-by-ten spaces with gray, fabric-covered, five-foot dividers, built-in desk surfaces, the same five-legged office chairs, and Post-it Notes and thumb pins holding up calendars and pictures of their pets. At least the bathrooms had stalls if I had to talk to Kevin in private.

Kevin wasn't used to morgue-quiet facilities like this. Full carpeting, padded dividers, and no ringing phones. Weird. There was no laughing, and no one got out of their chair to shake his hand, although a few said hi. There were just a few squat windows at ceiling level. Natural light from these slots helped the mood a little, but because the windows were so high, there wasn't much to look at from the inside except tree limbs, blue sky, and clouds. The building probably started as a sweat factory of some sort back in the twenties or thirties. It was old-school Chicago.

There were only two private offices in the front half of the building, one at each front corner. One was Raj Matesh's, and the other was Yalina's. Kevin guessed Bay was assigned to a cubicle. The back half of the building was separated from the front half by a solid wall with an airlock marked "Semiconductor Testing." Bay explained that because semiconductor testing requires a Class-100 or better cleanroom environment, no one could go in there without a sealed clean suit, booties, and loose hair tucked under an expanded cap. Bay should have known that Kevin already knew all that—another indication of inexperience. Cleanrooms are a great place to work if you had allergies, and wafer probers were always in clean rooms, so Kevin told Bay they didn't need to go in there until TJ showed up.

Bay explained there was a back entrance with its own airlock, so Terry Jana might already be in there. They might as well suit up and go inside. Once inside, Kevin saw another enclosed office in a back corner with a door labeled *T. Jana*. The audio was spotty, but I was able to hear some of what was going on, which surprised me. Bay introduced Kevin to a few people who operated the test equipment. These were production people. Bay asked if they were doing any wafer probing. That question made it clear that Bay wasn't really in the loop.

The female operator, Darla, must have looked directly at Bay when she said, "Where have *you* been? All the damn machines are shut down. That's why we're waiting for this guy to show up. Sorry, Kevin, nothing personal. We're just twiddling our thumbs here."

Obviously, Bay did not have the level of respect from the operators that would generally go with his position, but Bay didn't seem to be bothered; he just moved on and said they were waiting for Ms. Jana to return. Again, Darla excused herself to Kevin for her blunt comment.

I went offline with Kevin so I could explain to Jeff and Greg what exactly a wafer probe machine is so they would understand its importance.

"Hey, guys. Just some info for ya. Depending on the size of the individual chip, which is also called a die, a large wafer can hold thousands of chips. The prober drops a set of contact probes down on each chip and tests it by using a computer, then the machine steps over to the next die. If the chip fails the test, the computer maps the failures so they could be sorted out later. They used to mark each bad chip with a drop of ink, but sometimes the ink dot was larger than the die itself, and the ink could be a source of contamination, so today's systems just keep track of where the bad chips are located. Later, the entire wafer is scribed and cut apart. It all goes by pretty quickly, without ever being touched by a human."

Jeff said, "Thanks for the details. I've watched the process on YouTube. It's mesmerizing."

I went back online with Kevin.

We could hear Darla say, "While we wait, I guess I can show you our wafer extractor, which is a modified Zietech design. Great probers, but your extractor not-so-much. These are faster, and they can handle larger wafer containers."

We guessed that Darla was setting up a demonstration.

"These are test wafers, not production stuff. Notice I didn't have to line up the container or anything. I just put it down. The robot's AI figures it out. Then a wafer is automatically extracted from the carrier box by the robotic arm without touching the surface. The extractor automatically rotates the wafer too, so the rows and columns are almost perfectly aligned before the prober even sees it. Then the prober does its thing, which I can't demonstrate because the damn thing is broke."

It sounded like Darla would be fun at a football game.

Darla continued, "Anyway, this saves a lot of time because the prober doesn't need to correct the orientation much. Then the step-and-repeat process takes over. After the wafer is probed, our extractor removes the wafer, again without touching the surface, and then stacks it in an exit carrier. When everything is working, all I have to do is watch the test results get printed. Right now, I can't even do that."

I assumed Kevin liked Darla's spunk. "What were you testing before the machines shut down?" Kevin asked. "There seemed to be a lot of chips on that wafer."

"This is our D-Chip. There are over five thousand D-Chips on a wafer."

At that point, Bay said, "Here comes Ms. Jana."

Kevin finally was going to get his first upfront view of the infamous TJ. From the photo, he knew she was good-looking, but Kevin whispered that now she had her hair pulled back, wore no makeup, and had on a full-length lab coat that covered any hint of a female figure. A one hundred percent high-tech business posture that I could tell Kevin immediately liked.

Bay said, "Terry, meet Kevin, our latest Zietech support guy on his first visit here."

We could barely hear TJ as she said, "Hello, Kevin. Where's Bill? He knows everything there is to know about how we operate. I don't have time to train a new person in the way it works around here."

The audio was spotty, so I asked Jeff if we could do anything to improve our communication. He mouthed, "Probably not."

Kevin explained, "Bill is out for a few days on personal business, but he wouldn't be called in on this anyway. Bill's a mechanical guy; he knows the ins and outs of how the machines work, but from what I could see on your network, and since all the machines shut down at the same time, you are experiencing a software issue. That's my area."

TJ said, "Sorry I was not here when you arrived, but this was crazy town around here when all the probers just stopped and could not be rebooted. I needed a break. We need to find out what the hell is going on."

Kevin replied, "Once I log into the network, I should be able to see what has happened."

TJ was obviously frustrated. "They all quit at the same time. I have never seen that before. This is a disaster. Since you have not been here before, do you know the chip we are testing, or trying to? It's the industry-standard D-Chip, and we're already behind schedule."

"Bay Anderson gave me a rundown. Very impressive device."

"Do you know anything about semiconductors, or is your expertise limited to prober software?"

TJ was coming on very strong, but I knew Kevin could handle it. In fact, he probably liked it. She spoke with a slight accent, but I imagined she probably had a firm handshake. From her voice, I could tell that she was definitely an A-type manager. Kevin had to be careful not to react negatively to her aggression. He had to be polite yet firm without being macho. So far, things were moving along just fine.

Kevin pushed the "be firm" button a little harder. "I'm glad to be here, and no, I don't know that much about semiconductors, but I know how to write the programs that test them, and I know the Zietech software is the best out there. I should be able to find out what's going on quickly. I say we get on with it."

The A-types had met. It got quiet all of a sudden while TJ was probably giving him the visual once over. I'm sure he did the same in return while most likely maintaining his erect posture and trusting TJ was okay with that. I could almost smell through the wire that there was a biological and physical link in that first twenty seconds. Pheromone sandwiches, anyone? And it didn't hurt that Kevin was strong enough to hold his own.

Meanwhile, we could hear that Bay wisely and gracefully exited as an observer of a situation where he was outclassed.

I could tell that TJ liked the way Kevin was handling himself, because, after a slight pause, she was obviously much closer to the microphone when she said in a low, almost sexy voice, "Software makes hardware happen, you know. You can't do one without the other."

Kevin might have been stunned for a moment when he heard one of his own catchphrases spoken back to him. He scrambled for a nanosecond to assemble a response.

Kevin replied, "But software is only a dream, and the dream can't be satisfied until something moves." Kevin hoped the sexual innuendo was apparent without being brazen.

I said softly, "Careful, Kevin."

The sparring contest was recognized by both players and caused a few seconds of mutual silence, and I assume quiet admiration in what would otherwise be a chaotic scene due to the shutdown. TJ decided to break the spell and query this new person a bit. "What's your software specialty?"

Kevin responded quickly, "My software history is a little boring. My first job out of Berkeley was programming game chips in machine code. The chips didn't have enough memory for compiled high-level programs, and the chips had to run as fast as the hardware was able. The drivers in the Zietech machines all use machine language too, because even a ten-microsecond delay will accumulate to a much larger delay over an entire wafer. Then, at Sony, I used C++ for specific applications until the last four years, when I began writing test programs for microprocessor chips that were being probed by the Zietech machines. I guess that's how Zietech found me because I could support the Zietech software as well as the test routines for the chips being probed, and Zietech needed someone willing to work in the Midwest. That was a perfect chance for me to move back to Chicago, which is my hometown."

TJ abruptly asked, "Coming back to a girlfriend?"

Kevin responded humbly, "No. It's just that I never seemed to have much personal time in California. In Silicon Valley, the pressure to move forward was extreme. Sometimes I slept at the office, and working over the weekends wasn't uncommon. Don't get me wrong, it's a vibrant and exciting environment; it's just not for me. I like technology, but I won't kill myself to be in it. Also, I did a lot of coding at the machine level, in binary, which put me into a different class than most software people."

Posed as more of a statement than a question, and deliberately putting the current shutdown of the probe machines aside, TJ said, "So coding in ones and zeros doesn't put you off."

"I like knowing what the hardware needs in real time, without being isolated by a compiler in between. Tell me what a chip needs, and I can usually figure out the best way to do it. What's the software like in your chips?"

TJ redirected, "Before we talk about our chips, we need to get these damn probers running. We're burning mega dollars every minute."

"Set me up at a table for my laptop near the prober network, and I'll see what happened."

Kevin connected his laptop between the prober network and the building's network. Then he ran a fake diagnostic routine we had prepared that displayed all sorts of lines and progress bars and seemed very impressive but was actually doing nothing but looking good. TJ was looking over his shoulder, but the screens were going by too fast to interpret. After only fifteen minutes, Kevin bellowed, "Somabitch!"

TJ took the bait. "What? What?"

"I think I found a damn bug in our code. The counter that keeps track of the number of chips probed is supposed to report a number back to Zietech's tracking database, but this code will lock up the machine if the number comes close to an overflow of some stupid internal constant. It's just supposed to monitor the machines, not control them. When that happens, all the machines on the network are stopped, not only the one that caused the error. I don't know why we haven't run into this before. Maybe because your chip volume is higher than anyone else's. Either way, it's a dumb mistake. I'll fix this in ten shakes of a lamb's ass. Pardon my French."

Ten minutes later, after each machine was rebooted, the probers were back online and ready to run. TJ had Darla restart the two probers, and they all watched as the D-Chips were tested. It sounded like TJ was impressed and thankful, but the audio was cutting in and out. I was concerned that the quick fix might put Kevin out the door too quickly before he had found out anything specific about TJ's history, so we needed to find a way for Kevin to spend more time with her.

I told Kevin, "Stay with her if you can. Come up with something."

Kevin said to TJ, "I need to watch for a moment and verify that the software won't glitch as it passes an upcoming milestone."

There was no talking for a while, so I assumed that Kevin was watching a Zietech probe analysis when he said, "It's interesting that the M300 is spending less time per die than the test routine itself. That is unusual for a small hardware-only chip, where the prober is usually the slowest part of the process. That suggests the chip's test routine might be inefficient. A test routine can get complex if there's an embedded CPU on the chip, but that isn't the case here, right?"

"Nice one," I said to Kevin. "Quick thinking."

TJ said, "First, Kevin, I apologize if I came on a little strong before. I guess I was just feeling the pressure. Now . . . what are you asking?"

Kevin continued, "I was just curious if there is an embedded CPU on the chip, which might cause the extended test time."

"We make many semiconductors with onboard CPUs, but this is our D-Chip, which is a pretty simple device; there's no onboard CPU. Our test routines are developed using simulation software when the chip was designed. That's the way we flush out potential problems before we commit to silicon. Other devices that have onboard CPUs are much harder to simulate and take much longer to test."

Kevin said, "Yeah, testing anything that has an embedded CPU from the outside with another computer is challenging."

TJ added, "It's like locking a laptop in a room, where the only way you can talk to the laptop is through its USB port, and you have to verify that the laptop is working properly."

Kevin quipped, "Can I look through a window while this is happening? That's a Bill Gates pun."

I moaned, loud enough for Kevin to hear me.

Kevin continued, "I don't mean to be picky, but without an onboard CPU, the test routines seem to be taking a long time for a hardware-only device."

TJ explained, "You don't know what the D-Chip does yet. The D-Chip is like a receptionist sitting at the front door, sitting between the Internet and its host. The host isn't bothered until someone knocks at the door. The host doesn't watch the Internet twenty-four seven in real time; the D-Chip takes over that burden. It waits to detect its host's unique address and then tells the host that someone's at the door. It must ignore all the other addresses."

"Okay. I see that. So, I'm guessing the test routines are sending mega addresses at the D-Chip and verifying that it ignores them?"

"Not quite, but close, and of course it must recognize the correct ones too."

I could hear Kevin say, "Hmmmm. I can see from the dates on the test routines they are going on almost ten years old. Maybe I could speed things up?"

From what I was hearing, it was clear Terry Jana, or TJ, was getting more comfortable with Kevin by the minute. She obviously could carry on a conversation with just about anybody, but talking with Kevin made it seem like she had met someone of equal or perhaps superior intelligence, and someone who had a great personality and a great body too, and apparently he was not in a committed relationship. She was probably wondering if Kevin could really help with the D-Chip test routines. The Zietech machines were the best and the fastest probers available, but if Kevin was correct, the test routines themselves might be limiting production.

TJ had to ask, "Are you interested in looking at the test routines for the D-Chip?"

Kevin jumped at the opportunity. "I'm not saying there's anything wrong, but I am curious. I'd love to spend some time looking at the routines after I take a pee break."

"Absolutely. Restrooms are just outside the cleanroom. I'll wait in my office."

Once Kevin was in a private stall, he was able to talk more freely. "Richard, her office is in the far corner of the cleanroom. I may lose you there, but I was thinking I'd remove the earpiece anyway. It's uncomfortable, so how about we get together later tonight, say eleven p.m. or so?"

"Okay. Eleven it is at my place."

I logged off. I wondered if the Air Force had been flying over the AMIP offices with a heat-monitoring drone, would the image show a cold, gray Chicago building with one office displaying measurable sexual heat?

***

We broke up to check in with their offices and said we'd be back together at 11:00 p.m. for a debriefing. I invited Roger to attend.

At 11 p.m., Greg took the opportunity to tell Jeff and I that they had a lead on one of the people who'd entered Brad's office. Close inspection of the security film footage showed one of the invaders had inadvertently placed his right hand high on the right side of the elevator frame as he entered. This was possibly an area the cleaning crew may not have wiped down. Sure enough, they pulled a partial palm print as well as two fingers. Thirty minutes later, they had a picture of an assassin who was based out of the Middle East but no knowledge of where he was now. Greg sounded bleak.

Roger showed up a little late as usual.

When Kevin arrived, I said to him, "Well, you're still here. No wounds. That's a good sign, and no lipstick on your collar either, but you are smiling. Don't tell me—you had to change your shirt and maybe your underwear too. Right?"

Roger said, "Braddock, you do know you can be very obnoxious sometimes!"

I responded, "What's your point? Do you want another drink, Rog, or not? Besides, you didn't hear how well TJ and Kevin were getting along."

I said, "Kevin, you have the floor. Bring Roger up to speed."

Kevin kicked back in a recliner with a satisfied, smug look on his face.

"Well, everything pretty much worked as planned, except the wire was intermittent at best. The clean room's shielding made it tough to stay connected. Anyway, I got the wafer probers running again. They were running the high-volume device they call the D-Chip. Richard wanted me to stick around a while and dig some more, so I made up a story that the test routines seemed a little slow and that maybe I could speed them up. TJ took me up on that offer. We spent the next few hours reviewing the test routines until everyone other than the production people had left for the day. Then we went to her office, where she relaxed and admitted she was Vietnamese, born during the war, educated in Russia, and so forth. We shared a glass of wine or two, or maybe more, and we didn't talk about the test routines at all. TJ is something else."

My plan to get Kevin into AMIP had worked perfectly, but I wasn't as relaxed as Kevin about the risks. Sure, TJ's background fit the story, but it was still too early, and there were plenty of unanswered questions. After a few drinks, I discussed our next move.

I started, "Kevin, I can see that you liked TJ immediately, but let's not forget that there's an awful lot about this lady that doesn't make sense. How did she get here, and why is she covert? Why is she totally off the grid? That little man inside me is telling me that she's hiding something. I assume you have set up a situation where you will be seeing her again."

"Yes, I'll be seeing her tomorrow at AMIP."

"Keep your antennae up—waaay up. Greg. Jeff. Any thoughts?"

Greg said, "I totally agree; we can't be slack, if for no other reason than we may have an illegal immigrant here who has her hands in America's intellectual property, and this might be somehow related to Dempsey's death. And we still don't *know* for sure if she's the president's daughter."

Jeff said, "We'll keep the phone redirect going for a while more."

Kevin jumped in, "Well, other than a DNA match, I'm pretty sure Terry Jana is President Elliot's daughter, so it seems to me that we have met the objective. One secure email to the president and we pass the baton. Don't get me wrong—I like TJ a lot, so I'm in no hurry to terminate the mission, but where do we stop?"

I answered, "We stop when we *know!*"

Roger said, "I agree with Richard for a change; we are not one hundred percent sure Terry Jana is Thi Thom, the infamous Russian immigrant, and we have to know if there was any connection to Brad Dempsey's death. That, on its own, should be the overriding priority here. And why can't I find any documentation? I think Mr. Braddock here is correct. Let's start doing some real detective work. This may not be the time to mention this, but it looks like I'm not needed anymore, since surveillance is no longer required. Old guy Braddock here knows his way around the DHS with Greg's help, FBI Jeff is right here, and you, Kevin, are only a few days from getting your hands in TJ's pants, or maybe that's already happened. So, I go home now, right?"

I had to chime in quickly, "Okay, okay. Let's just relax for a moment. No, Roger, you're not going anywhere. I'm sensing increased activity, so you need to stay in the loop, and there's a lot more as well. Where did the seed money come from? And you have to admit, the AMIP corporate profile is strange. Kevin has made great progress, but we should use this opportunity for Kevin to get closer to Ms. Jana and get some real data, so we have something more concrete when we talk to the president. He will want to know as much as we know. Did I miss anything?"

"Yeah. You're buying dinner."

"Crikey, Rog. Yes, I'll buy you guys a goddamn dinner!"

Meanwhile, TJ and Raj Matesh were about to start checking up on Kevin Dupree.

Chapter 9

The next day, I called Greg and Jeff and set up a meeting at 9:00 a.m. Just the three of us. I asked for some additional help with following up on TJ's immigration, as well as who I could talk to about AMIP's funding sources. Jeff and Greg both knew a contractor named Bob Gretch, who seemed to be the preferred go-to guy when you had to "follow the money," so to speak. Also, Greg said that he had explored the immigration question in more detail and had some additional information.

"There's no doubt that she's in this country illegally," Greg said. "We can't find any record of her getting a visa, or green card, or being the guest of a sponsor, or anything. We also checked for a K-one visa in case she was getting married to a US citizen. Brad Dempsey had a link in his Russian history file about her, but those records are missing. Our database manager software only records *when* files are created, viewed, moved, copied, or deleted. The only date associated with the name Terry Jana is the date Brad was killed. I know that seems suspicious, but anyone with the access codes could have done the deletion. It didn't have to be Brad, and if you remember, Brad's terminal showed no activity on that date. Of course, Brad could have used another person's terminal, but video surveillance doesn't show him leaving his office around the time of the deletion. If Brad was part of this link, then he may have been forced to give up the access codes before he was killed."

"That seems like the most probable scenario to me," I commented. "The only time I saw the name Terry Jana was in that secure text message from Brad that your system would not have known about. And if that's the case, then we have a lot more on our hands than a female computer scientist who illegally emigrated to the US. We have to find out more about the timing and who was behind all this. I was about to write off Brad's death as an unrelated event, but now it seems someone wanted Ms. Jana's presence held secret at any cost.

"But what really bothers me is this AMIP place. No reputable company would have hired an illegal immigrant to do such important work. Therefore, the company must be part of the coverup. Millions of dollars to design and produce such a critical chip and with the help of illegal aliens? That just doesn't make sense. Jeff, I need the FBI to get more involved."

Jeff Shaw added, "I too felt the company was connected, so I took the liberty of building a more in-depth solid cover on the redirected Zietech line, just in case anyone starts checking up on Dupree. We'll keep that in effect for a while. I also plan on visiting Zietech later today. Ironically, the CEO is in town for the week. I will make sure that he understands what we are doing and ask them to keep their distance until we reach a conclusion. Of course, I won't disclose why."

We terminated our meeting, each with a list of action items.

Next step for me: call Bob Gretch and mention Greg Dillard and Jeff Shaw. Mr. Gretch answered the phone on the second ring. Bob explained that he was an independent contractor who follows the money flowing to and from overseas accounts, which could be an indication of illegal money laundering. He was very willing to help, but of course he needed data. I explained that I couldn't answer his questions over an unsecured line. Bob didn't have a phone with a secure link, so we decided to meet at my hotel at about 7:00 p.m. Bob was vetted by the concierge, and I picked him up in the lobby.

"Bob? Richard Braddock."

"Which celebrity's money are you trying to track?"

"No celebrity. A company, one that may have been funded from an overseas source."

"Nothing illegal about that. Happens every day."

"The money may have come from Russia or Iran, but we don't know. The company's activities are suspicious, as you might expect with both the FBI and DHS involved."

Bob answered, "Well, we probably won't be able to find the exact source of the money, but we can start by looking at the European banks that favor, or cater to, Russian and Middle Eastern countries. Any large transfer of funds into the US might give you the clue you're looking for. I assume because we had to meet here, that this inquiry needs to stay under the radar?"

"Yes, but the money is just part of the puzzle. All I need is information to help understand what is going on, but we will not be taking any action. There's no reason to call attention to ourselves."

Bob noted how to contact me securely and politely excused himself. I had not discussed any relationship to the president.

Meanwhile, that little man inside of me was beating on the walls and trying to get out. Things seemed to be moving along, but I had the feeling that I was walking down a quiet street without knowing that the street had no outlet, and people had me in their sights ready to pull the trigger.

Chapter 10

Bob Gretch began his exploration, and totally unknown to our group, Raj Matesh was immediately notified that there were inquiries into the financial background of AMIP. Apparently, the AMIP organization had links and capabilities no one knew about. This organization suggested to Raj that they monitor their security and keep their eyes and ears open for changes and anomalies in their company's operation. Both Raj and TJ considered the recent arrival of Kevin Dupree, so they decided to meet back at Raj's office.

Raj started, "You met with that Zietech tech man, and apparently he got everything back online quickly. Did you learn anything that moves the sun higher in the sky? Any reason to suspect he's related to this financial inquiry or our security?"

"His name is Kevin Dupree. Very sharp and pleasant, but I think he's blameless. Did you have him checked out with Zietech?"

"Yes, and they think highly of him, but he hasn't been there very long either."

"I was able to talk to him for a while. He's single, lives alone, and knowledgeable yet humble, even self-deprecating in a nerdy sort of way. I like him. He found a software glitch in the Zietech prober network and fixed it in fifteen minutes. We mostly talked about the technical details of his visit. He has some exposure to semiconductors, knows who you are, likes coding, and spent several years writing test routines for microprocessors. He didn't seem all that interested in the company—at least it didn't come up. He mentioned that our D-Chip testing algorithms seem slow by comparison with his prior experience for such a small die. He offered to look at the routines and maybe speed things up."

"What else did you find out about his background prior to Zietech?" Matesh asked.

"I talked to him for quite a while. He went to Berkeley and then worked for Sony and has both software and some semiconductor experience. He's a perfect fit for Silicon Valley, but he's from this area and prefers to be here. I think Zietech is lucky to have him."

"Does he know anything about the D-Chip?"

"Only what everybody else knows, and I would like to know why he felt our test algorithms were slow. I'm thinking of hiring Kevin as a part-time contractor for a few days to assist with speeding up the test routines. I think he could help, but that in no way exposes him to what the D-Chip can do."

Matesh said, "Between us and our second sources, we have shipped millions of D-Chips over the years. Since the encoded date is coming up soon anyway, is it even worth the effort? What's our backlog look like?"

"We still have about a hundred thousand in wafer form waiting for testing, so it's worth getting those shipped as soon as possible. Yes, there are millions in the field overall, but who knows how many are actually installed? With this new Internet protocol, our customers are expecting shipments. I think we need to operate in a normal manner right up to the trigger."

Raj added, "You're probably right. No change of plans. But the mere idea that customers have no idea they just purchased a Trojan horse that's not even a tenth of an inch on a side excites me. We are getting close. I can't wait."

"Yes," said TJ, "the same day as my mother's murder. No one will have any idea of what just happened to them."

Despite her words, Terry was internally melancholy when she thought about how many people would suffer worldwide because of her D-Chip. An inner part of her psyche hesitated for just a fraction of a second. Sure, when this project started a decade back, the United States government was a foe, and yes, the US was often behind the deaths of hundreds of civilians, probably more. The original idea was to affect the government, but it was clear now that the effect on necessary infrastructures could only be estimated as catastrophic with many innocent civilian victims.

There was no point in going over all these feelings again because there was nothing she could do about it now anyway. The ball had been set in motion years ago. Back then, TJ felt the president of the United States must be called to account for letting the country carry on with such violence. She also felt the US had to learn its lesson for being so lax when it came to simple security and protection of its people. At the time it seemed to TJ that the US didn't really care about its people. Virtually every country in the world provided health care for everybody, regardless of stature or poverty level. Yet to her, the US only took care of people who could afford it. Supposedly, it was the land of opportunity, but only if you had the means to take advantage of it. The US also ranked at the bottom half of the world in education, and it was dropping every year. Undoubtedly, the United States was spending its massive wealth on war and capitalistic leadership. TJ's D-Chip was all about putting a stop to that.

"Has this Kevin fellow asked about your background?" Raj asked. "Where you came from or education?"

It took a moment for TJ to shake her head clear and come back from her depressing thoughts.

"You ask this now?"

Matesh explained, "It only makes sense. We've been told there been inquiries."

TJ noticed Raj's demeanor was suddenly quiet and thoughtful. He just looked at the wall, not making direct eye contact. He wasn't keeping any secrets from her, but he wasn't sure what their next move should be either.

Raj added, "Someone has been asking questions. We've been told to keep a low profile, but why now, so close to the date? We've never advertised our existence. We're just a semiconductor company selling a popular chip to server and Internet customers. I can't imagine why anyone would start looking at us now. I can't shake the feeling this is somehow related to Kevin Dupree and his coincidental arrival. I think you should get to know Kevin a little more and see if you get—"

Before he could finish the sentence, his cell phone notification pinged. All his notifications were turned off except those from his superiors, so it had to be important.

DHS operative Brad Dempsey has been eliminated.
Thi Thom's arrival and location may have been compromised.
Suggest she leave the country immediately.

Raj held up his phone so TJ could read it.

TJ stammered, "How the hell is this Dempsey fellow related to me? And if he was looking for me, why did he wait until now? I've done nothing special to arouse suspicion."

Raj said, "I think our superiors may be overreacting. It wouldn't be easy to arrange for you to leave right now, given the heightened state of US security. I'll suggest we proceed as planned and make no quick adjustments. Besides, the fuse is already lit, and it cannot be extinguished. We are too close."

Raj formulated a short but direct response to his superiors, reviewed it with TJ, and clicked "Send." It took several minutes for verification feedback showing the encrypted message was successfully sent and received. The response acknowledged they could proceed carefully, but frequent updates were required.

Raj got back to the point. "Now, what's the status of the shipments again? I know your test systems were down right at the time demand had increased by a factor of three."

"The final shipments were supposed to go out by the end of January, but we still have that backlog of wafers waiting for testing. That's why decreasing our test times would really help. Everybody thinks this new version is required to take advantage of that new Internet protocol. No IP providers or new laptops and cell phones would want to be caught with their pants down when the new super-fast Internet is brought online in March. Our timing for this last foray is perfect."

Raj asked, "How has the encoding been going? Any changes to the rate?"

TJ responded, "No problems so far. When we started the process over a year ago, the rate was about three million per month. We are holding at that level."

TJ continued, "More than fifty million encodes so far! Talk about having an impact! Systems will crash at precisely the same instant. I get excited just thinking about it. A single pull on the trigger hits millions of targets with only one shot, and no one can stop it, not even us. There is no Nobel Prize for what we are about to do, but if there were, we would win it."

"Okay. I can see you're excited. Now, how do you plan to use Mr. Dupree?"

"Kevin is sharp, so I'd like to see what he can do to speed up the D-Chip test routines so we can make those final shipments, and I need to do it quickly. We may even run three shifts. The wafers are just sitting there waiting for testing. Right now, it's taking almost a full hour to probe a wafer, so I'm hoping we can make up lost time not only with extra hours but also with faster testing. A game programmer like Kevin might be perfect for that task. I think we would be okay without this effort, but I wanted to get ahead of the game and have excess inventory ready just in case."

"I like the plan because that gives us extra time to be long gone before the D-Chips trigger. I'll be back in India. Where will you be?"

"I haven't decided. I know it'll be anticlimactic, and I'll probably be a little depressed when it's all over. I might even go back to Russia. I haven't decided."

Raj continued, "It still would be a good idea if we found out more about Dupree. Where did he come from immediately before Zietech? What does he do in his spare time? Hobbies, etcetera. I'll make some more inquiries. Meanwhile, you're sure that exposing him to the test routines is not a threat?"

"Absolutely."

"We should know more. Since he's friendly and single and good looking, he may ask you out, so I'd call that an opportunity."

It was music to TJ's ears. She had already planned on seeing much more of Kevin Dupree.

Chapter 11

After a few days, Roger, Greg, Jeff, Kevin, Bob Gretch, and I met in my room to review the current status. I provided the adult beverages and bonbons for Roger.

Roger had nothing to add other than his two surveillance people felt they may have been detected, and one even thought he was followed. Rog assumed AMIP must have had some way of knowing about the surveillance, perhaps as a result of the DHS investigation, but there hadn't been any physical contact. As uncomfortable as that was, I felt it was probably not a priority right then because there was no overt contact.

Bob had already stopped the financial exploration into the company, and Roger's people were no longer tracking TJ, but it did beg questions about the body of the beast and how long were its tentacles. Bob reported that AMIP had several million dollars in a US bank; they paid their taxes on time and appeared to be on the up and up. The source of the initial funding had been distributed through several European banks, but as he suspected, he was unable to go beyond that.

Jeff's FBI activity showed that semiconductor shipments to and from Kansas City were often inspected at state border checkpoints, and shipping manifests always checked out. AMIP employees had clean records with positive work histories, and several were clearly family oriented. As best they could tell, of the twenty or so semiconductor products AMIP manufactured, most of the company's revenue came from the D-Chip, which was used by the majority of companies that supply products that connect to the Internet. This information came from an independent electronics research firm, as well as feedback from interested investors who were basically told the company was not looking for investors.

Bob added, "Nothing piques market interest more than when you offer a company money and they say they don't need it."

I thanked Bob for his data and follow up, and politely asked him to leave since the rest of us were going to discuss confidential information.

After Bob had left, Greg said that they were not able to determine the current location of the two assassins. As serious as that issue was, the likelihood of closure seemed minimal. It was beginning to look like a cold case to the authorities. The DHS managed to keep the reporters and public at bay, and with Jeff Shaw's help, Brad Dempsey's family was moved to an undisclosed location. Greg reiterated that Terry Jana was not in the DHS database. She had over a hundred thousand dollars in a separate bank account under a different name and, as we expected, she had never filed a tax return. She must have been getting paid in cash. Bottom line: TJ remained off the grid.

Jeff Shaw added that her cell phone showed frequent calls to and from Kansas City and Moab, Utah. Kansas was no surprise because that's where their semiconductor facilities were located. Jeff tracked the Utah number to a private party.

Bob and Greg's information was undoubtedly important, but Kevin was the real key to this effort. We were lucky; his first few days had gone very well with Kevin and TJ spending more time together. I could see it in Kevin's eyes. TJ was sharp, and her good looks made it easy for Kevin to flirt, and she obviously reciprocated. They were starting a personal and intimate relationship. She liked having him around, and they usually lunched together. Was it love at first sight? Soon it would be time for Kevin to delve into TJ's past more deeply.

TJ's first assignment for Kevin had been to look over the test routines for the D-Chip and see if he could actually speed things up. Since this was such an important device, he was pleased with the responsibility and was eager to help, and it offered more quality time with TJ too. Kevin said she would often gently touch his back while she looked over his shoulder as he typed. Women don't usually touch men while at the office. He said that she often wore a subtle perfume and was careful to keep her makeup professional but not overdone. Their late evenings at the office were more personal than professional.

Upon hearing this, Roger just groaned, "Jeez, Dickey! Are we playing *The Dating Game* here?"

I responded quickly, "Hang on, Rog. You shouldn't feel left out just because you're not getting any lately. Let Kevin do what he has to do. It's all part of the strategy."

I could tell that Kevin was feeling conflicted because TJ was starting to fall in love with a mole. The post-mission follow-up would likely present emotional turmoil for both of them. I had to make sure we were all on the same page.

"Kevin, I'm happy for you that your romantic relationship with TJ is progressing, but the time has come for us to know *for sure* who TJ is and her history. Now, let's make the most of it."

"Okay. I get it. That will be easy," said Kevin. "She's a workaholic, we like one another, and since the D-Chip market demand has been so strong, we are together most of the time. AMIP is now running three shifts and still not keeping up. I have been intentionally dragging my feet, but I'm sure I can speed up the test routines quickly."

I jumped in, "If you can pull that off, that would be a good time to share a dinner as sort of a celebration. Then the time might be right to delve a little deeper."

Kevin said, "For what it's worth, I'm pretty sure she doesn't have any idea who her father is. I've brought up President Elliot several times since he recently visited Chicago, and she had no reaction at all. She dislikes the office of the presidency and the government in general, but I haven't pursued that yet."

"Some animosity doesn't surprise me," I said. "There's no telling what she was taught in her early years under communism. Her mother died when she was very young, and she probably knows almost nothing about her parents. And even if she knew she was the offspring of an American soldier, who would make the connection to the president now?"

"Well, she's going to find out sooner or later!" said Kevin. "If she doesn't like our government, that would change her life. And how would the president handle that? She seems fairly well adjusted and very confident now, but that information would revamp her future. Not that she has any immediate plans, because these D-Chip shipments have got all of us in high gear with the throttle to the floor. If I can establish that she is the president's daughter, then how do we tell her?"

I responded, "That's not up to us. That's Paul Elliot's problem. Meanwhile, that's another reason why we have to move forward quickly. Do what you have to do, but don't let it drag out. This Zietech thing might blow up in our face if any more prober problems show up. Zietech knows about Kevin, but we can't keep it under wraps for too long. Ask her out and start filling these voids. Given your intimacy with TJ, we should forgo the earpiece. If she noticed that, you'd have to make up another story, but I'd like you to continue wearing the wire. I'll be listening if you'll let me."

Kevin smiled and gave me a thumbs-up. Roger sighed out loud as he lowered his head and touched his brow with his hand.

I said to Kevin, "I'll leave it up to you to set up our next meeting. Meanwhile, Jeff, we need to continue the redirect of AMIP phone calls to Zietech. No reason not to, and I'd like to review the scripts we're using just in case. Until then, drink up, and who's betting on the Bears?"

Chapter 12

While I was listening, Kevin seemed to stutter to TJ, "Please don't take this as being too forward, but would you like to share dinner . . . maybe a pizza . . . with me?"

"When?"

"How about tonight? I actually do have some questions about testing the D-Chip, but it's hard here at work when there's so much activity, and things seem to keep happening so fast that we never get to breathe. And I see your initials everywhere, not only on the test routines but also on the silicon itself. It's not often I meet a software person whose initials are included on the chip, and who is also . . . well . . . you know."

TJ had to smile. With a hint of excitement, she said, "No, I don't know—and sure, I'd love to have dinner with you. Where would you suggest?"

Wow, that was almost too easy, I thought. Kevin had already considered that if TJ was okay with pizza, it would be Nino's on North Avenue.

"How about Nino's?"

"I don't know where Nino's is, so you'd have to drive. Is that okay?"

"Sure, my car is the silver Accord. Meet me at my car at six?"

"See you then."

I thought to myself, *don't be late, Kevin!*

Kevin was at his car a bit early and commented to me quietly that when he held the car door open, TJ had changed her clothes, dropped her hair down, put on heels, and had on makeup. This was the TJ he'd seen in that first photo. She didn't look like she was ready to discuss software test routines or semiconductors. She slid in provocatively, pulling her skirt to cover an exposed leg while smiling directly at Kevin. I'm sure Kevin had to work his mind's gray cells hard to stay on point and not let his emotions, or hormones, get in the way. Since they were outside, I could clearly hear both.

Kevin started the Accord and said, "Nino's is just a small little place that was here when I was growing up. It has to be a hundred years old—at least it seems like that—and it has that special Italian smell and red checkered tablecloths and great Chianti. I hope you'll like it. I'm not Italian, but when in Chicago as they say."

Was Kevin hoping she would say something about her heritage? She didn't.

As they drove off, she said, "A Honda Accord. Not what I would expect a single thirty-something to be driving."

"Too geeky, huh? Perhaps a Corvette then? I could get one on order, or we could test drive one at a dealership I know."

"Could you afford it?"

"Probably. I've been one of those lucky SOBs who had the opportunity to work for some great companies and get paid very well, and until I returned to the Midwest, I lived very inexpensively in a small house just outside Silicon Valley that I paid for in cash. I didn't spend much time there because I was busy at work most of the time, so I was saving most of what I earned. That small house quadrupled in value in only a few years. It seemed you couldn't lose money in California real estate, at least back then."

Both Kevin and TJ knew the best way to get people to talk about themselves is to be interested in them. Unless they are introverted, a person will gladly tell you almost anything you want to know. It's basic psychology that if you are interested in them, they will probably warm up to you. Ask them where they grew up, did they have animals, what was the best part of school, hobbies, etcetera. The irony, in this case, was they were both trying to do the same thing at the same time. They also had similar agendas, so they were inclined to notice if the same psychology was being used on them. This meant it might turn out to be a long night at Nino's.

Kevin felt pleased, though cautious that their relationship was moving so quickly. TJ, on the other hand, had not had the benefit of learning all the street smarts of US culture. This meant that Kevin probably would have a slight upper hand in discourse dynamics while drinking Chianti at Nino's.

Kevin parked the car and got out thinking he would chauvinistically hold the car door open for her, but she was already out. He whispered to me that this made him feel even more at ease. She was an independent woman who probably wouldn't want any subtle subordination. They walked as briskly as possible through the light January snow to the front door, never touching except once where it was slippery, and Kevin held her by the elbow. Everything was starting out very well. He took her coat, hung it on a rack, and they sat down at a table directly in front of the main window. Then he said mockingly, "This is a very romantic view of busy North Avenue. Okay, scratch the romantic North Avenue part."

He quickly moved on before she could comment, "I didn't ask if you drink before I went off and started talking about Nino's Chianti."

"I'm not much of a drinker. I'm what you would call a light touch. I do occasionally have a sake, however, or a mixed drink when the mood suits me."

"Damn! And I brought up Chianti. What was I thinking?"

He was trying to be cute but clear about his intentions.

She said, "I'm willing to give it a try. Does Nino's have a full bar?"

"Yes, they do, so you can get whatever you want, except sake." He laughed. "If I may ask, do the Vietnamese drink sake?"

"What?"

Kevin said, "I need to warn you. From when I was very young, my mouth would say whatever came through my mind without a filter. Sometimes that's interpreted as funny, but sometimes it's outright embarrassing. Please excuse my mental deficiency if you could. Your good looks have got me flustered."

Another well placed but unexpected compliment.

It was clear that TJ was starting to like Kevin more and more. He was good-looking, intelligent, witty, friendly, and even modest. What's not to like? These were traits she appreciated, and that might allow him to share more information about himself. She may have also felt that she was the one in control. I have heard other women say, "Men are just like that. The priorities of the male mind are sex, food, and money. Food and money may change places, but sex is always at the top." She might be using her attributes to find out more about Kevin.

TJ didn't answer the Vietnamese sake question, and no waiter had shown up yet, so Kevin moved on. "They have the absolute best Italian sausage here. I'm thinking we could share a pizza."

"I'm a vegetarian. I should have mentioned that."

"But you're not allergic to gluten, are you?"

"I'm good with gluten."

I could tell that informal conversation was not coming as easily as it had back in her office. In her office, they played the you-show-me-yours-and-I'll-show-you-mine game, but now there were competing agendas. Thank goodness the waiter showed up asking if there were any drink orders or if they would like to see a menu. Kevin ordered a Chianti, and TJ ordered a JD over ice. She wasn't much of a drinker? Like the ice that would come in TJ's drink, the tensions were still chilled. When the waiter finally brought the drinks, Kevin offered a sip of his Chianti to TJ. She took a sip, gave the glass back, and picked up her JD. They clinked glasses and took a healthy drink.

To help break the ice, so to speak, TJ asked Kevin directly, "I assume you are not Chinese or Japanese or Milanese, whatever that is, either, but I am curious; if you don't mind—what's your heritage?"

Kevin saw it as an opportunity because once he answered that question, the door would be open to her. They clinked glasses again and had another hit.

"Actually, my mother was Czechoslovakian, and my father was French. Weird combination, eh? I was born in a Chicago suburb next to that cornfield we're famous for. I went to school here and never left town until college, and then I went west. I'm just a Midwest country boy who happened to live near a city. How about you?"

Direct but timely, I thought.

"I was born in Vietnam, schooled in Russia, educated in the US."

Wow, that was quick. It's almost like she had rehearsed that response. With every sentence, it seemed even more likely this was the TJ we were looking for. Gold star on that one. She wasn't hiding much, or maybe she knew exactly what she was doing. And what did she mean by "schooled in Russia, educated in the US?" I figured her precise choice of words was meant to prompt a discussion. She was playing with him, but what the hell? She started it.

Kevin didn't miss it. "What do you mean schooled in Russia but educated in the US?" Kevin avoided the obvious topic of how she got to the United States, figuring there was no point in putting her on the defensive.

"Schooling is just that," she said. "You go to school to learn things, but that doesn't mean you can function in the world. Education is the next step, where you learn how to apply what you learned. A schooled person always works for an educated one."

Kevin said, "I love that! I think I understand. Then what educated you in the US?"

"I learned to code in the Soviet Union, but it wasn't until I got to the US that I saw how software can be used. In the Soviet Union, you did what they told you to do. Mostly problem-solving projects, but here you have options. My education was finding that out. Now, where were you schooled?"

TJ was slick to pick up on this. Her answer would allow her to essentially ask Kevin the same question. Kevin was quick to realize this, so he had to come across as an honest guy with nothing to hide.

"I went to Carnegie Mellon, same as Mr. Matesh, and later Berkeley, as we discussed before. I guess you could say I was schooled and educated at the same time. US universities are like that. After graduation, I went to work out west. I made enough money and came back home, although I can't say I had any real plans once I got back. I admit it—that was not good planning, but it worked out for me, as things normally do. I'm one of those lucky guys who seem to be in the right place at the right time. Had I not come back, I wouldn't have found AMIP nor have been lucky enough to work with you."

That was a gratuitous flirt, but what the heck; a little flirting never hurt anyone. I could imagine a little cringe in TJ's eyes, possibly followed by a smile and a slight turn of the cheek that could be interpreted as shyness, maybe a little blush as well.

TJ asked, "You don't mind working for a woman?"

"Never did, never will."

"How's that?"

"I don't know. Maybe it's because women have to work harder to get recognized. You know, the old glass ceiling. I've had two female bosses, and they both were very focused on the task at hand. No personal agenda, no small talk about football or any locker room banter. They were simply direct: 'Here's our objective. Here's the plan for achieving it. Now, get to work.' I liked that, and no one was looking over my shoulder or questioning my competence."

Actually, I knew that Kevin had never worked for a woman, but his ad-lib answer seemed to hit the mark pretty well. They both clicked glasses again, finished their drinks, and ordered another. She was a light touch? Hmmm. I felt the dinner might work out after all. Surely he could outdrink her since she was drinking hard liquor while his was just wine. Kevin ordered a small personal-size sausage pizza, and TJ ordered cheese lasagna. Insignificant small talk ensued until the food arrived with another drink for each.

Kevin said, "Looks like I get the whole pie rather than just a piece, like out west."

"Whatsss do you mean?" TJ slurred. The alcohol was talking.

"Sorry. I had stock options at a company I worked for in California. Sometimes getting a piece of that pie is worthless, but sometimes you make out."

"You owned part of the companysss?"

"No. I wasn't an owner. I had some stock options."

"Uptionsss?"

"Options! Meaning you might own part of the company later if things go well. You have the 'option' of selling the stock if there's a buyer, and you aren't restricted. It can be valuable if the company does well. Most high-tech companies offer stock options. Doesn't AMIP?"

"Uptions were never brought up. But these uptions are real munney you didn't really earn by working?"

Kevin overlooked the tipsy language. "I guess you could view it that way. Call it an incentive to do a good job. It's a possibility for the future, but not actual cash."

"Americans need insssentivess to do a good job?"

Her voice suddenly had an unpleasant edge to it, but Kevin didn't back down. "Excuse me, TJ, but that sounds divisive. What's wrong with getting a little extra money if things go well with something you contributed to?"

I sensed Kevin was about to make an issue with how a capitalistic society can work to one's benefit, but he had touched a nerve. *Easy, Kevin.* I guessed he was hoping this dialogue might shed some light on TJ's value system, but unfortunately the conversation got quiet all of a sudden. After eating for a while longer, and after TJ's last drink, her words were slurring even more.

"Don't you think dat dis money that flows across the topss might never get to the peeeploe that need it? I see homless and perverty here. And where does all dat money goes? From what I've seen, it ends up in the pockets of the peeeople that don't need it."

TJ was drunk and getting wasted. Clearly, she had formed a position on American life and policy that Kevin hadn't noticed before, but she sounded like she cared about people. Kevin had to call off the dinner, let down the defenses, and take her home. He wasn't going to get any more information at this point anyway, and hopefully she would forget most of what she said by the next day, or the tensions from the evening could backfire. We had time, and he had found out what we needed to know for now. He concluded she was a well-schooled, probably lonely, good-looking fifty-year-old with a heart who could use some companionship and understanding. For a well-educated professional, she seemed to need more than the usual emotional support.

"Come on, TJ, let's get you home and in bed," said Kevin, assisting her with her coat.

"I like the 'in bed' part . . . but no home. Siiit with me for a while."

"We can't stay here."

"At your place then? Would you?"

At the beginning of the evening, Kevin had been looking forward to the possibility that they would get intimate again as they had back in her office, but not under these circumstances. If they had sex while she was drunk, there was no end to the possible ways that could be interpreted. He might even be accused of sexual misconduct. Nevertheless, he had to take care of her for the evening.

Outside, Kevin quipped that the January cold didn't seem to affect her much, but she didn't make it to his car before vomiting. He cleaned her up and brought her to his place and positioned her softly on the sofa. I think Kevin had forgotten to turn off the wire, so I turned up the volume on my headphones in case I heard something and went to sleep myself. They slept peacefully, apparently in each other's arms, probably fully clothed and under a blanket, until after ten the next morning. I had already been awake for several hours.

Chapter 13

Kevin was up and fixing breakfast. Bacon and eggs for him, yogurt and OJ for her. She was waking up slowly—very slowly.

In a very low voice, TJ said, "I apologize. I'm sorry. I didn't handle that well. I hope I didn't mess things up too much."

"Relax. It's more important you get your rest and get rehydrated. Maybe even take the day off."

"That's impossible. We're on a schedule. Those wafers need to be tested and shipped. Am I dressed?"

Kevin laughed. "As far as I know."

She looked under the blanket to check her current status. "Thank you for being a gentleman. Raj will not be pleased."

"What's Raj got to do with anything? You're an adult. You can do what you want, and what Mr. Matesh doesn't know won't hurt him."

"I suppose you're right," TJ responded meekly.

Kevin added, "We don't have to tell him, because he would probably assume the worst. I vote for keeping quiet."

As if wanting to change the subject, TJ asked, "What's that smell? Are you cooking?"

"What you smell is my breakfast. Yours is more on the healthy side so you can maintain your energy level."

"I went off on all the problems with America, didn't I? I am not as negative as you might think. When I came here,

I was convinced American policy was to control the world, but after being here for a while, I can see good people are the same no matter where they come from. Do you mind if I try that orange juice?"

"It's got your name on it. Want some coffee too?"

"Sorry, I don't drink coffee. Maybe I should have told you that too. I just don't know anymore."

I could hear TJ start to sob, almost as if she were breaking down. Kevin put down his fork, moved over to the sofa, sat beside her, and put his arm around her. He never said a word. He just swayed silently while humming. She slowly turned her head up as high as her neck would allow and made it evident she wanted a kiss. He tenderly obliged with a soft peck on the forehead, that was more like father to daughter than a lover. TJ couldn't remember the last time a kiss was just a sweetness. She must have felt in good hands.

They sat there for fifteen minutes, saying nothing.

Then Kevin asked softly, "Last night you mentioned you were schooled in Russia, but you didn't say anything about your parents. Are they still living?"

Good job, Kevin. Let's get some data!

"I never met my parents. My mother was killed during the war when I was very young, and no one seemed to know anything about my father. I lived in an orphanage until I was old enough to go to school. Then I stayed wherever the school was."

"So, maybe your father is still alive."

"There's no way I could know that. I'd rather not think about any of that if that's okay."

Then Kevin said, "Maybe we could go to a museum today. Someplace warm with no stress."

"No, I think we should go back to work. It would be good to get my mind back on the topic. I'm feeling better now. Besides, you were going to start speeding up the test routines, and we haven't even talked about that. My work clothes are at the office anyway."

"If that's what you want to do, I'm okay with that. Get something to eat first, and if it stays down, we'll head in."

Before they left Kevin's place, he mentioned to me that he would take off his wire when they would be working in the cleanroom, so we should all meet in the evening at about eight o'clock, and he would fill us in. Thirty minutes later, Kevin and TJ were back at work with no one the wiser. The test machines and probers were running, but the wafer inventory was growing instead of shrinking from new shipments that had arrived that morning. Kevin still had his wire on because the test review would be done outside the cleanroom in a small room with a terminal.

I could hear TJ say, "You've looked over the test routines before, but take your time and look over all the data and see if there's anything we can do? Call me with questions, and maybe later today we can review what you find."

Kevin said, "Will do. You mentioned you use a simulator to help generate and verify these routines. How can I get to that?"

"The simulator software is on the server. I will add you to the authorized list. Give me about five minutes, and you should be able to just log in. I'll assign you the password K-Man."

I knew Kevin didn't expect to find anything enlightening by modifying test routines, but it was a way to keep their dialogue open, not to mention a chance to find out just what the D-Chip did. After a few hours, he managed to write down a myriad of questions.

He called TJ's office and asked, "You had told me that the D-Chip was basically a receptionist between the host and the Internet. From what I could tell, the test routines pass Internet IP addresses to the D-Chip while the test system watches to make sure the D-Chip only acknowledges the ones assigned to it. So essentially, when the D-Chip sees the correct address, then it signals its host and opens the door to the Internet. That's all it does, right? We need a chip for that?"

TJ responded, "Basically, yes. The host CPU would slow down if it was looking at the Internet all the time. The D-Chip offloads the host CPU by waiting for a knock at the door—the host's IP address. It responds by opening the door so the host can take over. It really is that simple."

Kevin said, "The test routines seem simple enough. I haven't dug into them completely yet, but it seems we could do better fairly quickly and without much work, if I'm seeing this right. The current routines send addresses that we know the D-Chip should ignore and several good addresses to make sure it sees those, but we could change the approach by first testing the addresses that it should respond to first, because if the chip doesn't respond to that right up front, we might as well mark the chip as bad and move on. Then, only if the chip responds to a correct address would we proceed by testing the exceptions. Does this make sense?"

TJ responded, "Changing the order of the test seems obvious. Is that what's really happening. So, today we test wrong addresses first?"

"Looks like it."

I could hear some disbelief in TJ's voice when she said, "That sequence might have been a carryover from when we simulated the design when sequence didn't matter, but it sounds very inefficient to me now. Are you sure of this?"

"I'm pretty sure, but it wouldn't take much to test the hypothesis. Also, I had assumed there was no CPU onboard."

"Correct. There is no CPU on the chip. It's all done in hardware, not software."

"Hmmm. But the host's address needs to be stored somehow. How does it do that?"

"The functions are locked in by the basic design, but there is also a small amount of electrically alterable ROM memory, like a flash drive, that stores variable data such as the host's address. I guess you could say that the chip is semi-smart, meaning it can store data, but there is no actual CPU processing going on."

"So, when the D-Chip powers up, it's ready to go, just like an on/off switch. No software to execute or boot from, and it doesn't need power to remember?"

"That's right. So how long will it take for you to verify your modified test sequence?"

"Since I'm not altering the actual tests, only the order in which they are applied, maybe a day or two at the most. Do I have time to test this before you put me on the second shift?"

I guessed Kevin was trying for a little humor.

TJ was pleased with Kevin's creativity and humor and quick comprehension of the issue at hand. She said, "I'd like to have this approach verified as soon as possible. This is very important. Maybe then we can have another dinner without the drinks this time. Should I assume we'd be ready for a small celebration about Thursday?"

TJ was asking Kevin out on a date.

Chapter 14

Later that day, Raj Matesh called TJ into his office.

Raj started, "Kevin checks out. Zietech is glad to have him on board. They feel lucky to have found an engineer who has both hardware and software backgrounds but prefers to live in the Midwest. What did you find out when you went out?"

"We just went to dinner and made some innocuous small talk. He seems like a nice kid from the Midwest. He hasn't moved around much, and he moved back here just because he likes it here. This is his hometown. He's never been married, and he doesn't currently have a girlfriend. I couldn't detect even a single egocentric gene. He's already come up with a possible way to speed up wafer testing."

Raj said, "I think we have him followed."

"Followed? No. I'll be spending more time with him, and I wouldn't want to do anything that might cause a negative reaction."

"If he's the All-American boy you think he is, he would never suspect he could be followed. We don't want any loose ends. I think we'll do some more checking."

"Even if he was subversive, there's nothing he could do about it anyway. Ninety-nine percent of our commitments have already shipped, and most are already installed. We could almost lock the doors, go home, and watch it all on television as the US crumbles, taking most of the rest of the world with it."

Raj asked, "Any change of plans for what you will do afterward?"

"Change of plans? Ha. How could anyone plan anything after infrastructures start to fail? People will still take it for granted that the toilets will flush, the water will still be safe to drink, and the lights will stay on. It'll be educational just to watch from a safe distance."

"We will have to arrange travel and exit contingencies anyway. It won't take them long to figure out what happened, and when they figure that out, they'll be knocking down the doors. I'll be gone on February twelfth. I suggest you do the same. Do you want to return to Russia?"

"As I said, I haven't given much thought to that. I'm in a malaise. Although the US has been our enemy, I'm getting used to this place. Russia trained me and gave me information about the US, but I don't see the people reacting that way. I see this country fighting a spiritual battle of good and evil with Islam, but I don't see an actual threat from the US to the rest of the world. The curious side of me would like to stay and watch how the US population as a whole reacts to the D-Chip event. We know the government will become irrational and probably try to pass on the blame, but what will the people do? I think I'll stay somewhere close and just watch."

"When you're found, you'll be arrested. They can't try you for treason because you are not a citizen, but international espionage can carry the death penalty."

"Look closely at the D-Chip under a microscope and you'll see my initials are well-defined in the traces. I guess a part of my psyche actually wants the world to know. Sounds like a suicide note left at the scene of the crime, doesn't it? I'm fifty years old; more than half of that has been learning, but remember, the US was behind the murder of my mother! Since then, and after Adrian's accident, I was assigned only one mission, so I might as well sit back and learn something from it. I won't kid you. I have been getting comfortable in the US while this plan was already well on its way, and I admit I had second thoughts, but dying with a legacy is better than dying young with nothing. The US will be shocked to know how a relatively small device can do so much damage."

TJ made it sound good, but Raj could tell her heart really wasn't in it. Her tone had been changing for months, but they were so close he had to just move ahead.

Raj said, "In the beginning, you were clear on the mission, but over the years you have been softening. I can clearly see that, but we must stay the course! Is that understood?"

"I'm not going anywhere. When I said I was committed, I meant it!"

Chapter 15

The group assembled in my room that night, with everyone chomping at the bit to get the TJ update. I was tempted to spruce up the meeting with a little levity and adult beverages, but I held off. This was going to be an important meeting. See, I do have some control over my actions. Sometimes. Well, maybe one gin.

Kevin started, "First, I managed to see a way to speed up the testing. This will be a reason for a celebration. Second, I can say with ninety-nine percent probability that TJ is in fact the president's daughter. She was told her mother was killed in the war, and she has no idea who the father is. I know you lewd, frothing-at-the-mouth peeping toms want sex images and details, but I must first ask the obvious question: haven't we completed this mission? Finding the president's daughter was what we were supposed to do, and we did. TJ is a good person, and I hate deceiving her anymore."

I said, "I'll decide that later when we get more data. It should be obvious to all of us that to be absolutely sure we need to run a DNA paternity test. Jeff or Greg, do we have access to the president's DNA?"

Jeff replied, "That's a damn good question. At one time, there was a movement to supposedly protect our leaders and collect their DNA, but after the sexual activities of Clinton and Trump, this has not been a welcome topic. The author

Ronald Kessler said that Navy stewards gathered bedsheets, drinking glasses, and other objects so they could be sanitized or destroyed, but we really don't know for sure. It has been asked many times, and the Secret Service would neither confirm nor deny if the president's DNA is on file."

"Sounds like political bullshit to me," I grunted. "This was Elliot's idea, so he must be willing to give it up. I'll take it upon myself to call Tanner and the president and get this done. If he argues with that . . . I'll quit!"

After a few seconds, I said, "Kevin, please continue."

Kevin, who had been boisterous and proud of himself, was not expecting to be rebuked. He had been on a roll before I forced him to step back and slow down. He continued with his update in a much lower voice.

"Well." He stopped and took a breath. "I had my first dinner with her, as you heard Richard. We got along well, and I'll be seeing more of her, that's for sure. And I won't lie to you guys; I like her a lot, and I don't want her to be hurt when she finds out what we're up to."

I said, "Get off that horse for a bit. Aren't you the least bit curious about this AMIP company and the secrecy around TJ being here illegally? And Brad Dempsey was killed, remember? It appears it's not an open-and-shut case, with all that's going on around here."

Kevin said, "Of course. I don't mean to be callous, but we don't know if Brad's death was related, and I admit the AMIP funding does look suspicious but is that our job? Isn't this international security shit above our pay grade? It is for me anyway. I'm just a mole digging in the dirt, hoping someone isn't planning on playing Whack-a-Mole when I stick up my head. I'm sorry, and damn, I had the opportunity to get her DNA over our dinner. I just didn't think about that."

Roger jumped in, "I think Kevin had something else on his mind and is getting a little more than just sweet on our TJ—and after only *one* dinner! Our mole is obviously in heat. I see a family of little moles in Kevin's future."

Kevin defended himself. "That's not fair. Yes, I like TJ. I admitted that, but just because I didn't dig up some dirt doesn't mean I'm backing off. In fact, we're meeting again on Thursday night after we see the test improvements. All I'm saying is, so far I haven't detected anything negative other than her past feelings about American politics. That would be expected from someone who spent so many years in a communist environment. I'm sure many exaggerations and lies about the US were pounded into her head, but it seems to me she now sees the discrepancies between what she was told and what she's been experiencing. The United States is growing on her. She likes it here. Anyway, I'll have plenty of her DNA after that next meeting."

Rog added, "But we should still find out why and how she was brought here undercover in the first place, and what about her friends? She can't just be a loner."

Greg added, "And what about AMIP? Did you discuss the company details with her at all?"

Kevin answered, "Sorry, guys, we didn't get into any of that yet, but she'll talk to me. She had much too much to drink, so we had to cut our dinner date short. And, no, I didn't take advantage of her either."

"Okay, okay," I added. "It looks like we're in a holding pattern until after Kevin's next meeting or date. Did she say if Raj Matesh knew about your dinner?"

"It didn't come up. I know she didn't want Raj to know she got drunk, but I don't think she told Raj we were going out."

I said, "She would have had to tell him if there was even the slightest hint or curiosity about you. And they did call the Zietech number to check up on you. By the way, the FBI gave you a glowing reference, thanks to Jeff here. Since AMIP followed up on you, we should assume things may not be as neat as you seem to think. What would we do in the same position? We would track this guy Kevin and find out either way. Kevin, keep your antenna up and your radar screen on high. Let me know immediately if you suspect anything. Okay?"

"Got it."

"Until Friday then."

Chapter 16

By the middle of Thursday, and wearing the wire without the earpiece, Kevin was ready to try out his new re-sequenced test routines. The audio was clear while they talked outside the cleanroom.

Kevin said to TJ, "I think I'm ready to run some tests on a wafer."

"How much time does the simulator say we're going to save?"

"That depends on how many bad chips there are. A wafer full of bad chips will go through very quickly. The longest possible test would be a wafer of all good chips, but still, the simulations show a savings of as much as forty minutes per wafer."

TJ gasped, "Currently, we're at one hour, so that would be a massive improvement. Did you run into any issues?"

"Well, we can't test every possible combination of addresses, so I can't know precisely what we'd be missing. I can't predict if increasing the test algorithm thoroughness by throwing more addresses at it would be worth the extra test time. It boils down to mathematical probabilities. If we just had some unique test modes where I could jump around the addressing part . . . maybe if I reviewed the logic schematics I could see a way to test the chip in sections rather than just a black box."

TJ responded quickly, "That's not possible. The schematics are classified."

Kevin said, "Okay, I get that. Do we have any feedback about field failures when the chip had to be replaced?"

TJ responded, "D-Chips are not replaced in the field. Chips are mounted directly on the host's printed circuit boards using surface mount or embedded technologies; there is no room for anything else. Customers test their PCBs as a system, with the D-Chip as just another internal component. Customers cannot repair boards in the field anyway. They just don't have the time or the equipment to do so. If something fails and the host can't talk to the Internet, they can't tell if the D-Chip was the cause or not, so we have minimal field failure data. A board swap is the only way to get back up and running. These shipments are probably for inventory replacement PCBs anyway since most of the D-Chips were installed years ago."

"There are that many out there, huh? Any idea how many? I know that with the second source suppliers it would be difficult to predict, but you must have some idea."

"I'm not sure anyone knows the answer to that, but it's well into the millions. The D-Chip has been in production from multiple sources for years with few changes. It's a slave 'doorman' that just opens the door to the Internet. It's small, it's simple, it's inexpensive, and has been very reliable."

"Is that where it got its name? Is the D-Chip the 'Doorman Chip' or the 'Decoder Chip?' And is it patented?"

"There's not much that can be patented, and if there were, it would still be better to keep it under wraps. Patents just expose your ideas to the competition, and we really don't have much competition. Between us and our second sources, we essentially own this market! And at less than twenty cents a chip, who's going to want to compete? There's no incentive to do that."

"I had no idea the D-Chip was so ubiquitous. What's the possibility that my Internet provider or my laptop or my smartphone use this chip?"

"Ninety-nine percent!"

"Well, we'd better make sure they work then, right? Let's run a wafer with these new routines."

I lost the audio when they went into the cleanroom to run the tests.

I found out later that testing went well with yield results that correlated with historical data, but with a net time saving of more than fifty percent. TJ was elated. The dinner celebration seemed appropriate and on target. AMIP was planning to ship everything they could before the weekend, so later that day, after Kevin ran several different algorithms on the wafers, they switched to the new test routines, and production took over.

I was wondering what was going on because the audio was spotty, but I trusted that Kevin knew what he was doing. Soon they were out of the cleanroom, my audio was back, and the testing must have gone well, because TJ and Kevin decided to celebrate by going on that dinner date an hour early.

***

This time it was a cozy and quiet restaurant near midtown. Kevin drove. After they were seated in a private area, Kevin asked, "Hot sake?" She had previously said she didn't want any alcohol, but feelings could change. "I checked. They have it."

150

"Sure." As they waited, TJ broke the ice. "So, Kevin, I don't think you told me how you found Zietech. Care to fill me in?"

Kevin answered, "I don't remember who told me, or maybe I saw it in a mag, but somebody said there was a semiconductor testing company right here in Chicago. I had already moved back here without a full-time job, so I had to check it out. I guess because I had both software and semiconductor backgrounds, they hired me quickly. Then when I found out one of Zietech's customers was AMIP, where Raj Matesh was the CEO, I couldn't wait to visit."

To move on quickly before TJ had a chance to ask another question, Kevin said, "By the way, I found something interesting as I was experimenting with different algorithms today."

"What was that?"

Kevin said, "First, the warm bread and olive oil look great, and our drinks are here, so here's a toast. Here's to the D-Chip!"

They clicked their sake cups and snacked on the bread. Kevin's task was to get a piece of her bread.

Kevin diverted back to her question, "Just for fun, I ran some routines that generated random data patterns once the chip was accepting its correct address. I ran this approach on both the simulator and on the chips themselves. The simulator results didn't always match what the chips did. Occasionally, a chip would be passing the test with flying colors and then all of a sudden stop. That's to be expected when a fault is detected, but the interesting part was that once the chip failed, I couldn't rerun the same test and get the same result. Don't get me wrong, it was still a bad chip, but it was like finding a fault somehow changed the way

151

the chip worked. I found only one or two chips that failed that way, but those that did exhibited the same symptom. The chips just stopped accepting addresses. The simulator showed I could rerun the same test and find the same fault, but the chip itself didn't do that. That's weird, huh?"

"Probably just an anomaly. Who can say how a bad device would fail anyway? The possibilities are astronomical. Remember, there are a lot of transistors in there. I need another sake."

After a few hours and several drinks, I could hear that TJ was again very tipsy. Kevin whispered to me that he had already palmed several pieces of bread and her first sake cup. With her defenses down, she came right out and asked to go to Kevin's place, and Kevin was more than willing to pursue that opportunity. He drove slowly so as not to agitate queasy stomachs. There was no more talk about chips and tech bullshit. He had her DNA. Kevin hit the remote on the garage door opener and helped her into the house. TJ wanted to keep the conversation going, and it seemed that TJ was searching for an outlet for sharing. She would probably not remember what they talked about anyway, so why not continue the conversation before she was totally out?

He gently laid her down on the bed and lay down next to her, but she wasn't having that. She sat right up and yelled, "What are you trying to do? I think I love you, but I can't fall in love with an American."

Kevin didn't say anything. They had had sex in her office before without any issue, but in those cases, she wasn't wasted. Maybe this was an excellent time to keep her talking and get some information about her immigration and AMIP. I could listen in as Kevin went on the offensive. Without his earpiece, all I could do was listen.

Kevin said, "Is it okay if I fall in love with a Russian?"

"Probably not!" TJ roared.

Kevin said, "Well at least let me ask you a few questions, such as when did you get to the US? And how? And are you even legal? And has living in the US really been that uncomfortable?"

The flood of blatant unexpected questions seemed to overwhelm her for a bit, before becoming suddenly coherent.

"I'm sorry. Americans killed my mother during the Tet! They told me all about it before sending me away to school. I listened, learned, and started to despise capitalists. They tried to tell me what was really going on."

I could tell Kevin was losing his patience as he said, "I understand that your mother was killed, and I don't mean to be cruel, but that happens during a war. You were very young when that happened, so young that you don't even remember her. And they never told you about your father either. It had to be years before you even knew your name."

"I was told my mother's name was Hau, Hau Thom, and I should be very proud because she was an important leader during the war. My father was never discussed."

Wow! That was it. She IS the president's daughter!

Kevin didn't back off, "So how did you end up coming to the United States?"

"It was Somenski who offered me the chance to come here, and I took it!"

"Somenski? Who's Somenski?"

"A great man, that's who. He brought me here. I had nothing, but Som paid my way, set me up, and asked me to help design something that would stop the United States' aggression. I had many ideas, but I eventually proposed the Doomsday Chip."

I could clearly hear Kevin as he gasped, "The Doomsday Chip? That's what the D stands for?"

TJ responded slowly, "Raj has said many times 'At world's end, we will raise our glasses, and God, if there is a God, will no doubt have trouble with the benediction.' Are we going to have sex tonight or what? And will you be my Valentine? We might as well; there's not much time left."

With TJ slowly slipping into oblivion and unintelligible, mumbled speech, Kevin tried to comprehend what he'd just heard. At world's end? Not much time left? How could a small chip less than one-sixteenth of an inch on a side become such a weapon? He tried to talk to her, but she was unable to communicate.

Kevin said out loud to himself, "There's not much time left? What the hell?"

Then Kevin really screwed up. Without realizing that all he needed to do was to talk to me, he instead called me on an open line, "Braddock, we need to get everybody together ASAP!"

I yelled into the phone, "Why the *hell* did you call me on an open line? That's really stupid! I could hear what was going on, you know."

Kevin continued as if he didn't grasp the issue, "Oh, sorry. Anyway, TJ told me she knew her mother was Hau Thom, so that clinches the president's search in my book, but I have her DNA too. But that's not why I'm calling. Just before she passed out, she told me the D-Chip stands for Doomsday Chip. I have no idea what that means. Make sure Jeff Shaw is there. Open line? Crap. I wasn't paying attention. We're at my place, and she's passed out. We'll stay here until the morning, I guess."

I was pissed. Kevin sounded like an inexperienced, overexcited, confused cop on his first case.

I yelled, "Hey, stupid! You have a secure wire. *Use it*, or call me on the secure line. Don't screw up again!"

Sometimes youth is not all it's cracked up to be.

I hung up and called Roger, "Rog, send your guys to watch Kevin's place right now. Kevin's there with TJ, and shit is hitting the fan. Kevin was freaking out, and he even called me on an open line. Tell your guys to watch but don't interact. We need to meet here tomorrow unless something happens sooner."

Roger said, "In my gut, I felt something was going to happen. I'm on it."

Chapter 17

In the morning, TJ woke even more upset with herself for her lack of control. Kevin had the wire turned on. Finally, she said, "I guess you're starting to see who and what I really am?"

Kevin responded, "I see you are a beautiful woman that I am falling in love with. You just sounded a little confused about America, that's all."

"Confused? This is all happening so quickly. Who did you call last night?"

Kevin didn't answer that question. Instead, he said, "I understand your mother was killed, and you'll carry that for the rest of your life, but that happened during a war everyone wants to forget and benefitted no one. As you said, you were very young when your mother was killed, and you can't possibly remember her. So, where did this anger and vengefulness come from? Surely you don't believe everything they told you about the United States, do you?"

TJ said, "The mission was to teach the United States government a lesson, a lesson in restraint and not taking things for granted, but unfortunately, innocent people will have to suffer too."

A few minutes later, Kevin's front door was breached by three armed European-looking men who said nothing. They looked at TJ and, using the tips of their rifles, waved TJ and

Kevin with their arms raised into a corner of the kitchen. They were not dressed as soldiers—only jeans and T-shirts. They would look right at home strolling through the mall. TJ spoke to the men in a language Kevin didn't recognize, but it wasn't Russian. The men took Kevin's cell phone and keys, then found and removed the wire, and prodded him out the door.

I heard TJ say, "Oh my god. You're wired?"

I knew the shit was, in fact, hitting the fan.

They were ushered into a nondescript SUV and taken to the back of a building not far from AMIP. Raj Matesh was waiting inside.

***

When the goons had removed the wire, I immediately called an emergency group phone meeting so I could bring everybody up to date.

I started, "First, we have the president's DNA. I talked to Tanner and the president last night, and the president agreed quickly. That part was easy. The bad news is that Kevin called me last night on an unsecured line, told me he did his part and has TJ's DNA, but he also said the D-Chip was short for *Doomsday Chip*, whatever that means. I immediately called Roger and asked his team to watch Kevin's place. So, Rog, what's the feedback from your team?"

Roger reported, "This morning, we saw three armed men go into Kevin's house. A few minutes later, the five of them left in an SUV and went to a vacant multistory building about two blocks from AMIP. We did not see any weapons, but it's clear they were abducted."

Jeff would contact the police, but we all agreed not to react until we had a better idea of what was going on. Kevin's cell was turned off, so we couldn't contact him, and the building where they were taken looked unoccupied. I decided to inform President Elliot and Tanner of our situation. I didn't talk one-on-one to Paul Elliot, only Tanner.

"Tanner. Let me start by saying the good news is we're ninety-nine-point-nine percent sure Terry Jana is the president's daughter, and we have her DNA. She was told her mother's name was Hau Thom, so that almost locks it up, but no one knew who her father was. The bad news is there is some sort of conspiracy at AMIP, where she works. This morning, three goons—probably from AMIP—took TJ and our undercover man, Kevin, to a vacant building. We're working with the FBI and the local police on a plan."

Tanner said, "Don't do anything until I get there! I'll be there in a few hours."

The four of us sat in my room, trying to understand the turn of events until the concierge called about two hours later to say Tanner was in the lobby.

Although I had contacted Tanner many times via secure email and talked to him on encrypted phone lines, I'd never met him since I started this search. I exited the elevator and saw him standing next to the concierge. Tanner was tall and black and looked like Samuel L. Jackson with hair right out of *Pulp Fiction*.

By the time Tanner had arrived, we were all back in my room. The four of us went over everything we knew while bringing Tanner up to speed. Tanner was bothered that the building where they took Kevin was so large. Finding him in a multistory building was not going to be easy, and we would have to do it without attracting attention. Tanner also told us that President Elliot was aggravated by all this late-breaking intrigue and conspiracy talk. I should have talked to Paul Elliot myself. He just wanted to find his daughter, but anyone would get confused by all these developments. Tanner added that the DNA discussion made the president feel much better that I might actually find his daughter.

I took control of the meeting. "Remember, without Kevin, we still don't know what the hell is really going on here, nor where TJ's DNA is. I think Jeff Shaw needs to put a team together, and we just go in and get Kevin out."

"Hold on, hold on," said Roger. "People are going to get hurt. There were five people in that SUV, including Ms. Jana and Kevin. We can't risk hurting her or Kevin, and his cell phone now has some vacation message bullshit, so it's clear AMIP sees Kevin as a real threat, and we don't know if Kevin knows much of anything. He may suspect something, but what does he really know?"

I almost yelled, "It doesn't matter what Kevin really knows or doesn't know. I heard what TJ told him, and right now we just need to get him out. Jeff, let's get a team out there ASAP. Remember, no mention of TJ being the president's daughter to your team."

Chapter 18

Meanwhile, Raj Matesh was talking. "Well, Mr. Dupree, if that's really your name, welcome back. I'm not sure, but I think you probably know more than it's safe for you to know right now, so we have to take care of that. You will have to stay here while we decide what to do with you."

Kevin had never been exposed to physical violence on his projects, so this capture caught him off guard. He was undoubtedly terrified. TJ just stared at the floor and said nothing, as she was probably considering that she might lose Kevin for good.

Raj continued, "During your short stay here, we will ship the remaining D-Chips, which, with the help of your new test routines, will get rid of our backlog. We can't let you go and have you cause a disruption before certain parties have left the US. Oh, we took the liberty of posting a vacation notice on your email and cell's voicemail."

Raj respected Kevin as possibly the only tech guy out there who could understand the beauty of their plan, so he said, "I can explain that testing anomaly you stumbled over if you're curious."

Kevin fought to regain some composure. "Of course. I see there's no TV in here, so what else have we got to talk about?"

"You Americans are impertinent down to the last minute, aren't you? But you still don't see the big picture."

"Then why don't you educate me?"

"Be glad to. We are proud of our D-Chip. It has special circuitry that we encode with a date and time over the Internet. When that date and time happen, the D-Chip turns off access to the Internet. It's just that simple. This is done using hardware instead of software, so even a Chinese hacker cannot get around it. It's designed in! You can thank Ms. Jana for that."

Kevin looked at TJ.

TJ said, "You stumbled onto this with your random testing."

Raj continued, "After the chip closes the door to the Internet, it can no longer be accessed. The chip stores this shutdown condition, so turning off the power doesn't reset the chip. In other words, the D-Chip's host, as you call it, is cut off from the Internet . . . forever! Nothing can reverse this because the chip is no longer listening. It's as if it blew a fuse. Of course, not all D-Chips do this, so it looks like only the US and maybe a few of your allies will be suffering. Maybe twenty million at most." He laughed.

"I get it. You *use* the Internet to send a date that causes the D-Chip to disconnect *from* the Internet. That's a bizarre idea, but it would take much too much time and require millions of addresses, and it would be fairly straightforward to buffer around. Yeah, it would cause some panic, but doomsday? Come on."

"Very insightful. I commend you. Encoding each D-Chip one at a time does take hours, days, or even months to get to the millions of chips that are out there, and many networks are not even online all the time, so you're correct; the encoding process takes a long time. That is why we started the process over a year ago. We have been encoding every D-Chip that's already installed in servers, laptops, and cell phones throughout the world. Once encoded, even we cannot disable the chip. It is armed and ready for the trigger. We don't do anything except wait."

"The trigger is the date?"

"More than that. A specific *time* on a specific date."

"And if it worked, you feel this would that put the entire United States back into the Dark Ages?"

"Imagine if you will when people lose the basic necessities of their life, and they have the United States to thank for it. Because when the United States loses the ability to communicate via the Internet, your systems and infrastructure break down. No more infrastructure, no power, no streetlights, no television, no bank transactions, no radio, no gasoline— nothing. You have been ignoring the fragility of your decisions. You have had it too good for too long and have taken too much for granted. People will soon know that this inevitable catastrophe started in the United States. But the beauty of this plan is it all happens at *exactly the same time*! That by itself will be like a shockwave taking out the country in one fell swoop."

Terry Jana was listening and fully aware her efforts were going to hurt a lot of people, not just the ones at the top, and she may also lose her only love since her husband's death. They had engineered an encoded trigger mechanism that could not be disabled or undone. And to what end? Merely to make the US look bad? Her remorse was wasted, because there wasn't anything she could do about it anyway. She wished she had met Kevin years ago.

Raj Matesh added, "I'm sure a smart fellow like you is thinking to himself that this approach might not work because all these encoded chips couldn't possibly be triggered simultaneously, so there might be ample time to isolate the government and other high priority networks. Am I correct in anticipating your thinking?"

"It doesn't matter what I'm thinking. I'm sure you're not through bragging."

Raj just smiled broadly. "To have the appropriate effect, it *must* happen simultaneously. You see, every Internet server is synchronized to the Internet time as established by NIST, the National Institute of Standards and Technology. At precisely noon Central Standard Time on February fourteenth, Valentine's Day, most D-Chips in the world will disconnect their host from the Internet. The precise date and time were encoded years ago. The trigger is the UCT time, Universal Coordinated Time, which is independent of the time zone. Noon Central Standard Time is the same as one p.m. Eastern and ten a.m. on the West Coast, but it's all the same instant. Genius, isn't it?"

Kevin argued, "But a server or host or computer may not be online at that particular time."

"True, I admit, those that were not online would be missed, but I'm guessing those would be relatively insignificant numbers, and more likely to be in third-world countries and rural areas. All the major cities, companies, servers, systems, and infrastructure would be online twenty-four/seven. But even if you were one of the lucky ones who missed it, seeing what has taken place and thinking you might be next is almost as frightening as the event itself. And what happens to those when they go online and there's no one to talk to? What good is that? And we still have the submarines if we choose to use them."

Kevin said, "Submarines?"

"You don't know about our submarines? I'm surprised. But it doesn't matter, because the D-Chips will be thorough enough without the subs, which if deployed, might shift the focus away from the US anyway."

Kevin thought, *TJ never mentioned submarines.*

Kevin continued, "So, some boards fail. New boards would be swapped in immediately."

Raj said, "And they would fail too!"

"But according to your explanation, they haven't been encoded yet."

"True, but those swapped in D-Chips are listening for their encoding, so we just keep sending later encode dates. And if you think because of the Internet chaos caused by the initial trigger that we can't send the encode sequence, you'd be wrong. The Internet itself would still be there; you just couldn't talk to it. Only the vulnerable ones could log on and then get disabled later. People would assume the problem was just a bad board, because their replacement board would work for a brief period, not realizing it would go offline later. No one could anticipate the long-term aftereffects."

Raj continued, "We do not intend to kill you unless we have to. We just have to wait until after Valentine's Day. Then, if all goes well without interference, you'll be free to go, but good luck on making a phone call, scheduling a cab, or booking a flight."

Kevin said, "This process would take down the Soviet Union as well."

Raj said, "Not really. As I said, we have our own D-Chip."

PART 3

Chapter 19

Jeff Shaw went to tell the police to stand down and wait for further instructions; the FBI would take it from here. When Jeff got back, I talked to him. "Jeff, the captors don't know what we know. It seems like a small team could do this expeditiously."

"I concur, but we might have to wait until some technology tools arrive."

"I may already have what we'll need."

Due to the size of the building and its multiple floors, a small, quiet, covert team with the right technical equipment should be able to do the extraction without causing much attention. Tools such as through-the-wall heat scanners, metal detectors, night vision goggles, and frequency scanners might be all we needed. Between what the FBI already had on-site and the equipment I had sent to myself from California, we had the latest tech.

Jeff Shaw assembled two of his best agents trained in SWAT.

Jeff asked me, "Do you plan on going in with us?"

"Absolutely," I said. "The president would want that."

That was total bullshit, of course. Paul Elliot just wanted what he wanted. At this point, I imagined that he could care less if I was a casualty, but I had lost the depressing feelings of self-pity and aging. I hadn't felt that good in years. The activity and mental stimulation were invigorating. I was definitely going in!

We were armed with assault rifles. We watched the building for activity, discussing possible plans, when Raj Matesh and TJ left in the SUV. That was a pleasant surprise. They obviously didn't have a clue. I made sure the police took them into custody quickly.

Jeff talked to his guys via radio, since they wore helmets with headphones. "We have made no move on the building, and we have allowed two of the contributors to leave without interaction. They are now in custody. Therefore, the remaining perps do not know that we know where they are. Our mission is to recover a Mr. Kevin Dupree, who we assume is the only Caucasian. There are at least three other men, but there may be other armed guards as well. We are authorized to do what's necessary to safely recover Mr. Dupree. Under no circumstances are we to allow an injury to Dupree."

Jeff and I went with the other two to the back door of the building.

Being in closer proximity, I was able to use my somewhat illegal frequency scanner/jammer (Jeff just smiled) to establish the frequencies the perps were using for their communications. That part was easy, and jamming those frequencies was also a simple task. If they tried to use their radios, they would assume that they just had a bad signal. Since the building was quite old, all a team member needed was a simple lockpick to unlock the rear door. The pick made almost no noise.

There were four of us: Jeff at the door, two swat members standing close behind with weapons ready, and me, crouching, making sure I would not be in the way. We were prepared for the worst, but when Jeff slowly opened the door a crack, there was no one directly on the other side. Through the narrow crack, and through dense cigarette smoke, he could make out two men sitting in the hall lobby about twenty-five yards away. The exiting smoke smelled like camel dung. The thugs' rifles were just sitting on the floor. SEAL Team Six they were not!

The goons must have noticed something, because they scrambled for their weapons. Jeff flung the door open while ducking low, thereby allowing those two team members with silenced rifles to take out both men. There was barely a sound.

The first floor of the building was nothing but hallways and offices, which was good because the structure helped muffle any noise. We were taking no chances that we may have been heard, so we laid low, just listening. I was impressed by how Jeff's men communicated with hand signals, no talking.

Several minutes went by without a sound or movement. So far, so good. It was apparent this building had been used for small businesses, with its simple offices, floor-to-ceiling non-metallic walls with simulated oak doors, and dropped acoustic-tile ceilings. It was also cold, so the heating system was obviously turned off.

We entered the building. Being non-metallic, it meant we could scan each wall using through-the-wall heat and sound detectors, and we could detect metal movement as well. The walls might as well not even have been there. No interior doors were locked, so it was obvious that that the first floor was vacant. Bathrooms were located in the center of the floorplan next to the elevator, and stairs that were intended for service access had steel treads on a concrete base. These stairs were not going to creak! There were no guards at the stairways either. Someone needed some more training in security methods.

The second floor was also vacant.

On the third floor, my scanner showed multiple body heat signatures in a room next to the elevator. That room had no windows and only one double door. Heat profiles showed there were four people, with the weakest heat pattern coming from someone sitting in the middle of the room. Two others were walking around, and another was leaning against the double doors. Moving metal, assumed to be rifles, was detected as well. The weakest pattern that showed minimal movement was probably Kevin sitting, with the other three being the heavies. We couldn't be sure of that, but it was a likely bet.

We fixed microphones to the walls to listen in. No one was speaking English. Breaking through would put Kevin in jeopardy, so Jeff suggested we use gas. Gas never knocks people out in five seconds as they show in the movies. The odorless gas they brought caused nausea and diarrhea, enough so that, once exposed, you would want to find the bathroom. With the heating system off, it was easy to leak the gas under the doors via a small rubber hose that the team taped to the dark baseboard. The FBI team handed me a gas mask.

After about fifteen minutes, the talk was slowing down, a signal that physical discomfort was starting. Two of the FBI team were already waiting in the adjacent restroom; Jeff and I were nearby in a hallway. The first man came out and rushed to the bathroom, loosely carrying his rifle at his side, and was quickly, quietly, and lethally dispatched. The second showed up only a minute later, and Jeff's team was again very efficient. Not a shot had been fired. The third perp opened the room's door and started to yell something that I assumed meant he couldn't leave his post until one of those two assholes got back. Jeff shot him as he held the door open. He was dealt his *death sentence* before he could finish his *verbal sentence*.

Kevin was unharmed and displayed a prominent shade of Shrek green. We gave him an antidote and an oxygen mask and moved him to the nearby toilet. He spent the night at the FBI.

Chapter 20

The next morning, I called Lara to tell her that things were moving along quicker than I had expected, but it wasn't the right time to explain the details. She understood and just told me to be careful. I felt a little dishonest, acting like everything was good so far when the previous day could have ended poorly. I didn't mention the word doomsday. Lara did not know my real involvement.

About an hour later, the team was gathered in my room. When the team brought in Kevin, I quipped, "Is this any way to feel after a successful dinner date?"

Kevin said, "If I feel like this, I should have had much more fun than I remember. If I make a fast break to the can, please don't stand in my way. And don't offer me breakfast or anything to drink."

The FBI team brought Tanner, Greg, and Roger up to speed on the "mission" (their word) and asked if they should stick around. I offered them a drink, which they refused. Roger suggested they should stay because we might come under siege shortly and that we should relocate to a more secure location. Jeff had the perfect spot—the same secure FBI building where TJ and Matesh were being held. We packed up a few things we might need. I was a little disgruntled about us moving, because I knew the FBI wasn't going to have an open bar like I had.

***

After our short trip, and after Kevin made two more visits to the restroom, I had to get the conversation started. "Well, Kevin, where do we stand and what do we know?" Tanner, Greg, Roger, Jeff, and I were hanging on every word.

Kevin started, "I've been thinking about how I would explain this. It's complicated and pretty techy. I wish we had a software or IT guy here just so I don't get something wrong, but we don't have time for that. I would first like to say that, although TJ is the key to all this, I'm sure she's had second thoughts. She was motivated in her earlier years to do something against the United States government, but I know she's sorry now when she thinks about what may happen as a result of what she's done."

Roger said, "Bullshit. You're just trying to protect her!"

Kevin was quick and angry in his reply. "You can't know how others feel until you walk in their shoes."

I said loudly, "No time for arguing! Note taken, Kevin. Now, you had said on the phone that we didn't have much time. What do you mean by that? And before I forget, where is TJ's DNA?"

"TJ's sake cup and two pieces of bread she was eating are in a quart freezer bag at my place on the second shelf next to the fridge. I'm sure it's still there, unless someone went back to get it. TJ is not aware that I did that."

"Nice work," I said.

Roger had left his surveillance crew at Kevin's, so he immediately called and had a guy recover the DNA bag.

"So, what's this time crunch all about?" I asked.

Kevin replied, "From what Raj told me, we have until noon on Valentine's Day."

I said, "So, we have a little time if the US is not in imminent danger. Are you sure you really know what's going to happen?"

"Mr. Matesh was very willing to tell me what they've done over the past few years. He even answered my questions. He was very boastful, even proud, and I believe him. The CliffsNotes version is something like this: TJ was brought to the US to engineer a way to embarrass the US. I'm not sure who came up with the approach, but it's insidious. The plan was to take down the Internet in one fell swoop—all of it except Russia and their allies. TJ's background in software and semiconductors gave her the tech tool kit to engineer the D-Chip. The push to do it came from her superiors. She figured out how to do this by encoding this function in the D-Chip's hardware design that cannot be changed or hacked via software.

"She did this years ago, so for a long time now, AMIP has been shipping D-Chips to virtually every company whose products communicate over the Internet. This chip exists in everything! The volume was very high, and AMIP has licensed the design to other semiconductor suppliers. No one needed to reverse engineer the design, because it does what it's supposed to do. It's all the same design that came from AMIP. They call it the D-Chip, it costs less than a quarter, and millions have been shipped. I've been told that ninety-nine percent of all printed circuit boards that connect to the Internet use this chip."

Greg jumped in, "So what does it *do*?"

Kevin answered, "It sits between the Internet and its host, the host being the computer or laptop, server, cell phone, or whatever. Every host has a unique Internet IP address. What it is supposed to do is wait for the host's address, and then it tells its host that someone is knocking on the door. The D-Chip offloads the host, so the host doesn't have to spend time looking for its address. It's like an electronic doorman to the Internet. That's why I thought D-Chip meant 'doorman' or 'decode,' but it really means 'doomsday.' The D-chip has been encoded to disconnect from the Internet on Valentine's Day, February the fourteenth, at noon Central Standard Time."

Tanner asked, "So the D-Chip is waiting for a particular date?"

"And time," added Kevin.

Roger jumped in, "So people don't get emails for a few hours, and not logging on to Facebook could be perceived as an overall benefit to mankind."

I added, "But companies use the Internet for their main communication and infrastructure. Even phones other than cell phones are VOIP."

"VOIP?" Tanner asked.

I explained, "Voice Over the Internet Protocol. Who has a real hardline phone connection anymore? Our entire infrastructure is based on Internet technology. Face it, shut down the Internet and you shut down the country."

Roger's eyes and mouth were wide open. He said nothing for a change. Greg continued to be quiet too. Jeff, who never said much anyway, squinted his eyes and stroked his chin almost as if he wasn't buying the story. I must admit I had been concerned for years about our blind dependence and complacency on technology, ever since the first time I lost power at my cabin and the phone went dead too. In years past, the telephone was not dependent on house electrical power.

Ma Bell was always there via the landline. Lose the Internet now, and you lose the phone and probably the TV. Many new TVs can't even receive over-the-air signals anymore, and even if they did, who would be transmitting? All nonlocal content is sent to the station via the Internet. During a recent forest fire out west, the only reliable communications were volunteer amateur radio operators running on generators. I could envision the White House and the Pentagon having to use walkie-talkies.

Then Kevin dropped another bomb. "Raj also implied that since they had so much faith in their D-Chips, their submarines probably would not be needed. What the hell is that all about? TJ had never mentioned submarines to me!"

Jeff finally had something to say. "I know a few things about that. For years, we have been well aware that the Soviets have submarines directly over our transoceanic cables. They come and go all the time. This was a major concern when the cables were real cables, since they could tap in, and if they could decrypt the signals, they could listen in on our global communications."

I jumped in. "I have been aware of this as well. Heck, newspapers have written articles about it. I think it was even on CNN. But I wasn't too concerned because these cables transitioned from hard cable to fiber optic. You can't just tap into fiber. But if that is what Raj was referring to, I might see a link. If the overall objective is to shut down communications, cutting the fiber would disconnect the US from the rest of the world.

"My problem with that is two-fold: First, fiber cables go down all the time, and we never notice it because the Internet just finds another way. All the cables would have to go down at the same time, and that would mean the deployment of multiple detonation devices. We would know if that happened. Second, blowing up our cables would not be a quiet, undercover operation. It might even trigger a war. Knocking out our Internet is one thing, but detonating explosives is something else.

"Jeff, we need to see how many cables are vulnerable and how many subs may be parked over them. Can you do that?"

Jeff responded, "I'll find out who we can talk to."

Obviously very upset, Tanner yelled out, "Well, let's go get those sons-a-bitches! There has to be a way to shut this crap down. This can't happen on President Elliot's watch! And his own daughter is part of this? That would destroy him."

Greg asked, "Going back to the D-Chip, from what you say, the D-Chip would shut down everybody, Russia as well."

Kevin said, "I was told that somehow the Soviet Union and their allies are exempt. There might be two versions of the chip, but I'm not sure I believe it."

I said, "What makes you skeptical about there not being two versions?"

Kevin said, "I don't know. Just a feeling. I guess because I never saw any indication that there were two test routines, which there would have to be."

I said, "Well, in any case, we need to interrogate both TJ and Matesh and get some more information. Kevin, you seem to be the only one that TJ might talk to. She must be confused by you as much as you are by her. A personal discussion might shed some light on this and perhaps give us an opening. Ask about those subs! Meanwhile, we should block any shipments from AMIP."

"Do you think it's time to tell her who her father is?" asked Kevin.

Tanner said, "We can't do that without President Elliot's approval. I don't pretend to know what the president's plans were if we did find his daughter. He may not know himself, and we are not really sure until after the DNA results. I'll talk to him tonight and see what he thinks."

I'm the guy in charge, right? So, I jumped in. "I think we should all talk to the president right now! That way we are all on the same page with no interpretation errors. If this Valentine's Day crap is real, then we have no time to lose, and this submarine surprise can change everything. Time's a-wastin'. The fourteenth is five days away!"

Roger tried to be funny by adding, "Easy for you to say, Braddock. You're retired, over the hill, and have nothing to lose. We have jobs and careers."

I said, "Rog. I know your sarcasm comes from a basic internal insecurity, so I'll overlook it. Do you agree or not?"

Everybody except Tanner felt listening to the president himself was a grand idea, if it was even possible on such short notice. I think Tanner was protecting his position as a key intermediator to the president, but this was no time for such trivial concerns. To help his ego, I let Tanner make the call. President Elliot answered quickly.

Tanner said, "Excuse me, Mr. President, but I'm here with Braddock, and the other four are in the room. They are Greg Dillard from the DHS; Kevin Dupree, our technical mole; Roger Hest, who did the surveillance; and Jeff Shaw from the FBI. We're pretty sure we have found your daughter and will be interrogating her and commencing the DNA test as soon as we can. We have not told her that you are her father."

I cringed at the word "interrogating." Couldn't he have said "interviewing" or "talking to?"

The president said, "You're sure you have found my daughter?"

Tanner said, "We're pretty sure, sir, but the DNA will verify. If you don't mind, sir, I'd like to put you on speaker so the six of us can hear you. We are in a private and secure FBI facility."

"Go ahead."

The president asked, "Are you calling to ask me if you can tell her about me?"

I jumped in quickly before Tanner could say anything. "Braddock here, Mr. President. We don't intend to tell her about you until you say so. We are calling because of other pressing issues we need to discuss."

President Elliot said, "Okay, but before we get to those *pressing issues*, is she okay? How did she get here? And what name is she using?"

I said, "We think she illegally entered the United States about ten years ago, dropping the name Thi Thom in favor of the more American sounding Terry Jana, but that name barely shows up on our radar. She's been going with the abbreviation TJ. She works for a semiconductor company here in Chicago and is healthy and doing well, but we have uncovered two other issues that I feel are a higher priority right now."

There was a period of silence while I expected the president to say something, since I just moved locating his daughter down in the priority list. None of us could add anything, so we just waited. The ball was obviously in the president's court. I interpreted the delay as a sign that Paul Elliot really didn't know what to say.

Finally, he responded, "What the hell is going on here? What *issues*? You mentioned some sort of cybersecurity thing before, and now you're in a secure FBI facility. Why all the precautions? Has there been any violence? I think you people need to speak straight with me right now!"

That was a quick backhand return that clearly put the ball back into my court.

"Mr. President, Braddock again. It's difficult to communicate over the phone as to what we think is going on, because specific details are still unclear, but here goes."

I took my time and went over all the details as best we knew them about the D-Chip. I added the issue of the submarines, ending with the unsavory point that TJ was the critical player in all this, and although we think we have located his daughter, the D-Chip and the submarines needed quicker action. I explained that Kevin felt she had been brainwashed while being educated in the Soviet Union and that she has had a change of heart.

"Are you trying to tell me my daughter is a terrorist?" the president said with an air of disbelief.

I quickly tried to cover by saying, "One could view it that way, but she hasn't been an instigator of any violence, and we have not yet verified if the supposed threat is real. I think we also need to find out what exposure we might have to those submarines."

The president said, "I know about the subs. We've been watching them for years, but I'll get an update before we meet. In the meantime, is that Internet sabotage you refer to even possible?"

I kept going. Everyone else just listened. "Technically, yes. AMIP is a high-volume supplier of a simple, inexpensive semiconductor chip that most systems seem to use to connect to the Internet. It cannot be hacked or overridden. If it activates and a high percentage of the Internet is compromised, it will affect our basic infrastructure."

"When you say a high percentage of the Internet, how high are we talking?"

"Greater than half, maybe more."

"And TJ did this because she hated the US?"

"We don't know who originally orchestrated the plan, but we do know that TJ was the principal architect of the technical way to do it. When AMIP got wind of our efforts, they kidnapped Kevin, our mole. That's when we quickly brought in the FBI to retrieve Kevin and capture TJ and her superior, Raj Matesh, the AMIP CEO. Both are in custody, but we haven't started any interrogation. In the recovery process, several armed gunmen, who we assume worked for AMIP or its conspirators, were killed. That's why we all had to move quickly to a secure location. So far, all this has been done covertly and kept out of the press. As I said, Kevin thinks TJ has had second thoughts about all this, and maybe if she knew about you, she might be willing to help us stop this Internet bomb before it goes off."

The president asked, "And you said Valentine's Day?"

"Noon Central Standard Time on Valentine's Day."

"Why that day?"

"Supposedly, Hau Thom, TJ's mother, was killed on that day by US activity in Vietnam."

"And you're sure of the precise time?"

"Yes. Millions of these chips have been delivered and already installed, just in time to take advantage of the new Internet protocols coming online. They've supposedly already been armed and encoded with that date and time."

"How can I help?" asked President Elliot.

"Authorize us to inform TJ about you," I said. "Kevin feels this may give us an advantage if she really has had second thoughts, and perhaps she can give us the information we need to circumvent the attack."

President Elliot said, "If she's anti-American, it may make things worse."

"Kevin Dupree would not agree she's anti-American today. There are risks for sure, but what else can we do? It's Friday the ninth, and Valentine's Day is only five days away. This is a high-tech attack that needs a high-tech defense."

"Braddock, go ahead and talk to her, but all of you, including TJ, need to come to Washington now so we can meet with our technology people. Tanner, set that up!"

Tanner jumped in, "Will do, Mr. President. We'll be in touch."

We hung up.

I barked, "Shaw! Get Kevin in to see TJ ASAP. Meanwhile, see what you can get from Matesh. See if he's had any second thoughts, and try to find out who's sending the encode commands. Round up all the AMIP employees, detain them for as long as we can, and get statements. TJ may not be working alone here. Let me know if you suspect anyone else. Then, send in your IT people and see what they can find on the computers and the servers. It's Friday, so we have only a few days before the fourteenth. Greg, can you help with this? Roger, any ideas? Tanner?"

I was feeling very feisty in my old age, and it felt good!

Tanner said, "Either way, we're going to Washington. I'll get that set up."

Jeff said, "I'll get a small team of briefers started on the interviews."

Roger said, "Since Braddock here seems to want to run the show, I guess I'll have a coffee in the private investigator lounge."

I said sarcastically, "Thanks for your support, Rog. Kevin, get started while I find some *Mr. Rogers'* videos for Rog to watch while he drinks his coffee. Kevin, we'll be listening."

Chapter 21

Kevin was led to a room where TJ was waiting behind a nondescript military-looking gray table. She wore a dull-blue jumpsuit. A female security guard was also there, a call button was on the table if needed, and there were no windows or phones. Several hidden microphones and one camera allowed us to watch and listen.

TJ sat there in an upright posture, hands folded on the table, fingers locked. There was no sound other than the ventilation system. Kevin motioned to the guard that she could leave. Now, it was just TJ and Kevin.

"TJ," he said, "I hope you're being treated well. I want you to know I'll make every effort to protect you and keep you comfortable. You probably have a lot of questions. How about something to eat or drink?"

"Questions? That's an understatement, and I'm not hungry. Even if I was, I don't think you'd want to share this room with me if I had a fork."

"Well, you started it when you called in those gunmen. Otherwise, we'd still be at my place."

"I doubt it. You were wearing a wire, and your attitude toward me was about to make me leave anyway."

"Attitude? I just wanted some respect, and all you were doing was bitching about the US, our policies, me, and even the president."

"I was brought here to do a task, and I did it. Consider it a military mission successfully implemented. Now, can I go?"

"Surely you realize what the potential fallout will be if what Raj told me is true. How many innocent people will be affected through no fault of their own? Why are you so bent on hurting the United States as well as all those people? Did something happen to you while you were living in the Soviet Union that sent you on this path? Obviously, there was a lot of international tension back then, but a plan like this, with all the costs involved, had to come from a source that had some serious financial capabilities. And correct me if I'm wrong, but I was getting a feeling that your heart wasn't really behind all this. Is the D-Chip threat real, and if it is, is there anything we can do about it? Please, talk to me."

There was no response for a while. Then TJ asked, "What's your role in all this, and what were you doing at AMIP?"

"From your point of view, it probably looks like I was brought in to uncover your plans about this Internet Armageddon, but you'd be way off the mark. I had no clue. I was hired by Richard Braddock, a private investigator, to find a girl. You. Braddock was asked to find a girl named Thi Thom, whose mother, Hau Thom, was killed during the Vietnam War. Braddock traced you from Communist Vietnam to the Soviet Union and eventually to the United States, where you changed your name to Terry Jana and eventually TJ, ending up in Chicago at AMIP.

"When the information on AMIP looked sketchy, and with Braddock still not sure if TJ and Thi Thom were one and the same, I was brought in to see if I could get some more information. I had absolutely no clue about the project you were working on. I was drawn to you from the first time we met. That's the truth, you know that, and honestly, I think you were drawn to me as well. I'm emotionally committed, technically impressed, and confused all at the same time."

"Why was this Braddock fellow trying to find me?"

"Are you sure you don't want a drink or something?"

"You know how well I handle alcohol."

"I was thinking more like fruit juice or water. You may have a hard time believing the answer to your question, but I'll get straight to it. You are the daughter of a US military officer who served in Vietnam. We don't have many details, but we can assume he was in love with your mother."

TJ perked up. "So you know who my father is."

"Yes. The officer's name is Paul Elliot, and he's now the president of the United States."

So far, TJ hadn't looked at Kevin at all, but now she moved her hand to grip Kevin's and turned her head to look directly at Kevin's eyes, trying to deduce if he was telling her the truth. She saw only warmth and honesty, with nothing to suggest he was lying. She said nothing.

After a few moments of silence, Kevin continued, "President Elliot hired Braddock to find out what happened to his daughter. It's a father trying to find his daughter, as you can see. Nothing political or military about it. By the look on your face, I can tell you had no idea."

There was another long silence. Previously, Kevin thought TJ had perhaps already known who her father was and that it may have added to her motivation, but unless TJ was a fantastic actor, she was seriously stunned. Her facial muscles relaxed, she released her grip, placed her arms on the chair's armrests, gazed forward at nobody in particular, and sat back in the chair. Then she said, "I'll take that glass of water."

"I'll get that for you, but just so you know some background, Braddock and the president went to school together. Braddock was doing a favor for the president. That's how President Elliot has kept this from the media. He didn't want politics to be involved, but if what you have told me about the D-Chip is true, we are about to face an entirely different series of problems, all of which are heavily involved in politics. President Elliot did not anticipate or deserve any of this."

Kevin pushed the call button and asked for the water. One minute later, with her hand on the water glass, TJ didn't seem thirsty. Kevin waited for some feedback, but none came. Finally, he said, "I'll let you alone for now, but if you need me, just push that button. I really do want to help. I care for you deeply. Please, trust me."

He got up slowly to leave, looking to see if there was any indication or clue for him to stay. There wasn't, so he left as the female guard returned.

The five of us were all in the next room, waiting for Kevin's personal take on all this. We were all quiet as he asked, "Can I have a drink now?"

Before we had a chance to say anything, the call bell from the room rang. Kevin immediately went back to the room, and TJ spoke only two words before Kevin was halfway in.

"Prove it!"

***

Back outside, Kevin asked, "Hey guys, got that drink coming? She needs proof."

I said, "You don't look beat up, and we heard no yelling, and before you ask again, no booze for you or anyone!"

Kevin said, "TJ obviously wants some proof that the president is her father. Other than that, she didn't say much, as you heard."

"Crap!" Tanner said. "Why didn't I think of that? Of course she would want proof, but we don't have time for a DNA check. We have all the president's notes and photos if you think that would help. I'm sure it would be okay if—and it's a big if—you think she might be willing to help us. Otherwise, why are we answering her questions when she should be answering ours?"

Roger jumped in, "Why do we want to tell her anything? She represents the enemy in my book! Lock her up, and let's get on with it."

"Relax, Rog," I said. "We have nothing to lose by pursuing this a little further. Kevin, are your emotions disconnected? Can you be objective here? Can we really trust her?"

Kevin said, "Absolutely. I'm curious as hell as to what led up to this D-Chip, and I feel she'll tell us everything we need to know."

"Well then, let's get on with it!" I said.

Back in the room, with documents in hand, Kevin sat down close to TJ. He felt that sitting across the table would be impersonal. Kevin wanted to communicate with his body language that he was there to listen and help. He put his hand on her wrist. She didn't seem to mind, turning to see if Kevin's eyes were still truthful.

Kevin started, "I can't provide one-hundred-percent proof that Paul Elliot is your father without a DNA match, but that would take time that we might not have. For now, I can show you the information the president provided to the PI, Braddock."

Over the next twenty minutes, Kevin exposed the history and showed TJ pictures of her mother he was sure she had never seen. TJ was crying when she finally took her first sip of water. She leaned against Kevin's shoulder while sniffling.

Kevin asked, "Can you tell me about how you got involved in this? I'd really like to know for my own personal reasons. At this point, I don't think either of us has much to hide."

TJ dried her eyes, took a deep breath, and started, "I was aware of what happened to my mother before I went to what you would call a public school. I lived in an all-girls dormitory, wore a uniform, and had a pleasant childhood. When I was ten or so, I was moved to another school. During my teen years, we went to school every day, even weekends. While being educated, we were exposed to the political beliefs and structure of the Soviet Union. It was all very positive. I don't remember any animosity against the US at that time.

"I was very good at mathematics and was starting to do some programming. It was a stimulating time. After I was moved to another school, someone, I don't remember his name, said I was being selected to apply my skills at a higher level. There were six of us chosen. In our late teens, while we were being tested and groomed for college, we were told about how the US seemed to be using its power to control its access to raw materials such as oil and some other natural resources. They showed me films about what was happening in the Middle East, making it clear the US was in it for themselves. I had trouble understanding how a democratic society could function without more government control.

"On the other hand, it was understandable that capitalists would do what they had to do for their own good and leave society behind. At least, that was what it seemed. I met a few boys along the way, but it was hard to do any socializing, and most of the boys were not very smart, so they had trouble understanding what I was doing. I was swamped with programming. I was also being exposed to semiconductor chip design. After I graduated as a software engineer, I spent several years at a semiconductor laboratory, learning how to merge chip design with my software skills."

"How did you survive all that? Were you being paid?"

"I didn't need to get paid. Everything was taken care of for me, including a small house I shared with a few other female engineers. I was thirty when I met Adrian. Adrian was one of my teachers. He was an experienced semiconductor design engineer who was nurturing and teaching several engineers about semiconductors. We spent a lot of time together. We fell in love and decided to get married. We were married in 2002 when I was thirty-three. He was spending all his time understanding the Internet, which had exploded in the middle of the 1990s. We were both working very hard to keep up with the technology so the Soviet Union wouldn't fall behind."

Kevin sounded somewhat surprised as he said, "You never mentioned you had been married. Wow. Were both of you still supported by the government?"

"Yes. We had no worries except the increasing pressure to stay current in Internet technology and semiconductors. We worked at the same location for the next four years, then I became pregnant. I lost the baby at six months."

Kevin didn't know what to say for a bit. "I'm very sorry to hear that. Do you want to stop talking about this?"

"No, it's okay. We never found out what the problem was, and we were told that getting pregnant again would be risky. We were still talking about trying to have another child when Adrian was killed in an automobile accident. I didn't know what to do, so I just stopped working for a while."

"You could do that? Just stop going to work?"

"No one said no. I guess they figured I needed time to grieve, but after a few months, I was expected to go back to work. I didn't want to, so I was considering changing to a new career, but as you might expect, after all the years of training, that's not very easy. That was when I was introduced to Kliment Somenski. He goes by the name Som."

"That was the man you mentioned before. Was Mr. Somenski part of the government or the semiconductor lab or what?"

"I'm not sure. I never saw him before I was at the lab, but he seemed to know what he was talking about."

"Was he going to take over your training, like what Adrian was doing?"

"My training had already ended, and I already had my degree and credentials. I thought Som was going to ask me to take on the teacher role and start training new engineers, but instead, he wanted to know if I was interested in a research project. It was highly classified and would require that I not pursue a new marriage, because married people might present a security risk. He explained that married people were never allowed to do this level of work. It was essentially espionage against the United States and carried the risk of death if I were caught."

"That's overstated for sure. Was this research project the D-Chip?"

"Eventually, yes, but this was early. I was being recruited to find out what could be done. The concepts of what to do didn't exist yet."

"Then you were moved to the US?"

"Not right away. They had no idea what could be done. They wanted me to figure that out. It was clear this effort needed to be classified, so I wasn't going to get much help because they wanted to limit exposure. The fewer people who knew about this effort, the better. Som's underlying strategy was to take advantage of the United States' vulnerabilities in basic infrastructure because the US was arrogant and took things for granted. The US military was strong, but their cybersecurity was weak. The idea was to come up with a way to hit the American government. We never talked about taking down the entire Internet."

Kevin said, "So something like a computer virus that would infect government computers."

TJ continued, "That was considered, but the Internet was changing and developing so fast that most of those ideas would not work by the time we could implement them. The Internet was being plagued by virus infections and cybercrime, which is basic software hacking. The problem with software is there is always a decision point inside the code somewhere. You can have all the firewalls, virus checkers, and security gates you want, but at some point, the decision is binary. Yes and you're in, or no and you're out. All systems that have many levels of access security eventually ended up making a yes-or-no decision.

"I was able to hack these systems by ignoring all the levels, passwords, and encryption and going to the final yes/no decision point in the code. Sure, it was deep inside and difficult to get to, but it was always there, somewhere. All this hacking was calling attention to the lack of Internet security, so US systems were getting better and more secure daily. I mean that literally. Sometimes within hours. Any software-only approach might be found and mitigated before it could be implemented. So, I had to come up with something that could not be hacked, something designed in or encoded in the semiconductor itself rather than the software. It would just be wired that way."

"So, it was then you conceived the D-Chip?"

"No, that was still too early. Besides, no Internet service providers would buy chips from the Soviet Union. All microprocessors and basic random logic chips were designed in the US, and the popular ones were vigorously tested and multisourced. Although the concept of a hardware-encoded chip seemed like a good idea, we had no way to implement it."

"That was going to be my next question."

"That was when Som said I had to come to the US and go to work for an American semiconductor company called AMIP. There was no specific schedule, since we still didn't know what we were going to do yet. Call it continued research. I was smuggled into the US, set up financially by Som, and introduced to Raj Matesh. Raj is a genius and very open to almost any approach."

"When was this?"

"Almost ten years ago."

"Weren't you curious about AMIP?"

"Sure, but Som told me adequate funding had been arranged through European banks. He made it clear that many US enemy countries were eager to help. Iran was mentioned, but the actual financial sources were never shared with me. I didn't care because I was told I would be paid very well and could return to the USSR at project completion. Meanwhile, I didn't anticipate how my lifestyle would improve beyond my comprehension. To keep focused on the project, I kept reminding myself that my mother was killed by the US, the American government only cares about itself, Adrian was dead, my baby was dead, and the technical challenge was appealing. I had no other plans or future, so why not see what we could do?"

"So, the D-Chip was invented right then, right here, at AMIP?"

"Well, sort of. AMIP was already supplying a decoder chip to the marketplace. They were already making and selling other Internet chips as well. By the time I arrived, the company was already well on its way, supplying the Internet community with chips. Customers were comfortable buying from AMIP as long as they had second sources. It was a while before I realized that AMIP essentially bought that market with chips priced below their competitors. I struggled with how to make a new version of the chip that, once enabled, couldn't be disabled even when the power was removed. It needed a way to remember that it had been encoded yet continue to function normally until it was triggered. We considered just blowing a fuse on the silicon, but testing showed it was unreliable, and the process could damage the chip such that it wasn't able to do its primary function. The chip had to remain operational until the trigger point.

"It was about this time that there was talk about a new, improved Internet standard that was going to increase speed. This new standard was eventually approved, and everybody was starting to hustle to make whatever changes were necessary to take advantage. The old chip didn't have to change at all to support these higher speeds, but Raj saw this as a window for us to insert new D-Chips into government installations, since they would have to support the newer standard ASAP."

"How did you solve the fuse problem, and how were you going to infiltrate the government's Internet?"

RICHARD NEDBAL

"I discarded the fuse idea and went with EAROM instead. By this time, semiconductor technology was able to produce EAROMs. You know EAROM, right?"

"Yes, Electrically Alterable Read-Only Memory. It maintains storage after the power is turned off, like a solid-state flash drive."

"Yes. The chip design would contain a small EAROM memory section. We were concerned that our alternate vendors may not have the EAROM process technology, and without multiple second sources, we wouldn't be able to sell the new chip, but that turned out not to be an issue. The microprocessor market was forging ahead even faster than we were, so we actually had to catch up. By then, every semiconductor vendor had flash drive technology. Mind you, we didn't need EAROM for the chip's basic functions, but the market was due for an update anyway, so the semiconductor technology timing worked to our advantage."

"Didn't the implementation of that new semiconductor technology increase the cost?"

"Yes, but it didn't matter, because the original idea was to install the chip into only government servers. That would be only a few thousand laptops and servers at most. But after Raj saw what the chip did, he contacted Som, and the powers that be decided to make this new chip an upgrade to the entire global Internet market. If the new chip was an expected upgrade to the already industry standard, then the chip would get installed in government computers and servers by default. Once that was decided, Raj didn't want to increase the price for fear of losing market share, so he maintained the lower price. I'm sure the profit margins decreased, or the chips may even have been sold at a loss, but he didn't care about that. Plans like this have an implementation cost, and since AMIP is a private company, no one would know."

"I guess the new chip worked?"

"You saw it work when you threw millions of random codes at the chip and occasionally a chip that was apparently working perfectly would all of a sudden shut down. Then when you repowered the chip, the chip was still dead."

"Why are you willing to share all this information now? In other words, why the change of heart?"

"I have been in the United States for about ten years. My idea of what this country would be didn't match what I was experiencing. People treated me well, and everyone just seemed to enjoy life, maybe raise a family and watch football.

"Several years ago, after visiting our Kansas facility, I decided to take a road trip to see some of America's sites that I had heard about. Raj did not approve, but I did it anyway. I visited Yosemite, the Grand Canyon, and several other beautiful places out west. On my way back, I stopped in beautiful Moab, Utah, where I became very ill with some sort of virus. Because I was an illegal alien, I could not envision staying in a hospital that only has seventeen beds. Matie Benton, a nurse practitioner who's about my age, took me in and let me stay at her place until I recovered. Matie and I became good friends. We still talk all the time. Matie helped me understand the world I was living in.

"People are different everywhere, but your government lets them do whatever they want as long as it's legal. I admit that I have trouble with this country's haves-versus-have-nots culture that seems to start with the government itself. And although the United States is a world superpower, America hasn't done much to improve the world's situation. Meanwhile, its people are still free to live as they choose.

Your constitution actually allows dissention. That in itself is amazing, and probably healthy overall. It's an interesting mix of contradictions that I haven't totally figured out yet. Anyway, I like it here, and I assume you know I like you too."

Kevin said, "You already know I feel the same way about you."

She continued, "But despite the American policies and struggles with class separation, my original mission was to come up with a method to send a strong signal to the American government. Meanwhile, the Internet had infiltrated *everything*! Businesses and infrastructure could not run without it. All of a sudden, making the D-Chip an upgrade to an industry standard meant the entire population would suffer, not just the government. Millions of innocent people will be affected, not just the government. That is not what I signed up for.

"I was also getting pressure to finish the project and return to the Soviet Union. After I met you, I knew I didn't want to go back."

"I don't want you to go back either. Are you willing to help us then?"

"Absolutely, but honestly, I don't think there is anything I can do. The D-Chips are already out there; they have already been encoded. They're just waiting for the trigger."

Kevin verified, "Which is noon Central Standard Time on February fourteenth."

"Yes."

Kevin asked, "How did you pick noon on Valentine's Day?"

TJ said, "My mother was murdered on February fourteenth. Noon was just the middle of the day when a lot of people would be online."

Kevin went for the jugular, "Why have you never mentioned the submarines that Raj brought up?"

TJ almost screamed, "The first I heard about the submarines was the same time you did! I have no idea what he was talking about!"

"So, you don't know what Raj was referring to?"

TJ said quite loudly, "No!"

Kevin said softly, "Well . . . we're going to find out. I need to share your comments with the rest of us."

"Who is *the rest of us*?"

"Five other people know what I know, and the president makes seven, but we will have to bring other technical people into this, and soon."

TJ asked, "What do you think will happen next?"

"We need to introduce you to the other five and see if they believe you are willing to help."

TJ asked, "What about Raj?"

"I assume Mr. Matesh does not share your feelings?"

"Absolutely not. He has been very focused on inflicting harm on the United States for a long time. When we were communicating with his superiors, they actually became more excited when they realized the entire Internet would be affected."

Kevin said, "Then we keep Mr. Matesh and the other employees out of the loop for a while. Are there likely to be any ramifications or violence from your superiors when they realize they lost contact with you and Raj?"

"It's possible, but they are well aware the fuse has been lit, and we made it clear that even we can't stop it. Rescuing us would only attract more attention, and there's not much time. They would probably just sit back and see what happens."

"Then let me discuss this with the others. We'll probably have to jump on a plane to Washington to meet some technical people and also arrange for you to meet your father."

TJ asked, "Then, after we talk, maybe we could arrange for me to change into something more presentable?"

Kevin kissed her gently on the forehead.

Chapter 22

Kevin left the room and answered questions. TJ's change of heart was questioned, as you might expect, but her story was convincing, and Kevin did his best to convince us.

Greg had an opinion: "Obviously, you've fallen for Miss Pretty here, but she's no dummy. What makes you think she isn't just playing us along while the world starts to collapse? She has minimal incentive to help us. I say lock her up with Mr. What's-His-Name and let's get on with what we have to do."

I said, "From what we've heard, it seems to me we have no other options. I can't see what she could be hiding that would affect what we need to do anyway. Sure, she could be hiding something, but it seems obvious to me we can test her statements about the D-Chip fairly easily. All we have to do is connect a few laptops to a fake Internet and advance a temporary calendar to noon on February fourteenth and see what happens. We need to be in Washington anyway, so if she's decided to be cooperative, we bring her along to meet her father. You didn't talk much about Matesh."

Kevin said, "As you heard, he's against us one hundred percent. I suggest we leave Matesh here so the FBI and DHS can do a background check and start the interrogation. I don't think he's aware of TJ's change of heart, but it doesn't matter even if he was."

I said, "I seriously doubt that. He's no dummy, and he'll certainly figure that out in a New York minute when she doesn't show up. Roger, Shaw, and Greg might as well stay here. Tanner, Kevin, and I will take TJ to Washington as quickly as possible to meet some technical people and her father. Tanner, I suggest you contact the president and get a technical group collected and ready for when we arrive. I'll have the concierge at the hotel ship my stuff to Washington. It's February ninth, so we have five days. When can we leave, Tanner?"

"Within an hour, if we hurry."

Kevin said, "I'm sure TJ wants to look presentable when she meets her father. That's understandable. I think we can afford a little time for her to get cleaned up and dressed in something other than prisoner garb. If she is on our side, let's be as hospitable as we can. We will need her help while we try to figure out how to get out of this."

Greg and Roger both groaned, Jeff Shaw didn't show any concern one way or another, and one of Roger's team was on his way over with the freezer bag containing the DNA.

"Done. Let's get to it," I said. "Tanner, call the president. Kevin, we need her laptop, in any case. It's probably encrypted, but if TJ really wants to help . . . I'm just saying."

Paul Elliot was waiting for our call. He quickly rearranged his schedule to meet with us first thing in the morning. I asked that a tech team be collected and that we are brought up to speed on the status of those subs. The president thought his newfound daughter might not want to help as much as we hoped, but we might as well play along. He could also understand his daughter's emotional state. President Elliot was not only a great statesman but a cordial and understanding father.

I had to ask the president, "Does Nora know about your daughter yet?"

"Well, Richard, I knew this day would come. I'll take care of that tonight. That's the reason we should meet tomorrow instead of later today."

"I'm sure Nora will understand and trust you as she always has. We'll see you tomorrow."

An hour later, after TJ did her best to answer additional questions, we retrieved her laptop, and we were all on the same page. An hour after that, TJ was standing before us looking as good as ever, wearing a slim black skirt, a mildly ruffled white blouse, the dark-red heels that someone found for her, and a modicum of makeup. I realized it might be hard for some techies in Washington to believe this pretty woman could possibly be responsible for a potential worldwide apocalyptic event.

I said to TJ, "We need to bring some D-Chips with us. I'm sure the engineers will want to see the silicon. Also, to make sure we have it covered, let's get a small blood sample so we can start the DNA match process." I felt it would not help our situation if she found out that Kevin had already acquired her DNA covertly. I told Kevin, and he agreed.

I sensed a slight hesitation from TJ—not something most people would notice, just a hint that comes from years of working with all sorts of people. I will admit my mental intuition is wrong, maybe as much as fifty percent of the time, but that also means it's right in one out of two cases. If there was a nanosecond slip in the action, was it the D-Chip request or the blood sample? Maybe I was just paranoid in my old age.

Kevin, Jeff, and I took TJ back to the AMIP building, which was locked up and under FBI guard. Jeff made verification and entry quick. We left TJ with a guard while Kevin and I went to TJ's office, because we knew she had D-Chips in both wafer form and individual die, but we couldn't find any of the second version of the supposedly "good chips" that went to Russia.

I said to Jeff and Kevin, "We probably don't need them. All we are interested in are the schematics and the mask set, in case we have to reverse engineer the design. Without the schematics, it takes a long time to reverse engineer a design by looking at a chip under a microscope. That's very time-consuming. The Chinese do this all the time, but time is a quantity that's in short supply for us. We'll have to check TJ's laptop."

TJ's laptop was password-protected, so we asked TJ to gain access. She said, "Sure, but I don't have the schematics. Once we finished the design, the schematics were stored on our server, and hard copies, if there are any, might be stored in Raj's vault. My laptop has nothing that will help you."

"Certainly the schematics were necessary to develop the test algorithms," said Kevin. "You didn't keep a notebook or sketches on your laptop?"

TJ said, "Raj didn't allow that. One thing he is is security conscious. Back when we started, we referred to the schematics all the time, but after the chips went into production, we were told to upload everything to the server."

"I'm just trying to cover all the bases for when we meet with the tech staff in Washington," I said. "Opening the vault would probably require a warrant and maybe even explosives. We don't have the time for that. We'd better get going."

It seemed to me that Kevin didn't quite buy all of her story yet. Every design he'd ever worked on had schematics saved on multiple computers, but he let it go. Fifteen minutes later, we were back at the FBI offices waiting for Tanner to pick us up. I asked again for that drop of blood from a finger pinprick.

"I am deathly afraid of blood," TJ said. "Especially my own. I know I'll faint and be dead weight. Can we do that on the plane, so I'll have time to recover?"

Kevin was too quick to reply, "Sure. No problem. Tanner is out back. Let's get going."

Certain aspects of Kevin's personality were starting to bother me. He always tried to exhibit confidence and assuredness even when he did not know the answers. I have worked with people like that before, but quick decision making not based on solid information can cause complications.

I made a quick, unsecured call to Lara, telling her that I had to go to Washington, that there was nothing to worry about, and I loved her. I was lucky to be involved with such a woman.

We rode to Midway Airport in an armored SUV. Most people think O'Hare when they think of Chicago, but Midway is actually closer to midtown. It's just smaller, more private, and has limited military access. We were led through a private gate directly to a Gulfstream G500. The G500 runs just a shade below Mach 0.9, so our trip to Andrews Air Force Base would be just over one hour. Now that's flying! I have been on a G500 several times, but only in the presence of some very wealthy people. I have never had the whole plane for my team with a hostess to boot. Tanner had rented a private jet! Although this was going to be a short trip, I figured I still had time for a single, not-yet-celebratory drink for finding President Elliot's daughter. TJ didn't want any alcohol since she was a lightweight when it came to drinking and also prone to airsickness. Kevin gave her some gum to help with that, while he had a ginger ale. Tanner drank bourbon like it was his last day on Earth, and he was still drinking when we arrived.

I thought about the blood thing again but noticed TJ disposed of her gum in the wrapper just as we were deplaning. I deftly picked up the gum, figuring that would provide all the additional DNA we would need, and since I saw it, I was sure it came from her mouth. This way, I wouldn't have to bring up that unpleasantry again.

We were escorted to a small, guarded FBI building that looked more like a hotel inside. I guessed this was how visiting VIPs might be housed, but you would never know about the opulent interior from the outside.

Tanner called the president and was informed we were to have breakfast at 7:00 a.m. and meet with the president at eight. At the White House. The president graciously apologized for not being able to meet with us immediately. I knew this was Paul Elliot's last chance to talk to Nora.

I gave the freezer bag and the gum to an agent, with instructions to start the DNA paternity extraction process and crosscheck all the DNA sources. I knew the paternity DNA process could be as short as twenty-four hours, or even less with priority, which we had. I gave him Jeff Shaw's and Greg's numbers if he needed additional authorization. I did this secretively so TJ wouldn't notice, partly because I didn't want her thinking I didn't trust her, but also because I didn't want her, or anyone else for that matter, to know I took her gum. Sometimes it's better just to leave these things alone.

We were all asked about our clothing sizes because fresh clothes would be made available in the morning, and we would receive a wakeup call at 6:00 a.m. We were told we had to give up our cell phones and other electronics for the evening, but we would get everything back in the morning. We went to bed early, and I expected to sleep well, but that didn't happen. All this semiconductor mumbo jumbo, together with the international implications, was overloading my mental computer. I was asked to find a girl, which I did, but now I had a more substantial problem. Locating the girl might turn out to be the easiest part of all this. I hoped my name wouldn't be connected with an event that brought down the Internet. Al Gore would be pissed!

We had private rooms with no windows. We were told to just dial zero to ask for almost anything as long as it was legal. People were posted in the hallway in case we needed anything, but I knew they were probably guards, although no weapons were visible. I had no idea how thick the walls were, but they were obviously well insulated, because I don't think you would hear a shotgun fired in the adjacent room. It was like sleeping in the Helmsley Palace, but without the New York view.

Chapter 23

February 10

The White House

My phone rang at six o'clock exactly, and I was a little surprised that I actually did sleep a little. Several clothing options had already been delivered and were hanging in the closet. How they did that without me hearing anything bothered me a little. After a great shower, I dressed sport-casual, and as I stepped out of my room, I was immediately directed to the restaurant at the end of the hall. I was the first one there. I am always the first one there. Fashionably late is for losers, or as they say in the Marines, "If you're on time, you're late." The restaurant was exquisite, with a beautiful, thick burgundy carpet you could lose your shoes in if you weren't careful. Each table had tablecloths, crystal goblets, and upholstered chairs with armrests. Walls were covered with artwork, along with photos of prior presidents and visiting dignitaries. There were no menus. You just told the waiter what you wanted, and he would take care of it.

Breakfast was excellent but eerily quiet. The four of us sat at the same table, with Kevin and TJ side by side. We had much to talk about, but instead we all just sat there like we were waiting for the professor to hand out today's test. Four days until our day of reckoning, or the Rapture, and here we were sipping coffee at the Ritz. It felt very strange.

At 7:45, we were ushered to the White House and into the West Sitting Hall, the high-ceilinged private gathering room located on the second floor. A large lunette window looked out upon the West Colonnade, which was covered in several inches of fresh, wet snow. I fought off the urge to excuse myself and go build a snowman, but I said nothing because saving the world had to take priority. A sofa at the base of the window and nearby parlor chairs communicated a warm, unpretentious feeling of welcome.

Paul Elliot and his wife, Nora, were introduced at precisely 8:00 a.m. Two Secret Service men stood beside the president.

Paul started, "Gentlemen and lady, it is a pleasure to meet all of you. Please, Mr. Braddock and Mr. Dupree, make yourself comfortable." Elliot offered a sofa to the three men. He was suave if nothing else, and he clearly wanted TJ to remain standing.

Nora, leaving the president a few steps behind, was the first to approach TJ. She used both of her hands to softly embrace TJ's single outstretched hand as she said, "It is truly wonderful to meet Paul's daughter. It's Thi Thom if I'm correct?"

TJ acted like she hadn't planned on what to say. She just bowed her head, and after a several-second uncomfortable delay, said, "My friends call me TJ."

"Well then, TJ it is. Paul, come say hello to your daughter."

Presidents are supposed to be prepared to handle any situation, but Paul Elliot didn't appear ready for what to do next. He approached TJ and held his arms open, but no words were spoken. They hugged, but the hug was distant—

the way a man might hug his mother-in-law or his ex-wife at a neighborhood gathering. This was the I-guess-we-have-to-hug-but-I-don't-know-you-yet hug.

For the next thirty minutes, Paul, Nora, and TJ sat at a nearby table and shared stories. TJ shared her background, the same as she had with Kevin the previous day, but the Vietnam War wasn't brought up. Everybody listened, drank coffee, and stayed quiet. I can't talk for anyone else, but TJ's history dissertation seemed almost word-for-word from the previous day.

The president said to TJ, "We are very sorry to hear about Adrian. It must have been challenging to get back into the work."

He then turned to talk to everyone. "Speaking of work, this would be an excellent time to take a break, and then all of you can sit down with our technical staff. From what I understand, we have a major challenge on our hands and no time to waste. TJ, I genuinely appreciate your willingness to assist. I have a few things I need to attend to, but if time permits, we'll share lunch in the dining room.

"Meanwhile, we have prepared the Situation Room downstairs for the technical discussions. It offers a totally secure environment, has all the technology you might need, and you will not be disturbed there. I apologize for leaving, but there's not much I could add. Ralph and Gary here will be your direct link to me if needed, and they will introduce you to the technical staff, who are already there.

"Mr. Braddock, I have also arranged for all of you to meet with Vice Admiral Quincy Ratliff, the director of the Office of Naval Intelligence. He can bring you up to speed on our intelligence about the submarines sitting over our cables. He has been fully debriefed, so feel free to share all your information. I shouldn't need to emphasize that this is still classified. No one talks to the press, or anyone for that matter, until we have a plan. Until later then . . ."

The president shook everybody's hands, gave TJ another hug, and left us with Ralph and Gary, who didn't appear all that excited. Five minutes later, we were walking into the Situation Room. I had heard of that room before but had never been in it. I had heard sensors were in the ceiling to detect cellular signals and to prevent unauthorized communications and bugging by mobile phones. We deposited all our electronics in a lead-lined cabinet on our way in.

I said to Gary, "Is this where they keep the Kryptonite?"

Gary seemed confused by the question and did not respond.

Inside, there were two tiers of curved computer terminals, six flat-panel displays for secure video conferencing, and four enclosed phone booths at the far end of the room for private and secure phone calls. It made my little high-tech condo feel like a garage stuffed with video games.

The center table looked like something you would find in a boardroom. Not a very high-tech look. This was going to be a conference of nerds, yet as far as I could tell, no one was wearing white socks. Oh well.

Ralph and Gary introduced us to four young engineers. Two, Sam and Sol, were men who had semiconductor backgrounds, and the other two, Riley and Ada, were women who introduced themselves as crypto software engineers. I would estimate the men were in their forties, but the two women were maybe ten years younger. They were all very reserved, controlled, and ultra-professional in their manner. They made it clear the meeting would begin immediately, with them asking the questions. We didn't have time for niceties.

After we all sat down, Riley began, "Who can start with a brief summary?"

I spoke up, "My name is Richard Braddock. I'm the private investigator the president asked to find his daughter, but those personal details are not pertinent to what we need to do right now."

I again explained the history, the D-Chip, and the time-critical issues. I ended by introducing Kevin. "Kevin is a software engineer who is probably the best person to give you a better version of what we know, and TJ is the Soviet engineer who designed the D-Chip device. It's that device that is the subject of our focus."

Riley was quick to ask, "Is TJ under arrest?"

I responded, "No, not at this time. She has offered to answer our questions and assist in whatever way she can."

"Why would she decide to help now?"

"I'll let her answer that. TJ?"

TJ said, "It's a long story, but the quick answer is that a lot has changed over the last decade that has caused me to reevaluate my mission and my purpose."

Riley said, "Your purpose?"

"All I can do is offer to help. I will do my best to assist you in any way I can."

I jumped in, "Kevin, in the interest of time, can you please give everybody an overview of the situation?"

Kevin asked the technical people, "How technical do you want me to go? A full understanding requires knowledge of software, semiconductors, and Internet protocols."

Ada responded, "Feel free to go as deep as you need to. We can follow and will ask questions as needed."

I was already liking Ada.

Kevin stood up and explained what the chip does, how it was hardware encoded, and what would happen on Valentine's Day. That took about twenty minutes with a lot of technical Q and A. Ada did not disappoint.

Sol asked, "You said that millions of these chips have been installed?"

I decided to answer that question to drive home the point. "There are millions of these chips already installed in virtually every server and computer and cell phone that connects to the Internet. Companies worldwide rely on it. Kill the ability for a host to connect to the Internet, and the infrastructure of the economy collapses."

Riley asked, "TJ, is that description accurate?"

TJ said, "Very accurate."

Ada asked, "How was the enable date code sent to the devices?"

TJ answered, "The devices look for the date code when their host's address is recognized."

Ada took over, "So, someone puts the date code on the Internet, one address at a time, and one by one the date codes are accepted if the host is online?"

Kevin added, "Exactly. And someone who we don't know has been sending out these codes for months already to make sure the maximum number of installations were covered. Now the D-Chips are just waiting for the activation time to show up."

Ada added, "But if the host was offline at noon on the fourteenth, it would escape the event. Millions would be missed. Has any of this been verified?"

I said, "No, not yet."

Sam stated, "This is simple to test. All we have to do is connect a few devices to a simulated Internet, including a simulated UCT clock. We can make it noon Central Standard Time on February fourteenth in a heartbeat."

Riley said, "I agree. We have to test this in other parts of the world to see how far this chip has permeated. We should contact a few of our secure military installations, hardwire our simulated Internet to them, and see what happens. But if this chip does what it supposedly can do, how do we bring those affected hosts back online? Kevin? TJ?"

Kevin said, "You would have to replace the board containing the D-Chip."

TJ quickly added, "But that solution would be temporary."

Riley and Ada both said simultaneously, "*Replace the board?*"

Riley continued, "That would be almost impossible to do with a cell phone and would take a lot of time with any other installation as well. It would take months. And from what you're telling me, the replacement board would have the same D-Chip already installed anyway. Is that what TJ means by temporary?"

Kevin said, "What TJ means is that replacing the board would be temporary because that new D-Chip hadn't been encoded yet, so it would be vulnerable to a new encoding of a later date. As long as someone keeps pumping out trigger dates, new boards would eventually fail even though the original date and time have come and gone."

Ada spoke up out of frustration, "So let me understand this. If this chip functions as you say, all someone has to do is send a new date and time code. Newly installed boards that have not been encoded yet will still fail, just at a later date. Correct?"

I said, "That is our expectation."

Tanner commented to himself under his breath, "I never thought of the moving date thing. We're dead meat!"

Kevin added, "That's also what Raj Matesh, the CEO of AMIP, told me."

I must admit, I hadn't thought that out either. What bothered me was that TJ never made mention of that in prior discussions. We all just sat back quietly as each of us worked through the scenarios in our minds. I was getting a headache.

Kevin jumped in, "We could build an Internet simulation module that would allow us to preprogram the date code ourselves into new D-Chips. We would just send a date that has already passed. Never mind; that's a bad idea. The thought of requiring this extra step for every replacement board would be almost impossible to implement. Okay, here's another idea. We send safe date codes over the Internet ourselves 24/7. A new board gets installed, it sees its host's address, and accepts a bogus date. Possible?"

Ada said, "But if that someone was also sending date codes, we would have no way of knowing if the replacement board had already accepted an encoded date from the other source. The only surefire way would be to find that someone and shut them down. TJ, do you know who and where that someone is?"

TJ said, "No. We were never told. They just asked for the protocol sequence, which we provided via email, and the target email address always changed."

Sam said, "Either way, we need to know if this hardware virus/encode thing is really out there. We have to run the test *now*!"

Ada said, "We can't set up an Internet simulator from the White House, but we can do it from our lab in a couple of hours. Meanwhile, Tanner can line up some overseas sites for us to link to with the simulator. Let's shoot for a one p.m. test."

I jumped in, "Before we break up, we have another issue as well. TJ's superior had casually mentioned that since they had faith in their D-Chips, they probably would not need the submarines. No one knows what that means, and TJ says she was not aware of any discussion about submarines. The president and I have been aware of Soviet subs sitting over our communications cables for years, but this D-Chip episode may be related. So, the president has asked that Vice Admiral Quincy Ratliff, the director of the Office of Naval Intelligence, bring us up to speed on these submarines. Agent Gary, would you inform Admiral Quincy that this would be a good time."

While we waited, Ada, Riley, Sam, and Sol said that they were also aware of the submarines because it was almost common knowledge. Kevin and Tanner had no clue. It was coming up on lunch when we were told that Admiral Quincy was on his way. Admiral Quincy arrived soon after and looked the part.

The admiral introduced himself. "I can see we have a nice co-ed group here. I assume the president has filled you in on what we do, and your visit is judicious, so let's get to it. By the way, call me Quince."

He continued, "Russian subs have been exploring our international cables for several years now. They have made no attempt to hide their activity. I have here several reprints of public articles that have covered this. Here's a brief list."

Quince handed out copies and waited a while for us all to scan them.

New York Times, Oct. 25, 2015:
"Russian Ships Near Data Cables Are Too Close for US Comfort"

The National News Service, August 19, 2018:
"Russian Spy Submarines Are Tampering with Undersea Cables That Make the Internet Work. Should We Be Worried?"

CNN, Posted at 10:31 p.m., July 25, 2019:
"The Global Internet is Powered by Vast Undersea Cables. But They're Vulnerable."

CBS News, Posted at 6:58 a.m. March 30, 2018:
"Concern Over Russian Ships Lurking Around Vital Undersea Cables"

WIRED, Posted at 7:00 a.m., January 5, 2018:
"What Would Really Happen If Russia Attacked Undersea Internet Cables"

Quince continued, "As you can see, the subs are no secret. US Intelligence has been moderately concerned about this, but we have not raised the alert priority until recently, because there are only so many things anyone could do with the cables. These are the typical questions:

"One, could they tap the cables and listen in? With actual electrical cables, it *would* be possible to tap in and connect without us knowing. Conceivable but unlikely, because they would have to decrypt the bi-directional data in real-time. These cables are being upgraded to the faster fiber optic technology, which are impossible to tap into without breaking the link first. If an optic link is severed, we would detect it immediately, and we would be able to determine exactly where the break occurred, so there would be no doubt what caused it.

"Two, couldn't they just cut the cable? Sure. But cable flaws happen all the time, and current technology would find an alternate path, such as another cable, almost instantly.

"Three, couldn't they cut all the cables at the same time then? Possible, but they would need a submarine over every cable because the only way they could do that was to either: A) Place a sacrificial sub over each cable. Not likely because there are eleven cables to Europe and five to the Far

215

East. It doesn't make sense to destroy sixteen of their own submarines with their crews just to sever communications. B) They could deploy remote-controlled or timed explosive charges from multiple submarines and leave the area quickly. They would have to wait until the last moment to leave, since we would be aware of the deployment and could probably deactivate it if they left too soon."

Admiral Quincy took a deep breath and continued, "I implied your visit was timely because in the recent few weeks more Soviet subs have moved into positions over the cables. Before, submarines have come and gone one at a time, but now several submarines have parked over cables. We do not know why. Accordingly, we moved some of our own submarines nearby to watch and monitor the situation. Since we just found out that there was some covert activity related to cutting off communications, we have activated our alert system."

I asked, "What do you mean by the alert system?"

Quince replied, "With more subs being tracked all of a sudden, and not knowing why, we had to raise the alert status to red, meaning twenty-four-hour watch with preparedness."

I asked, "And you did this when you heard about the D-Chip."

"No, we were already going to the red status. This only heightened our resolve."

Tanner asked the admiral, in a weak voice for Tanner, "What do you mean by preparedness?"

Quince replied, "If all the submarines move off their position at about the same time, that would be our signal that perhaps explosive devices have been deployed. I would have to recommend to the president that we take appropriate action."

That short presentation from Admiral Quincy Ratliff stopped us in our tracks. No one had anything to say. Kevin held TJ as she started to cry. I could only imagine sixteen demolition charges all programmed to detonate at noon on the fourteenth. If they were simple timers, anything we did over the Internet to stop the D-Chip would be moot. Then what?

There were no questions. I thanked Admiral Ratliff and assured him that we will all stay in close contact. He gave me his direct line. I knew we were all feeling depressed, but we still had work to do when I said, "Well, it's time we get back to the task at hand, the Internet simulator, so we can verify what the D-Chip actually does. Ada, test results by five p.m. maybe?"

Everyone was ready to get their mind off the submarines anyway. Riley and Ada left the room, Sam and Sol went along, and they also took our wafers for visual inspection. The rest of us just talked about submarines. It had been a stressful, depressing, and informative day, but now it was a relief of sorts because the D-Chip was out of our hands—for a few hours anyway.

By 5:30, we hadn't heard anything. We had missed lunch, so a small dinner was delivered. We had just started eating when we were told all four were on their way back.

Ada summarized, "Our testing showed the situation is as you stated, only a little worse. We used the Internet simulator on a few local laptops and a cell phone, and when the simulated UCT clock hit noon Central Standard Time on February fourteenth, they all were cut off, and from that point on, we couldn't get them back on the Internet. Links to several overseas sites did the same thing. Clearly, this chip has proliferated worldwide. The only host machines that were unaffected were a few old laptops that were designated out of service years ago. They were probably built before the D-Chip was available."

Tanner asked, "So how is that any worse than what we thought?"

"For the most part, the boards cannot be fixed. Electronics such as cell phones and laptops are now so small that semiconductors like the D-Chip are surface mounted or embedded directly on the mainboard—what used to be called the motherboard. Inspection of the D-Chips under the microscope shows they were never intended to be a stand-alone device. In other words, these electronic devices are not repairable in the field. The D-Chip has turned these boards into garbage. Can you imagine telling someone they have to buy a new laptop or a new cell phone unless they don't need to get on the Internet? And what are the chances the new laptop doesn't already contain a D-Chip? If it was made within the last few years, it probably does!"

Tanner spouted, "Great! Do you have any *good* news?"

Sam replied, "Actually, no. We started to inspect the silicon itself to see if we could reverse engineer the logic's schematic, but the semiconductor process is a multilayer planar process that has multiple buried interconnection layers. The Chinese could probably do this in a day or two, but it would take us weeks. Sorry about the weak attempt at humor, but there's just no way we could have the schematics in time."

Kevin replied, "TJ says the schematics were probably locked up somewhere. She doesn't have a copy."

Sam said, "Excuse me, but that sounds like bullshit. No semiconductor engineer would lose track of a chip's schematic. Without that, you couldn't make changes, and engineering changes are common. TJ?"

TJ responded, "You are correct, I know that sounds strange, but Raj Matesh, my superior, made us work from our company's server. We were not allowed to keep private copies."

Sam continued, "And where is this server?"

"I don't know, but I don't think it was local to our office. I never saw a computer or server room anywhere in the building."

"Then it's off-site, but you can still log on to it, right?"

"I never tried to do that from a remote location, but I don't see why not. Each laptop has its own serial number, so if the server is online and I use my laptop, I should be able to log in."

Sam shouted, "So, go get your damn laptop! Why are you dragging your feet on this? Kevin, is she here to help or not?" Sam was obviously getting edgy.

Tensions were running high. I was starting to get the feeling that maybe TJ was just along for the ride and didn't seem to be a front runner in the field of creative thinking. For someone who'd spent all those years designing semiconductors and software, she should have had ready access to the schematics or at least anticipated what we would need. On that point, I had the same doubts about Kevin. We should have never left Chicago without the data.

This aircraft, with all of us aboard, was already looking more dismal by the minute when it suddenly took a hard dive straight for the ground.

Chapter 24

Secret Service Ralph came up to me quietly. "Mr. Braddock, a Greg Dillard needs to speak to you. You can take it at booth number one. It's secure."

I excused myself and entered the booth, which was so quiet that no one would be able to hear me scream if I had to. "Greg, what's going on?"

"Are you sitting down?"

"Crap, Greg. No one likes that phrase because it's always bad news. I'll stand right where I am, thank you very much."

Greg said, "Sitting down wouldn't help anyway, but there's good news as well as bad news."

"We're in crisis mode around here, Greg. New developments have got us running scared. What's the *goddamn* news?"

I never thought I would talk to a DHS agent like that.

"Calm down, Richard. You asked that we verify the DNA from TJ's sake cup, bread, and that gum you scrounged out of the trash. That took some doing because of the short time frame, but we managed to compress the normal five-day cycle to twenty-four hours since we were only going for a paternity match. The woman we call TJ is *not* the president's daughter. There just isn't a match."

Holy crap again. I was just starting to feel like I was getting somewhere, but now it looked like I'd made what a millennial would call an epic fail. The wrong girl, the clock ticking, and a WW3 possibility. I wanted Lara.

I forced myself to ask, "Is there any room for error or a chance someone made a mistake? This will blow up in our faces."

"Sorry, Richard. Of course, anyone can make a mistake, but we are ninety-nine-point-ninety-nine-percent positive. The DNA was the same from all three objects, and we made two parallel runs on the test. I started a longer verification run, but that will take a few days. If something comes up, I'll be sure to let you know, but I'll stake my career that there's just no way she's his daughter. But just to show you how the DHS and FBI are working together to assist you, I also have some good news, and the good news is worth sitting down for."

"You know, Greg. I really don't want to play this anymore. Just tell me!"

"Okay, okay. The good news is that we found the president's *real* daughter."

I gasped, "How is that possible? Now I *do* need to sit down. So, the president's DNA matched someone that *was* in your database all along?"

"Exactly. Remember Occam's razor? The problem-solving principle that states the simplest solution tends to be the right one. Well, what could be simpler than taking the president's DNA and running a match against our DDC (DNA Diagnostics Center) database? That's also our immigration DNA database. We got a hit on a fifty-year-old software engineer working near Silicon Valley. And guess what her name is?"

"More guessing?"

"Well, her current name is Suong Yurievich, which is her married name, but her maiden name is documented as Thi Thom."

With a queasy feeling coming from my stomach and under my breath, I said, "I think I need a drink!"

Greg continued after a short delay, "She's a legal citizen with two children and a great job. Talk about hiding in plain sight. I guess President Elliot will be glad to find out he's a granddaddy of someone who isn't a terrorist. Anyway, we have not done the background work to find out how her DNA showed up in our database, but it's there!"

"No one has tried to contact her, I hope."

"No. I assume you and President Elliot would talk that over. I assume we will sit on this for the time being?"

"If we know where she lives, and she doesn't know we're searching for her, we leave it alone for a few days. This distraction would derail our efforts right when we need to stay focused on the more significant problems."

Greg said, "Problems? As in plural for problem?"

"Yes, we found out that Soviet subs are parked over our international communication cables."

"We've known that for years."

"Yes, but we think they may be related to the D-Chip activation date. I don't have time to explain right now. Anyway, back to Thi Thom, if what you say is accurate, then this TJ person, who's sitting within my viewing range right now right here in the White House, is essentially a spy who probably hasn't had a change of heart like we were led to believe. Maybe I'll use it to flush out who she really is, but

I'll have to think about this for a while before I make a rash decision. TJ is tight with Kevin, and she knows where our heads are at, so I have to figure out our next steps without exposing our underbelly.

"Greg, what can I say? You may have just saved the United States from making a serious mistake, although I still don't know how we're going to get out of this D-Chip mess. By the way, to bring you up to speed, we have verified that the D-Chip does exactly what we were told it would do and that it has populated Internet hosts around the globe. We have about three days to figure a way out. Thank you again for your help and the call. I owe you big time."

"No problem. Keep Jeff and me informed."

"Will do."

I strolled back into the Situation Room, trying to act like nothing important had transpired and casually said to everyone, "Hey, guys, we need a short meeting so I can fill you in on Greg's call. Sorry, TJ, just us."

TJ knew she would never be part of all our meetings anyway. I asked Secret Service Agent Gary to take TJ out for a coffee or something, and we'd let him know when they could return. Tanner, Kevin, and I all sat down around the table with Ralph, Sam, Sol, Riley, and Ada.

I said, "Well, how's our day going so far?" Trying unsuccessfully to ease the tension.

Sam, Sol, Riley, and Ada didn't even smile or snicker at that remark. These people had no sense of humor. I, on the other hand, realized years ago that humor is good for the soul, lowers your blood pressure, and helps break down walls. I started to learn that when I was being bullied in school. If a bully was trying to pick a fight, I could often avoid direct confrontation with a quip and a smile. It was a mental game, and bystanders would often conclude the spunky kid with the quick wit might also be smarter. Don't get me wrong; it didn't always work. I have scars to prove that, but I was able to survive.

"Relax," I said. "Before I fill you in on Greg Dillard's call, let's remember the D-Chip is our number-one priority, so we mustn't divert our focus. For those of you we've just met, Greg Dillard is with the DHS, and we have also been assisted by Jeff Shaw from the FBI. Both are back in Chicago. They have been helping with this mission and are fully informed. So, to get right to the point, Greg Dillard says our TJ here is an imposter. Her DNA doesn't match the president's."

Tanner sneered and crunched his brow as if he just suffered a brain freeze. It would take a moment for his brain to process that information. Kevin looked like someone just ran over his dog.

I continued, "To make this even more interesting, the DHS has found the president's real daughter via their DNA database. Before you ask, the real Thi Thom has no clue about the D-Chip, or us, or the president, or anything else. She's a bona fide US citizen with a good job and family, and she lives in Silicon Valley. Her married name is Suong Yurievich."

Tanner immediately stood up from the table, simultaneously confused and upset. The lines in his forehead were turning red. He leaned forward, resting his weight on clenched fists. "Three questions. One: how the hell did you run a DNA match in one day?"

I responded slowly and clearly, "Greg pulled some strings, but paternity DNA checks are quicker if that's all you're looking for. Full verification will take a few more days, but they are ninety-nine percent positive. That possible one percent error might be more of an issue, except that the real Suong's DNA matched one hundred percent almost immediately. We have to assume TJ is an imposter and Elliot's real daughter is alive and working in California."

Tanner continued, "Next question then. Why is the real Thi Thom's DNA in that database?"

"I can't answer that. Greg and Jeff are doing the research to answer that question."

Tanner pushed, "But they're sure about the results?"

"They're sure."

The room was silent for a while.

Tanner continued, "Third, what the hell do we tell the president?"

I said, "The truth of course. Sometimes the truth is hard to explain, but we cannot let this defocus us either. The D-Chip is more important right now."

Kevin just sat there breathing shallowly with his mouth half-open, maybe a small drop of drool about to emerge. Tanner sat back down, flopping his head to the table.

Tanner then picked up his head like he all of a sudden knew what to do next. "We have to inform the president immediately, but we have to keep this to ourselves and not let TJ know what we know. She might have a plan underway that we don't know about, like those subs. She is hiding information, like where are those damn schematics? I'm getting more pissed off by the minute. I'm going to wring that bitch's neck!"

Kevin had to give his thoughts, "Hold on, hold on. The Russians *told* TJ that the US killed her mother and that her mother's name was Hau Thom. That's how they controlled her. After I shared the information from Braddock's investigation with her, which matched what she was told, she honestly thinks she is the president's daughter. She's not a traitor; she's an unintentional imposter who is ignorant of the facts. However, I will admit, in light of this new info, we can't rule out that it's a ploy to delay everything until after the trigger date. I'm wiped out. I have no wind in my sails. I'm very sorry, Richard, I may have let my emotions fog my thinking. What do you want me to do?"

I answered, "Kevin, don't beat yourself up. You've done a fantastic job. Without your work, we would have no clue of the Doomsday Chip's existence."

I stopped and said, "I need a minute."

It was silent again for a few minutes.

After everyone caught their breath, I continued, "We could go on the offense and announce, with TJ in the room, that Sam and Sol have reverse engineered the connectivity from a chip and have already extracted their first shot at the schematic. They think there might be a back-door entrance to the D-Chip. They are working on that now and should have something maybe as early as tomorrow. After she hears that, we just watch her reaction. That will tell us who's side she's on."

Kevin quickly chimed in, "I don't think that would work. She'll know immediately it's a trick. A programmer can insert a back door in software quite easily, but hardware, such as raw logic design, is something else altogether. It's not likely she'd believe we managed to pull a rabbit out of the hat this quickly. The only way a logic design would have an intentional back door is if the original designer put it there. That would be her, and if so, and if she's really a spy or traitor, she's not going to give that up."

Sol said, "Okay. Well, maybe she did, or maybe she didn't, but there's always a chance there's a glitch in the logic. That would be a nonintentional flaw in the design. Hell, I'm just throwing ideas out there."

Sam asked, "Kevin, for you to work on the test program, surely you had some documentation about how the chip functioned."

Kevin responded, "No, that wasn't necessary. TJ already had a test program. All she was asking me to do was speed it up. I never saw a description of how the device worked. It's a black box to me."

My mind was working this over, yet trying to stay calm to control the anxiety, since we were coming up on three days away. Tanner, who wasn't hindered by the technicalities, chimed in, "What about Raj or the other employees? They're all just sitting in detention cells. Someone has to know something."

I have been in situations like this before when stress made people feel like they had to act fast, but acting fast is usually not acting smart; that's when mistakes happen. I had to calm everyone down.

I said, "We need to use TJ's laptop and get into that server. So, we kill two birds with one stone. We just ask TJ to help get into the server and see what she does. That will tell us what we need to know about her. And second, we need the data anyway to move forward on resolving the D-Chip."

Ada said, "I agree. Any reasonable security firewall with encryption would take at least several days for us to break into. She's said she really wants to help. We may not believe that now, but that would be a quick way to test her motives. We'll just ask her to log on. Where's her laptop? Ask Gary to bring her back in."

"The laptop's here," Tanner said. "We brought it with us."

"I like this," I said. "We'll flush out what she's really doing simply by asking her to log on and get the data at the same time."

Agent Gary brought TJ back to the Situation Room.

I started, "TJ, we have your laptop here, and we need you to log in and see if we can get those schematics."

TJ said, "I've never tried to do that from a remote location, but it should work from my laptop because its serial number will match, though I don't think the schematics will be there even if I do get in. Raj would typically move design data to another server somewhere, but we'll try."

We all watched her body language as she complied. Riley and Ada observed closely, because they wanted to watch her login procedure and password, but before TJ even got started, we were presented with the message "Server Offline." Riley and Ada took her laptop, typed some commands, and quickly determined the server on the other end was indeed offline. With some diagnostics, they were able to find the server's IP address and location, which to no one's surprise was back in Chicago. I made a quick call to Jeff Shaw and gave him the address of where the server was located, but I knew in my gut that we were, as TJ said, wasting our time.

We talked to TJ about everything we had gone over before and even probed pretty deeply into how confident she was that she was the daughter of Hau Thom. She gave no indication she was lying. Kevin also went so far as to tell her that today's research suggested she was not the Thi Thom we were seeking. TJ looked astonished but innocent. She said, "All I know is what I've been told. I had no way to verify anything."

I said to TJ, "You were very hesitant to give a blood sample for DNA checking."

"So that's what you think I was doing? Bring in the needle. I'll close my eyes while you take all the blood you want. I'd need a towel and a bucket in case I get nauseous."

The seven of us (Gary and Ralph stayed back with TJ) went into an adjacent briefing room to talk. Kevin was convinced TJ wasn't lying or trying to cover up. He believed her, as I thought he would. I had to admit, if she was acting, she was pretty damn good at it. Tanner was only thinking about what the president was going to say when he found out. Ada and Riley also felt that she seemed willing to access the AMIP server and seemed truly surprised to see it offline. Sol and Sam had no comment. We agreed that, even though we weren't sure about TJ, there was nothing she could do to make things worse. We had to move forward.

It was getting late when we were told President Elliot wanted to meet with us and get an update.

I said to the group, "We need to inform the president about TJ, but I suggest we keep the new information about his real daughter to ourselves for now. Everyone needs to stay on the D-Chip problem, including the president. I'll take full responsibility for this decision. Everyone agree?"

No one dissented, not even Tanner.

It was almost midnight.

We were escorted to the president's dining room. Gary stayed back with TJ, and Nora joined us, as I expected. I assumed that Elliot was on the same page with Admiral Ratliff. President Elliot was calm and, in my opinion, not overly surprised when I told him that DNA testing suggested that TJ was not his daughter. It almost seemed like the Papa Bear could sense this cub was not his real offspring. I said nothing about finding his real daughter. He stayed calm and on point because he knew the D-Chip was the real issue. Nora didn't say a word. The discussion got very quiet.

President Elliot said, "That TJ information is unfortunate, and I will need to spend some time with Mr. Braddock here on what we really know or don't know, but the more serious issue is this doomsday device. Who can give me the most accurate status, other than Braddock this time?"

Sol stepped in, "Unfortunately, our efforts to reverse engineer the D-Chip would take more time than we have and might not yield a solution anyway. TJ appeared to be helping us get some documentation, but that seems to be a dead end because the server AMIP used was shut down and offline. Riley and Ada were able to confirm the D-Chips do what we were told—their host computers go offline. We've verified this globally. If we don't come up with something soon, we will be faced with some tough decisions."

"Such as?" Elliot asked.

Sol stuttered, "Please understand that I don't mean to tell you or anybody else what we should do, but we could warn the public about what will happen to defuse the impact."

The president responded loudly, "That would cause a panic! We can't do that!"

To my surprise, Tanner jumped in, "No worse than when everyone finds out our government knew but kept everybody in the dark. At least share what we know with the heads of our allied governments."

"Braddock!" President Elliot raised his voice. "You're supposed to be a sharp son-of-a-bitch private investigator, but I need your thoughts here. The president of the United States can't just go public about an apocalyptic event and then just walk off the stage. Roosevelt said, 'Complaining about a problem without posing a solution is called whining.' I'm not a whiner. I need a solution, or at least I need to give a clear direction. It's what a president does, for Pete's sake. Do you have *anything* constructive to say?"

Trying to bring down the tension a bit, I said, "I know it looks like our goose is cooked, but we need to stay focused and start doing some creative thinking. Admiral Ratliff did a great job bringing us up to speed on the submarine issue, but this group must stay focused on where we can do some good. I suggest we retire for the night and let our brains process subconsciously. Many times, I would rack my brain for hours on a problem, only to awake with a solution. It happens."

We were marched back to the Situation Room, and we retired to our rooms.

I decided I better not call Lara.

The worst day in my memory had ended.

Chapter 25

We had agreed to convene as early as we could with TJ in the room. I was glad we decided to include TJ, because she was actually the one who came up with a creative idea. She said, "What would happen if noon on Valentine's Day never actually happened?"

Ada was quick to jump in on that. "I was thinking along the same lines. There may be a way to do that. I need to do some research to see if what I'm thinking is even possible. Can we adjourn for an hour? I need to do some research with Riley."

I asked, "What are you thinking?"

It was TJ that said, "I think Ada and I are both thinking that we may be able to stop the clock or somehow skip over the one-minute activation window."

All I said was, "Hmmm. Call us as soon as you can."

We had missed breakfast, so we took the time to get some food brought in. I was going to ask Gary to move TJ to another room since I wasn't sure what we'd be discussing, but I decided to let her stay since she was actively participating. Tanner did not agree, but he acquiesced.

About an hour later, Ada and Riley were back. Ada had the floor, with all of us at attention.

Ada started, "We all know that every four years is a leap year where we add a day to February to synchronize our calendar with the Earth's orbit around the sun. There are other components to this. To be exactly in sync with the earth's rotation, and since the earth's rotation is always slowing down very slightly, the clocks might also need to be advanced slightly, denoting a later time. Before the difference reaches one second, a leap second is sometimes added to all the atomic clocks, thereby exactly synchronizing the clocks with the Earth. Universal Coordinated Time, or UCT, is determined by these atomic clocks, and as of today, there are about two hundred atomic clocks worldwide. That was a surprise to me. I thought there were maybe five or so."

I asked, "Who does this, and how is it done?"

"Riley found out that the requirement of an upcoming leap second is announced well in advance by the International Earth Rotation and Reference Systems Service, known as the IERS. The IERS is a body of astronomical geeks located in Paris whose job is to maintain global time and reference standards worldwide. This includes the clocks used by GPS systems as well. All the other clocks just do what they're told to do at the appropriate date and time. The atomic clocks, located at strategic points around the globe, tell a series of computers what time it is every second. Then, another set of computers receive the time, and those computers pass it on until the correct time propagates throughout the entire Internet.

"They also cross-check to make sure it all happened as planned and corrected if necessary, thus keeping every clock on the Internet in sync. All devices on the Internet are checking the UCT using a special network time protocol, even though you don't notice it. That sounds like a tough scheduling task if you ask me. Anyway, the new time, with that extra leap second added, becomes the new UCT time that the Internet uses."

"So, the Internet's time is essentially bumped up by one second," I said. "Am I jumping to a conclusion here, but are you about to suggest we bump the clocks past the noon activation time on February fourteenth?"

"Absolutely not! That would not work, because twelve noon would still occur; it would just go by faster, and one second plus or minus would still be recognized by the D-Chip as noon. We just tested that. No, what I am suggesting is that we completely *stop* the UCT clocks before noon, say at eleven fifty-nine a.m. Central Standard Time, and then restart them at twelve oh one p.m."

Kevin yelled out, "That's genius! No one would even miss that minute—sorry, those *two* minutes—and even if they did, the clocks would be back in sync only a minute later. We need to test this theory with the Internet simulator now and see what the D-Chip does."

"Hold on, hold on," I said. "Even if that worked, how would we do it? From what Ada has implied, the world is notified of an upcoming leap second, and I quote 'well in advance.' We may not have the time to do this. Sorry about the time pun—it wasn't intentional—but either way, we need to know if the D-Chip would respond as we hope. No point in killing our brains' gray cells if it doesn't."

I asked Riley and Ada, "How long would it take for us to test this?"

"Twenty minutes, maybe. Our Internet simulator is still set up."

"Well, get on it. Tanner, you and I need to find out how to contact the IERS and tell them what we're thinking, but we can't tell them why. This issue is still classified. We'll ask them if it's possible to actually stop the UCT update and then resync it two minutes later. Meanwhile, I see no reason to stop the chip reverse-engineering effort. Sam, Sol, you agree?"

"Absolutely."

"Then let's all meet back here at nine a.m."

Initially, Tanner and I were not successful in calling the IERS. Everyone we asked didn't know who to call. Time zones and the volunteer status of the members added to the frustration. It's not like people are sitting around watching the seconds go by. On top of that, we had to bring a language translator into the action without violating the security status. We were still trying to make a connection when nine a.m. showed up. We were running late.

Riley said, "Great news! The tests showed that skipping over twelve noon worked. Apparently, the D-Chip is looking for twelve o'clock to twelve o'clock and fifty-nine seconds. The activation window is, as TJ said, one minute long."

Then I interjected, "Even if we could pull this off, there are a couple of aspects to all this that would keep me up at night. First, the untriggered D-Chips would still be out there watching twenty-four/seven, like the Sword of Damocles waiting to chop off our heads. Second, newly installed systems that had not been encoded yet would still be vulnerable to activation at a later date and time, as we discussed. The first point doesn't bother me too much, because once time has passed, well, it's passed. But on the second point, we need to find a way to make sure yet-to-be-encoded D-Chips can never be encoded."

Sam said, "What's wrong with us sending the encode protocol ourselves as was suggested before?"

I responded, "Right now, that still sounds like the best idea, but there's no guarantee that the other Russian encode might still get there first. And remember, new installations might not happen for months. We could never stop sending the new dates until all the D-Chips were encoded. It would feel to me like we were being held hostage in the meantime. I don't like it at all, but it's all we have. Tanner, we have to get the president involved. We need to let the president know what we're thinking. We will need his help with France."

For the next few hours, Tanner and I stayed current with Sam and Sol, who were trying to reverse engineer the schematics by looking at the chips microscopically. Tanner and I ran into more obstacles trying to communicate with the IERS, so we had to meet with the president. We updated him on our status, including our unsuccessful attempts to talk to the IERS. He said he would personally call the French prime minister, Emmanuel Banet, to get the executive authorization skids greased in advance. There was no reason not to. We were running out of time.

Meanwhile, none of us had any idea what to do with TJ. Tanner suggested we just keep her under watch or maybe even ship her back to Greg and Jeff in Chicago, but Kevin strongly disagreed. He felt we still needed her, even if Tanner didn't think so.

Kevin said, "Hell, Braddock, this leap-second time thing was her idea! Why the hell would she do that unless she was trying to help?"

I said, "Okay. Okay. Calm down. I'll keep her in our meetings for now."

I called Admiral Ratliff, "Admiral, if the submarines are set to simultaneously blow up the cables at the same time as the D-Chip timing, how much ahead of one p.m. East Coast time on the fourteenth would the submarines have to leave their post?"

Quince said, "It depends on the size of the explosive devices, but one hour would give them enough time to get away."

I clarified, "So you don't get excited unless all the subs move after twelve noon Washington time?"

"No one knows for sure, but that's the way we see it. If they left much earlier, we would have time to find and defuse the devices. We know exactly where the subs are."

I clarified again, "And I assume that even though the D-Chip event is keyed off Internet time, the submarine devices would be independent of Internet time, right?"

Quince said, "Yes. We assume the devices would be internally timed. Once set, they would detonate regardless of what happens anywhere else."

"That's what I thought. Thank you."

The rest of the day was a fiasco. We were trying to get the proper IERS people on the phone via a translator, and one p.m. Washington time was already six p.m. in Paris. There was no one there to talk to. It was very frustrating.

Chapter 26

February 12

Halfway through the next morning, we were finally in direct communication with a representative from the IERS. President Elliot had contacted Emmanuel Banet, who gave the IERS people the authority to do what they could do. We managed to ask the questions without providing the full reason as to why we were asking. We had no other option.

Through a translator, I asked, "Is it possible to stop the UCT clock update and resume synchronization two minutes later?"

"Why would you want to do that? Systems around the world would falter, GPS systems would lose accuracy; the world would think we've lost our minds."

"But it would only be for two minutes."

"*Two minutes!* You really don't understand the importance of what we do."

I asked, "Please be patient with us for a moment. Is it technically possible?"

"I don't know the answer to that. We'd have to look into that and get back to you."

"How long would that take?"

"A few days."

"That isn't soon enough. Please stay near your phone, and we'll get back to you as soon as possible."

President Elliot had already talked to Emmanuel Banet, but we needed feedback before the end of the day. Tanner spoke to the president again. President Elliot informed us that since he was good friends with Mr. Banet and trusted him emphatically, he would confide in him and tell him everything he needed to know. We had a call back from the IERS within an hour.

"Mr. Braddock, please."

"I'm Richard Braddock. Thank you very much for your call back. We really appreciate it. Just so you know, several other of my technical associates are listening as well."

"We have not talked. Your call was forwarded to me. My name is Jacques. I am the director of technology here at IERS. I've been told you are asking if the UCT update can be halted for one or two minutes. I assume you are not asking to actually stop the clocks. Is this what you are asking?"

"Yes. We are only talking about stopping the update to the Internet."

"It is possible, but are you aware of the possible ramifications of such a move? They are potentially disastrous. Even life-threatening in certain cases. Satellites could drift off course, Global networks could lose synchronization, financial trading would stop during that time, and I'm sure there are many other situations that I haven't thought about."

"Believe me, we understand the depth and possible consequences of this. We would fully inform you well in advance as to what we are thinking and why. If we collectively agreed to do this, how long would it take to implement?"

Jacques seemed to be talking to himself. "We would have to create a short program that would be sent to all the atomic clocks. This program would establish a halt time. The clocks themselves would not be stopped, only the synchronization over the Internet. For all the clocks to be ready, we would need to send the commands at least one hour in advance. Any clock that didn't get the commands would need to go offline until resynchronization. It would take an additional day to prepare the local administrators about what was going to happen since a system operator could override a command like this. We would be deluged with phone calls."

I said, "Thank you for your openness and sincerity. Please remain near your phone. We need to discuss this with President Elliot. And just so you are fully informed in advance, our target halt time is eleven fifty-nine a.m. on February fourteenth, Central Standard US time. That's the day after tomorrow. We don't know what that is in UCT time. Clock resynchronization time would return at twelve oh one p.m., or approximately one minute after the hour and not a second sooner."

"The day after tomorrow! If that's the date, we must get started *now!*"

"Have you issued commands like this before that waited for a final go commitment?"

"Every time we do a leap second update. But that's different, because the UCT update is never stopped. The increment is minimal compared to what you are asking."

"I would ask that you go ahead and start communicating with the clock administrators. We could give the final go, or cancel, at least two hours in advance of the eleven fifty-nine time. Is this feasible?"

"I'll discuss this with the prime minister, but if he approves this action, we can begin the process. Please keep me informed."

"Thank you again for your assistance. Sorry this is so rushed; I'll be in touch."

I asked Gary to take TJ out of the room for a few minutes while I summarized for everyone else.

"It looks like we may be okay for the D-Chips that have already been installed. Frankly, once we heard that the skipped minute worked with our simulator, my mind switched to the D-Chips that have not been encoded yet. They are just as dangerous. We will need to know the protocol for how to encode those D-Chips ourselves. Kevin, although everyone but you was unsure about TJ's motives, this is the time she could really help. She's the only one who knows how the encoding protocol works. You still think she's on our side, right?"

"Yes."

"Then you need to talk to her and tell her how we know that she is not the president's daughter. She needs to understand that this is her chance to prove herself. Ada and Riley will be standing by. You have thirty minutes."

Tanner was aggressive. "I hope we're not wasting time by talking with the enemy! I wouldn't give a rat's ass if she knew about how we found out that she wasn't the girl we were looking for or not!"

I answered, "Please, Tanner. We need to know how to communicate with those chips when they are connected to the Internet, and she knows how to do it. Please, let Kevin do his job."

Kevin jumped up. "Gary, where can I talk to her?"

***

Ralph escorted Kevin to a small room that I could monitor, and Gary brought in TJ.

Kevin said softly, "TJ, please sit down. We have about a half hour to see if we can work something out. First, we know for sure that you are not the president's daughter."

TJ almost screamed, "How is that possible? Hau Thom was my mother, so Mr. Elliot must be my father! How could my real father be somebody else?"

"Your DNA just doesn't match. We extracted your DNA from the gum you had on the plane, and I took some bread you were eating from our dinner."

"So, you were planning this all along! Your love for me was an act?" She started to cry.

"Please, TJ, try to understand. All we were trying to do was verify that you were the president's daughter. You would have done the same thing. DNA was the only way."

Kevin waited for a few seconds before saying, "You said you wanted to help with the D-Chip. You really do want to help, right?"

TJ was still crying when she stuttered, "Of course."

"I believe you. You know that. It would help if we could convince the others by filling in your history a little. For example, how did you taking over Thi Thom's identity come about, and why?"

"I didn't take over anything! Som, Kliment Somenski, told me it was the reason the Soviet Union chose me. They told me the US killed my mother, who was famous for fighting for her people. I had no reason to think they were lying to me."

"When were you told this?"

"When I was a very young girl. From then on, I was Thi Thom. If I'm not Thi Thom, then who am I, and is there a real Thi Thom? If there is, I may have ruined her life because the Doomsday Chip will always be linked to her name. I'm to blame for everything that is about to happen."

TJ stopped talking. She linked her fingers, looked down, and started to break down again. Then she stood up and put her arms on Kevin's shoulders. She couldn't hold back, as if this sorrow needed a release. Then, she and Kevin embraced as they both dropped to their knees. It took several minutes for the emotion to settle down to where they could even think about talking again.

I thought to myself, *I believe her too.*

Kevin had to continue. "I believe you. You said you wanted to help, but nobody except me, and maybe Braddock, think you've been honest with them, so how do you expect them to trust you now?"

"Despite what they think. I don't want to hurt anyone."

"Then why the delay with finding the schematics, and where are those supposedly good chips the Soviet Union is using? Why do we have only the bad D-Chip version?"

"I didn't intentionally mislead you. There is only one D-Chip. They are all the same, even the ones in the Soviet Union. Raj and I couldn't get around all the United States' cross-checking requirements for us to get the required number of semiconductor second-source suppliers. The chips' serial numbers, the mask revision numbers, and all the test routines had to match. If we designed a different chip but left all the documentation the same, then just trying to keep them separated would be a nightmare that Raj felt was destined for problems. So, we had to figure a way to disable D-Chips going to Russia in the field."

Kevin almost yelled, "You can do that and you haven't told us?"

"No, no, no! I didn't lie about that, but remember that after a D-Chip is encoded, it cannot be re-encoded. The hardware closes the door so no one can get in again. All we had to do was pre-encode the Russian chips with a date that has already passed. So, every chip we made was both a good chip and a D-Chip."

"We were thinking along those same lines. That's why I'm here. We need to know how to do that."

She said, "I'll show you how the encode protocol works, but remember, this protocol will not work if the chip is already encoded. There's nothing we can do about those millions of encoded chips that are already out there waiting for Valentine's Day."

"How did you encode the Soviet Union chips with the old date then, since they haven't been installed yet?"

"We used an Internet protocol simulator, just like what you used, to set a past date."

"One board at a time? We know how long that would take. Why didn't you just encode the bogus date while the chips were being probed on a wafer."

"Well, for one reason, writing bits into an EAROM is much slower than writing and reading RAM memory. You know that. RAM can be written to in nanoseconds, but writing to an EAROM takes longer. Writing to an EAROM during wafer testing would take too much time and limit production. And even if we were willing to take the extra time, we still have the problem of not knowing what the wafer contained when we were done. Were those pre-encoded chips on that wafer or not? There would be no way to visually tell an encoded chip from a ready-to-be-encoded D-Chip. Another inventory nightmare. But the main reason was that the encoding protocol would be visible in the test program, which any second source could recognize if they examined the test routines. You would have found it as well. We had to keep that secret."

"So, you encoded the chips after they were installed."

"Yes. That's easier to do in the Soviet Union, where everything is controlled by the government. It would be impossible here. The manifestations are mind-boggling. You would have to physically do that for every computer or every cell phone or every Internet product made in the world, one at a time. Not possible here, but in the Soviet Union, everything went through the government first."

Kevin was in a hurry. "We still need the encoding protocol. Let's get to it."

"Of course. Afterward, do you think there might be a way where I could stay with you in the United States, maybe apply for asylum, and eventually become a citizen?"

"I doubt it if this D-Chip fiasco happens, but in any case, that decision is outside my wheelhouse. We'll take that up later if we manage to save the world. Come with me."

Kevin reconvened the group with TJ.

"TJ is here to help in any way she can. You just have to take my word for that. Meanwhile, as a clarification, there is only one type of D-Chip. There are no good chips versus bad chips. They are all just D-Chips. The Soviet Union just preprograms their chips with a past due date, as we have talked about. TJ will show you the encoding protocol. This won't help the chips already out there that have already been encoded, but it may be a way out for the chips not yet installed."

I said, "That's all well and good, because using the Internet itself to encode any new chip installation is still a viable option, as long as we can shut down the Soviet Union's attempts to encode these chips before we get to them. Let's talk about how to do that . . . TJ?"

"I don't know where the Soviet D-Chip commands originate," she replied. "There are probably multiple sites, but even if I knew where they were at the time, it wouldn't be difficult for them to just move to other locations. Flexibility like that is a basic characteristic of the Internet. I can't see a way of shutting that off."

I asked, "Ada, Riley, do you agree with that?"

Ada said, "I have to agree, but once we know the protocol, Riley and I have been discussing using Internet quarantine robots. They're called bots. These Internet bots would be out in cyberspace, supported by major server companies, looking for that unique protocol sequence. Once found, the encode commands could be quarantined before affecting the rest of the Internet."

Tanner said, "But those bots would find our encodes as well."

Riley was eager to get more involved and responded, "No, the bots would be programmed to only quarantine those that didn't include our unique date and time. The bots would ignore ours. It could work."

I asked, "How long to write a bot like that?"

Ada said, "Maybe a day, max, with testing."

"TJ, now's your chance to prove your commitment to helping us," I said.

She replied, "Bring my laptop back in, and I'll show you how to set up the encode protocol."

TJ really is on our side.

By the end of that day, we had a plan. It was time to talk to President Elliot.

Chapter 27

Later that day

I took the lead, "Mr. President, we're quite sure we have a solution. It will require that you call Prime Minister Banet and tell him what we're about to do. We've already talked to Jacques, the director at the IERS, about what we need to do and when. He has completed the preliminary work. All he needs is approval and the go-ahead from Mr. Banet."

The president said, "What's the plan?"

"We plan to stop the Internet time at eleven fifty-nine a.m. Central Standard Time on the fourteenth, the day after tomorrow. The entire system would resynchronize at twelve oh one p.m. The result of this deviation is that, as far as the Internet is concerned, noon in Chicago on the fourteenth of February never happened. Therefore, the D-Chips will not trigger."

President Elliot said, "How the hell do you stop the Internet clocks?"

"We aren't actually stopping the clocks—only how they update their time to the Internet."

The president added, "Who came up with this? And I can guess that this two-minute gap in the world's time is going to stress people out."

I said, "It was a collaboration between TJ and your tech people, and we can only guess at what the negative effects of this decision might be, but it's all we have."

The president asked, "After that two minute two-step, we're in the clear?"

I continued, "Sorry, no. It doesn't end there. We still have to handle those chips that have not yet been encoded. They would still be subject to encoding for a later date. So, in advance of the time hold, we would also start a few Internet robots, or 'bots' as they're called, to look for the encoding sequence the Soviet Union uses. These bots would recognize and quarantine Soviet requests. We would flood the Internet with our own encode sequence that would install a past-due date into those yet-to-be-encoded vulnerable chips. These bots would be programmed to ignore our own encode commands. These two steps should neutralize both current and future threats."

The president said, "Braddock, you might be worth something, after all. What's your percentage of success?"

"Any off-the-wall concept like this has a lot of variables and pitfalls, but we're confident at about ninety percent, sir. We're not sure of what the two-minute loss of time will do worldwide, since it's never been done."

The president asked, "What happens to all those people who were not on the Internet at that time?"

I responded, "There are two situations. First, the people that were not online would avoid the problem entirely, because when they do go back online, the trigger time will have already passed. They are safe. The real victims will be those who are online but part of a smaller stand-alone network that provides their own time and only synchronizes with the Internet periodically. If they're not synced with the atomic clocks, they miss the skipped minutes, and they will be shut down."

The president said, "Let's hope there aren't too many of those. I'll call the prime minister right away. By the way, since you didn't find my daughter, I assume you will not be providing me with an invoice for services already rendered. That sounds like some wiseass thing you would normally say. Just kidding, Richard. You and your team have done a fantastic job."

I took a chance to say the following before we were out of the woods, but we had to get to it sooner or later, so I said, "Actually Mr. President, I *will* be sending you an invoice because we think we found your real daughter. She's a legal US citizen, married, and living in California . . . surprise!"

I used the words *we think* because I had to leave the possibility open that we had not found her, and I didn't want to switch our focus until the D-Chip threat was neutralized.

"Braddock, are you being a wiseass again?"

"No, sir. We found her with a DNA search. I haven't talked to her because this D-Chip crap must take priority for now, but I will as soon as we get out of the woods with this Internet mess. By the way, her name is Suong Yurievich. She's been in the US for years, was married here, and has two children. That makes you a double grandfather."

The president said, "That's a lot to take in, but I agree we have to save the Internet first. Let's hope we can do that. I assume Suong doesn't know about me yet?"

"That's correct, sir. Plenty of time for that later."

President Elliot immediately called Prime Minister Banet, and Jacques called us back within minutes. He had already started the communications with the remote clocks both via email and with phone calls. As he expected, the number of return calls was overwhelming at various hours of the night, so he was bringing in volunteers to handle the phones.

But something was occurring that Jacques hadn't anticipated. Since this had never been done before, operators at the remote atomic clocks were not sure of exactly how to do it. Jacques had some technical people ready to talk about the process. It's was very straightforward, just different. The clocks would continue to run as they always had, only the link to the Internet was to be shut off. The Internet would see the UCT time stop at 11:59 and restart at 12:01. I cautioned it must not delay or reconnect even one second sooner. We were hoping most people wouldn't even notice.

I prompted Jacques, "We should start a few seconds sooner and wait a few seconds after to compensate for a possible delay in the systems. These clocks are all over the globe, and even at the speed of light, it takes about a second or so to propagate, and there would likely be other delays, so give or take two seconds should cover it."

Jacques said, "Of course. I have already taken that into consideration."

Riley and Ada were hard at work on the Internet quarantine bot. Large server organizations around the world were contacted and prefaced that we needed their help to launch these bots no later than 2:00 p.m. on the thirteenth, less than ten hours away.

Ironically, after all that rushing around with borderline panic, and Ada and Riley busy coding on limited sleep, all of a sudden, the rest of us just sat around, waiting. Kevin and TJ spent at least two hours in an adjacent room. I have no idea what they were doing. Sam and Sol were both hoping to get a good meal and maybe even a good night's sleep, but alas, I couldn't see myself going to bed without finding out more about the real Thi Thom. I called Greg, hoping to get some positive information for the president and his wife.

"Greg, how's the Windy City today?"

"Richard! What the hell is going on? What's this I hear that the Internet will shut down tomorrow? You must have some excellent compromising pictures of government officials to pull that off."

"Yeah, well, we aren't shutting down the Internet. We are just holding back the time a bit. If the D-Chip is waiting for noon on the fourteenth, we figured we'd just skip over that time. So, sorry, noon is not going to happen on Valentine's Day. Besides, this is small potatoes compared to what happened in the past. Heck, one of the tech people here told me that in the 1500s, Pope Gregory dropped ten days when switching to the Gregorian Calendar. After that, some months had only eighteen days. In North America in 1752, the month of September was eleven days short. So, what's the big deal about two freakin' minutes? But I didn't call you to talk about your Timex."

"If I had a Timex, it would just keep on ticking after the licking, as they say. Speaking of time, you're working late. Time and a half for overtime?"

"I was starting to like you, Greg, but you're picking up some on my sarcasm. By the way, this issue is still a secret. I hope everyone is still treating it that way."

Greg said without hesitation, "Secrets? I can totally keep secrets. It's the people I tell who can't."

"I called about the real Thi Thom. Did you dispatch anyone to the West Coast to check her out, and what additional information did you uncover?"

"Yes, I sent an agent just to have someone there, but he has instructions not to contact anyone. Since she's not hiding from anything, we were able to do a lot of research just using public information. She immigrated to the US about eighteen years ago, sponsored by the software giant Terradata. Terradata requires DNA and fingerprinting from their employees; that's how her DNA ended up in our database. She's been married for twenty years and became a US citizen five years after applying for citizenship. She has two kids. Her husband is also an engineer, and together they live in Saratoga, California, which is an affluent suburb in Silicon Valley. She has no criminal record, not even a traffic ticket. She's received recognition for her software work from two professional organizations, and she also volunteers at the local senior center. Looks to me like she's holding out for sainthood."

"Do you know if she's done any research into the death of her mother?"

"No, but if she did, that wouldn't show up in a public record."

I said, "If we manage to dodge this D-Chip bullet, I'll want to go out there and give her the news personally about her father. I almost wish I didn't have to, because I wouldn't want the information to disturb her life. I'll leave that decision to the president. Thanks, Greg. Seriously, you saved the show."

"Nice to hear good comments from a friend, even the ugly ones."

***

February 13

This was a strange day. Tech people were installing more monitors in the Situation Room, and Admiral Ratliff had installed a small, separate monitor. It had a nondescript printed label off on the right that said, "Alert Status." The display was blank until someone touched it, then an alert bar showed up. It was bright red. I asked Quince what it meant.

He said, "I didn't want the red bar to be constantly visible or upset anyone, so the screen will be blank until you touch it. Then it displays the current alert status for ten seconds. If no submarines are over communications cables, the bar would be green. If multiple subs are sitting over the cables, the bar shows steady red. If the red bar flashes, the subs have all moved off the cables at about the same time, with imminent detonation expected."

I said, "So the steady red we see now means the subs are still parked over the cables?"

"That's correct."

My heart skipped a couple of beats, but Admiral Ratliff showed no emotion at all. These guys are tough!

Everybody, except me, seemed to have a task, but no one was talking. Communications with the IERS showed that everyone was ready. I had no appetite for breakfast. Ada and Riley had worked with their software team and large server companies to oversee the launch of the bots. The bots were launched worldwide by 1 p.m. In only a few minutes, it was evident that the bots' quarantine functions were working as predicted. Results were easy to track because the Soviet's encoding scheme was still running, and TJ's protocol information made it easy for us to see the encode attempts in real time. Quarantine results were rapidly increasing.

Ada and Riley were reviewing statistics in the Situation Room with me, Kevin, and Tanner. After only an hour, the bots showed a dramatic decrease in the February fourteenth Soviet encode protocols being found on the Internet. In fact, the number was almost zero after only forty-five minutes. This would be a different story in countries where the Internet was controlled and restricted. We might never know what happened in those countries. Should we have informed major corporations and allies? It was already too late in the game to think about that. It would only cause stress.

***

It was time to spend some more time with Paul Elliot and Nora and talk about their real daughter. We talked for almost an hour. I shared the DHS research data on Suong Yurievich that Greg had sent me. They both said that after the current crisis was over, they definitely wanted to meet her and her family. Paul was already acting like a proud parent.

After a quiet moment, I asked, "Paul, before the trigger event happens, I would very much like to call Lara and tell her what's going on. I know she's worried about me, and I can assure you that she will honor our secrecy. I'd like to call her maybe later tonight or first thing tomorrow morning."

Paul asked, "Her phone is not encrypted?"

"Correct."

"Well, tell her as much you feel is necessary. As I said before, I trust you and your judgment, but remember, we still don't know what the repercussions will be."

***

February 14

Valentine's Day

Doomsday

12:30 p.m. EST

We were set to meet back in the Situation Room at 12:30 p.m. (11:30 Chicago time). Minimal sleep and no breakfast again! I needed to lose a few pounds anyway.

I had called Lara and filled her in on my current status. She was relieved just to hear me say that this would all be over by the end of the day.

At 12:30, we, including the president and his wife, were all sitting in the Situation Room quietly watching screens and monitoring the Internet with the local time displayed in the lower right-hand corner of each display. Many different machines, such as laptops, were all actively logged on, but the sound was turned off. Several phones were connected to overseas locations on speakers, but there was no talking. Televisions were monitoring all the primary channels, again with the sound off. After all that stress and everybody running around at full speed, the feeling in the room was mysteriously quiet. When Tanner refilled his coffee cup, the clink when his cup touched the coffee urn was heard by everyone. Other than some laptop cooling fans, the clink was the only sound. Was this the calm before the storm? On the screens, the technicians managed to show the time in hours, minutes, and seconds, with the seconds ticking by. Each display was logged into a different site. One was on YouTube, one was streaming a movie, another was logged into CNN.

At precisely 12:59:00 Washington time, the second's field on the display clocks all stopped. If you weren't watching the time, you would not have noticed. At 1:00 p.m., CNN stumbled slightly as it tried to switch to the next scheduled program, but nothing was said over the air. The local news station was giving a last-minute weather summary, as it always did at 1:00 p.m., but the time display on *their* weather map was stuck at 12:59:00. The show must go on.

Then, at precisely 1:01:00, all the clocks started up again. I felt like cheering. So I did, damn it! I let out a loud "Hooah!" as I raised my fist to the ceiling. Everybody joined in.

We were all subconsciously expecting to hear an alarm go off, a bell to ring, or some thunderous applause to come from somewhere, but there was nothing other than the noise we made. Instead, after the high fives, we moved from laptop to laptop to see if they were still able to surf the Internet. They all did. President Elliot and his wife Nora proposed a toast, but by that time it was anticlimactic. The phone rang about ten minutes later to report that, so far, negative results were minimal in the major cities.

I had to see the submarine status, so I touched the Alert Status screen. The alert bar was bright green, meaning the submarines had moved off the cables at separate intervals well before 1:00 p.m. Admiral Ratliff smiled and shook my hand.

The aftermath verified what Ada and Riley had predicted. Many local networks that had their own clocks and were not synchronized with the UCT had problems. Anyone connected to those networks at that time lost their Internet, such as Newcastle, Oklahoma; Wells, England; Kewanee, Illinois; and many other small networks. Tanner was trying to estimate the economic effect, but it was much too early. It would take days, maybe weeks, for all the smaller networks and related infrastructures to fail. For the moment at least, I breathed easier while I went to dinner with Paul and Nora in their private dining room.

Chapter 28

A week later

I had traveled back to California, and President Elliot allowed me much leeway in discussions with Lara. I spent a few glorious days with Lara, and she clearly understood that certain technical aspects of this project would remain secret.

I asked her, "Did you even notice what happened at ten a.m. on the fourteenth?"

She said, "I did because you had told me what to look for, but it didn't make the news."

I don't think I'm exaggerating in saying that Lara was impressed we could pull this off in such a short time. Some might not agree that we had minimal collateral damage, but the full effects might never be known.

Lara asked me, "You seemed to be right at home doing this type of work, even though you said you were retired. Are you going to stay active?"

I said, "I honestly don't know. I had to respond to the president—that was a foregone conclusion—but if something else comes up, all I can say is that I will treat each situation on its own. But if you don't want me to take on a project, your feelings will always have priority."

She kissed me and said, "For a man like you, that's all a lover could ask."

What a woman!

***

Lara and I don't live far from Saratoga, but before visiting Thi Thom (now Suong) and her husband, Dari Yurievich, I spent almost thirty minutes on the phone getting to know them and trying to minimize any anxiety. I also emailed them a letter, signed by the president himself, which introduced me. I explained the requirement for secrecy, and I went alone to their home in Saratoga. They were welcoming and gracious.

Suong and Dari were obviously very curious about everything that had transpired, and with both being technically connected, they were superficially aware there had been a hiccup on the Internet. I thought it was interesting that they were as curious about the Internet hack almost as much as Suong being related to the president. Nerdy tech people just need to know how things work. I reaffirmed that certain aspects of the attempt will stay secret; for example, I could not disclose how the D-Chip actually works, but they understood that the encoded date/time and skipped minutes were the significant points.

I wanted to know more about their past, so I could properly prepare the president. Dari explained that they met while getting their computer science education in the Soviet Union but didn't get married until they were in the US. They entered the US legally via H-1B work visas. Their US employer, Terradata, was their sponsor. They eventually received their green cards and were recognized as permanent residents. Five years after that, they applied for citizenship.

Suong said, "We knew that sooner or later we would become US citizens, but the actual day it happened became one of the best days of our lives. Terradata has been fantastic! That's when we decided to raise a family."

Being told she was the daughter of the president of the United States was obviously a bit overwhelming; however, they were open and eager to bring their family to Washington to meet with Paul and Nora. My initial concern about how it might affect their lives never came up. They were willing and able.

I asked Suong, "When did you find out your name was Thi Thom, and why did you change from Thi to Suong?"

"I don't know. Thi had always been my name, but I changed my first name to Suong because one of my best friends was named Suong. I just liked it, and since I was starting a new life in the US, I felt that was a good time."

"And you had no idea about your parents?"

"I was told my mother was killed during the war, but no one knew anything about my father."

I asked, "How do you feel, now that you know who your mother was?"

Suong responded, "That was a long time ago. I'm surprised, but I'm not going to dwell on it."

I continued, "So how were you educated? And how did you get to the US?"

Her story was similar to TJ's, except she had not been singled out for special education, nor was she anti-American. She arrived in the US a decade sooner and had never heard the name Kliment Somenski. She met Dari while in college, fell in love, and, as they say, the rest is history.

I put together a scenario in my mind where the Soviet Union took another orphan who was possibly better at technology and perhaps more manageable and told her she was Thi Thom. Then they gave her the background about how the US killed her mother. This would provide the additional incentive to get TJ to do the espionage work.

We talked for hours as I answered all the questions I could until they were fully informed.

I continued, "And you have a son and daughter?"

"Yes. Alan, thirteen, and Ada, eighteen."

Ada? What are the chances that I just worked with a software person also named Ada?

"Dari and I are both in software, so we chose Ada as a reference to Ada Lovelace, the math whiz who helped Charles Babbage develop his computer they called the Analytical Engine."

I said, "Yes, I know the Babbage history. Some would say he was the father of the computer. Should I try to guess why you chose Alan for the son's name? Perhaps another software reference?"

"It's unlikely you would understand, but please try."

I blurted it out, "Alan Turing?"

"Very good. You clearly have some background in software."

"A little, but my career has been private investigation. I did a little coding back in the day, but I was never very good at it."

I went on to explain how the president and I knew each other and how I was commissioned to find his daughter. I answered all of their questions.

"When you come to Washington, you will meet another software genius also named Ada. It was your stand-in, TJ, and Ada who came up with the idea for skipped minutes, and that idea has saved most of the world from Internet Armageddon. You will enjoy talking to her."

Dari finally said something. "Our Ada is very smart but not a genius—at least not yet."

We made plans to visit Washington. I knew it would be a waste of time to try and hide these family details from the press, so I set up meetings with the White House press agents to provide an accurate account for the American people. After all, there was nothing to hide anymore, especially with such a positive outcome and with Nora on board.

Back in Washington, the White House press agents created a chronicle of events for the media that was surprisingly accurate. Paul Elliot's concerns were put to bed, and once the public understood the history, he was essentially given a free pass. His public approval rating actually improved.

We were in the White House reception room waiting to finally meet President Elliot. The president was busy for a few minutes, so Nora was first to arrive and meet her stepdaughter and her two new stepchildren. They hit it off very well, to an extent that surprised no one. Everyone likes Nora. I had some anxiety about how Thi would be accepted into the First Family after that first false alarm, but those fears were soon eradicated. Thirty minutes later, all talking stopped the moment President Paul Elliot entered the room. He stopped and just looked at Suong, her husband, and his two grandchildren while holding the door open. Nora stood beside him, grasping and gently squeezing his other hand.

No one said a word. It was quiet for a few seconds, but that's a long time when you're waiting for someone to say something.

Suong stared at the president, took a step forward, stopped, and said only one word in a soft voice: "Father?"

***

Before I left the presidential family to themselves, I asked president, "Paul, has the Situation room been cleaned? Are the monitors still there?"

The president replied, "Good question, Mr. Braddock."

I took that comment as a compliment that I will always remember. The president called me "Mister."

He continued, "Richard, I wanted to leave the room exactly as it was so we could take some photos and document what had transpired for history. Someday the public will know how close we came."

I asked, "Any chance I could go there and take a look for old times' sake?"

President Elliot said, "Absolutely, but no pictures!" He actually laughed a little.

I was accompanied to the room by Agent Gary. I sighed a release while I wiped my hand over the table's surface. All the monitors were still connected and operational; they were just turned off. I touched the screen of the Alert Status monitor.

The Alert Status bar was bright red.

Epilogue

AMIP never reopened its doors. The employees were interrogated, and it was interesting that most had no idea what that chip could have done. The chief strategists were Raj Matesh, TJ, and two other engineers who had to know what was going on to implement the encoding protocol. They were all imprisoned, except TJ. President Elliot gave her a full pardon and arranged for her to go into the witness protection program under her new name, Rose Novak. That was necessary for her own safety. Kevin Dupree and Rose Novak were engaged to be married on the next Valentine's Day. That would hasten Ms. Novak getting her citizenship. She liked the way her new name, Rose Dupree, sounded.

The AMIP server was located and hacked, thereby extracting the schematics, the full photolithography mask layer set, testing algorithms, and the semiconductor processing information. With the help of a major semiconductor company, the chip was quickly modified, and a new version was provided to all the second-source suppliers. In the world of semiconductors, the revision level for each layer, or mask as they are called, must be clearly marked and visible under a microscope. This could be something as simple as Rev-B, but as a token and recognition to TJ, the revision level for the new chip was designated TJ214.

No public announcements were made that new D-Chips were being supplied to the industry because the United States' encode protocol had successfully deactivated the majority of the D-Chips already in the field. A recall of millions of computers and cell phones would have been disastrous to the economy and potentially lethal to the vendors themselves. The entire episode was suppressed and remained classified. There were rumors on Wall Street that something had happened because time stood still at noon on February fourteenth Central Standard Time, but nobody knew exactly what caused it.

Some speculations and rumors prompted the TV program *60 Minutes* to try to put together a story about the event, so they were aggressively looking for participants to interview, but to no avail. The story was going to be how this event may have been similar to the Y2K bug, also known as the Millennium Bug. Both were somehow related to the formatting of calendar dates within a computer. The Y2K bug did cause some public chaos because it was openly discussed, but companies worldwide checked, fixed, and upgraded their systems well beforehand. As a result, very few computer failures occurred, and for the rest of us, it provided a fantastic excuse to have a party on New Year's Eve 1999. Y2K was talked about because everybody knew about it, but the D-Chip February fourteenth episode dropped out of consciousness in less than a month because, for most people, nothing happened.

The assassins who killed Brad Dempsey were never found, nor was it discovered where the AMIP funding came from, or who was actually sending the encode commands over the Internet. High-level discussions with the Soviet Union were getting nowhere.

In the end, I was back in my condo, wondering if I was too old for all this. Lara convinced me that I still had a lot of spunk left in me. Actually, I did feel better than I had in years. I had nothing particular on my calendar, other than perhaps asking Lara if she would marry me.

***

Southern Power

Newcastle, Oklahoma

Mason Branner, Jesse Burke, and crew had worked feverishly to stop the natural gas leaks and shut down the plant. The only casualty was the technician, Jorge, but there were numerous other injuries. Jesse felt personally responsible, and as a result, suffered from a form of PTSD that required psychiatric counseling. Later, and on his own, he started a GoFundMe page to help Jorge's family.

Jesse quit working at the power plant and was known to have started drinking heavily. Mason was doing his best to pull Jesse back from the brink.

Mason lobbied publicly for better communications systems with backups, so an occurrence like this could never happen again. He never considered resigning, because he knew he was one of the few who understood how something as simple as the Internet could cause such a chain reaction. He started to travel, speaking to other plant operators about what had happened. He would end each speech with one statement: "Don't trust people's lives on things you can't control."

***

Wells, England

Hollis and Edna Buckley eventually got their money back from the bank, but Edna still clucked when she thought hard about anything worrisome. Edna always felt the bank was where their money belonged, but Hollis was adamant, at least temporarily.

While clucking softly, Edna said, "We have to trust something, Hollis."

"Balderdash! No one knows how all this crap works. It's bonkers, I say."

Eventually, they put all the money back into a secure account and paid a small fee to make sure it was 100-percent insured.

Word was out that the new high-speed Internet would soon come to Wells, but even under pressure from their children, Hollis and Edna never opened a Facebook account.

***

Kewanee, Illinois

The town's grouchy ham radio operator, Daryl Walker, with officer Ken Griffin's help to get temporary generator power to Daryl's radio gear, proved to be the only means for the residents of Kewanee to find out what was happening in the rest of the world. After finally getting Daryl's gear on the air, they heard other ham radio operators say that thousands were suddenly cut off from the Internet. No one knew for sure how many or what had happened. Individual issues were not significant, but some major infrastructures failed. Businesses were not able to stay open, fuel deliveries were in jeopardy, hospitals couldn't access patient records, and smaller water filtration plants shut down, as did most rural electrical power grids. Thousands more had lost telephone communications—at least that was what Ken, Butch, and Daryl heard from the ham operators.

Ken listened to the fear and panic in the ham operator voices, thinking that maybe it wasn't as bad as what they were hearing. Nevertheless, he was thankful for that lone hobbyist/ham who now had a backup generator, because that was the only means of communication for a while.

The town agreed to let Daryl keep the generator. Daryl said, "Thanks, now get off my property."

***

Although the events described have not happened yet, our culture is still vulnerable when we start taking the benefits technology has gifted to us for granted. The chilling part about this is most of us don't even know we are taking anything for granted. "We are all connected" means "We are all at risk" of infrastructure failure from the smallest of digital bits.

What will you do when your cell phone doesn't work (you canceled your landline years ago, remember?), your laptop won't log on the Internet, the number of online TV stations dwindles, gas stations start running out of fuel, grocery stores run low on food, water filtration is questionable, electric power goes from intermittent to gone, and a battery-powered radio and generator-powered amateur radio—albeit temporary—become your last resort for information?

And finally, what will you do as you sit there in the dark at your cabin where you went when you needed to unwind, perhaps a little cold because your propane delivery hasn't shown up, wondering if the water you're drinking is safe, and you realize that not knowing what happened is the worst part?

"We never know the worth of water until the well is dry."
—Thomas Fuller

"Worldwide connectivity means worldwide vulnerability!"
—Richard Braddock

The Alert bar was still bright red.

About Richard Nedbal

Richard was raised in the mid-west and was fully invested in electronics by the age of seven after receiving his amateur radio license. He went to the University of Illinois and later joined the USAF during the Vietnam war, where he taught electronics in the crypto field. After the USAF, Richard joined the Carnegie Mellon Institute and learned how to design integrated circuits used in microprocessor-based automotive fuel injection systems. Then Richard and his family moved to Silicon Valley, where he became the microprocessor engineering manager for a semiconductor company. He founded two software companies just as the Internet was about to take off. Although Richard has published numerous technical articles and has written several books, this is his debut novel in his planned Richard Braddock series. He lives in Northern California.

Review Requested:

We'd like to know if you enjoyed the book.
Please consider leaving a review on the platform from
which you purchased the book.

9 781952 269288